Radiant Days

BOOKS BY ELIZABETH HAND

Winterlong

Aestival Tide

Icarus Descending

Waking the Moon

Glimmering

Last Summer at Mars Hill (short stories)

Black Light

Bibliomancy (novellas)

Mortal Love

Chip Crockett's Christmas Carol

Saffron and Brimstone (short stories)

Generation Loss

Illyria

Available Dark

Radiant Days

Radiant Days

A NOVEL BY

Elizabeth Hand

VIKING

An Imprint of Penguin Group (USA) Inc.

VIKING
Published by Penguin Group
Penguin Group (USA) Inc., 345 Hudson Street, New York, New York 10014, U.S.A.
Penguin Group (Canada), 90 Eglinton Avenue East, Suite 700, Toronto, Ontario, Canada M4P 2Y3
(a division of Pearson Penguin Canada Inc.)
Penguin Books Ltd, 80 Strand, London WC2R 0RL, England
Penguin Ireland, 25 St Stephen's Green, Dublin 2, Ireland (a division of Penguin Books Ltd)
Penguin Group (Australia), 250 Camberwell Road, Camberwell, Victoria 3124, Australia
(a division of Pearson Australia Group Pty Ltd)
Penguin Books India Pvt Ltd, 11 Community Centre, Panchsheel Park, New Delhi – 110 017, India
Penguin Group (NZ), 67 Apollo Drive, Rosedale, Auckland 0632, New Zealand
(a division of Pearson New Zealand Ltd.)
Penguin Books (South Africa) (Pty) Ltd, 24 Sturdee Avenue, Rosebank, Johannesburg 2196, South Africa

Penguin Books Ltd, Registered Offices: 80 Strand, London WC2R 0RL, England

First published in 2012 by Viking, a member of Penguin Group (USA) Inc.

1 3 5 7 9 10 8 6 4 2

Copyright © Elizabeth Hand, 2012

All translation of Arthur Rimbaud's poems and letters by Elizabeth Hand

My thanks to Patti Smith for the permission to quote from her song "Land."

All rights reserved

LIBRARY OF CONGRESS CATALOGING-IN-PUBLICATION DATA IS AVAILABLE
ISBN 978-0-670-01135-3

Printed in U.S.A.
Set in Granjon

For my daughter, Callie,
Poetry in motion

There is no keeper but the key
[Up there there are several walls of possibilities]
Except for one who seizes possibilities

—Patti Smith, "Land: La Mer (de)"

My eternal soul
Seize your desire
Despite the night
And the day on fire.

—Arthur Rimbaud, *A Season in Hell*

CONTENTS

PART ONE: Alchemy of the Word   1

PART TWO: Strange Couple   103

PART THREE: Exiles   157

PART FOUR: State of Siege   185

PART FIVE: Farewell   225

PART SIX: Radiant Days   257

Author's Note   279

Select Bibliography   285

PART ONE

୨୧

ALCHEMY OF THE WORD

Seen enough. That vision everywhere.

Had enough. Chaos of cities at night, in
daylight, all the time.

Known enough. Sick of life, chaos and
visions—

Time to take off with a bang!

— Arthur Rimbaud, "Departure"

1

Washington, D.C.

CLEA WAS TWENTY–THREE, five years older than me. She was my graduate instructor for life drawing at the Corcoran School of Art.

"You're a girl," she said on the first day of the fall semester. She glanced, frowning, at the list of names on her clipboard. "Merle—I thought that was a guy's name."

"My father wanted Merle for Merle Haggard. My mother said Merle Oberon." It was typical that my parents couldn't agree on something, even when they seemed to want the same thing. "So I'm Merle."

"Merle." Clea didn't smile. She continued to stare at me as she read the rest of the class list. Three hours later, when the class was done, she asked me if I wanted to have lunch.

"Yeah, sure." I shrugged. The other students hurried past, paying no attention to us. I grabbed my bag, an old canvas mailman's satchel filled with my sketchbooks and charcoal pencils, notebooks, Magic Markers and spent Bic lighters and empty packs of cigarettes, and followed her outside.

She took me to a place called the Blue Mirror. I'd never been there—I'd never been anywhere. I was a scholarship student from rural Virginia, hours away in the Shenandoah Valley, living in a group house in Northeast where I had to pay only fifty bucks a month for a mattress on the floor and a single bathroom shared with ten other people, most of them students at other schools. My father had given me four hundred dollars to last the entire year, but I'd paid my rent several months in advance, which didn't leave much. I was broke, living on apples and whatever my roommates didn't finish of their own scraped-together meals. Spanish rice, mostly, which I hated, burned toast, hard-boiled eggs.

It felt strange, now, to be in a restaurant—a big diner, really, booths and, yeah, blue mirrors reflecting the narrow space, so it seemed like we were sitting in a railway car to infinity.

"So where you from?" Clea asked.

"Norville, Virginia."

Clea laughed. "Where the hell is Norville, Virginia?"

"Nowhere." I grabbed the sugar and started pouring it into my coffee. "That's why I left."

I ordered a Reuben—I'd never had one but I liked the name. When it came, I stared at it, an oozing mass of neon orange and creamy yellow on grilled rye bread, and finally took a bite.

"It's good." I pointed at the lacy pink fringe of meat. "What's that?"

"Corned beef. Or no, maybe pastrami."

"What's pastrami?"

"Corned beef with a fancy name."

The waitress set Clea's lunch in front of her: apple pie and vanilla ice cream. I said, "That's your lunch?"

"Apples are good for you. So's pastrami. Eat."

It was hard to focus on eating with Clea sitting across from me. She was impossibly exotic, not just older than me but married. The only married people I knew were even older, like my parents, though it was only my father, since my mother had left years ago.

But Clea hardly mentioned her husband. Her mother was black, a former dancer with Katherine Dunham's company; her father was a Swedish businessman. Clea had grown up in Manhattan and Stockholm, gone to boarding school in Geneva, then studied art in Paris before ending up here in D.C., teaching at the Corcoran while her husband attended Georgetown Law School. She was tall and lanky; her skin looked as though it had been dusted with gold. When I touched it, I half expected to see my fingertips yellow with pollen. Her dark hair was thick and curling, pinned back from her face with two combs that had black feathers in them; her eyes narrow, the pupils a gleaming liquid amber flecked with green. Later, when she came back to my place and kissed me, it was like pressing my mouth against an overripe fruit that split beneath my lips.

"Have you done this before?" She took a black cigarette from an alligator-skin case, tapped it against the floor, lit up, and exhaled. "With a woman?"

I shook my head. "Just guys. Well, my friend Lorna, we kissed once."

"Did you like it?"

I scrounged through my bag until I found a bent Marlboro. "Yeah."

I lit my cigarette from hers, then dug in my bag for a charcoal pencil. On the floor beside my mattress was a crumpled paper plate smeared with ketchup, like a lipstick kiss. I worked around this and drew Clea as she sat, eyes shut, smoke coiling around her unsprung hair like a nest of baby snakes.

"Let me see." Her eyes opened. Before I could stop her, she grabbed the sketch.

She stared at it for a long time, the way she'd stared at me in class that morning. I wanted to curse her out but didn't, and waited for what I knew would come next, what always came when a teacher saw my work: disdain or anger or, at best, impatience that I hadn't followed directions, hadn't drawn what was in front of me.

"This is amazing," she said at last, and stared at the paper plate. "I was on the selection committee—I saw your portfolio when you submitted it."

"You thought I was a guy."

She nodded. "It's good."

She looked at me, and I saw something flicker across her face. A sort of hunger; a terrible, helpless longing that I did not yet recognize as envy.

"No one ever likes it," I said. I didn't tell her that I'd been rejected by all the better-known schools I'd applied to—Pratt and

RISD, the Parsons School of Design. "My teacher in high school, she said I didn't show the real world. She just wanted us to copy stuff, bowls of fruit and shit like that."

"'Art is not a mirror to reflect the world, but a hammer with which to shape it.' That's Mayakovsky." Clea took the paper plate, touched the ketchup to see if it was still wet, then carefully slid the sketch into her leather bag. "I need to go meet Marc. See you Wednesday." She stood and dressed, and left.

WHEN I WAS THREE YEARS OLD, MY MOTHER WOULD GIVE ME A bucket of water and an old paintbrush, and tell me to go outside and paint the driveway. I'd carefully paint the cracked concrete, watch bewitched as the dark gray chunks turned white again. I didn't know the water was evaporating: I thought it was magic, something only I could do. I'd mix dirt with the water, or crushed dandelions, to see if the water would turn yellow. I'd take spoonfuls of grape jelly and Tang to make purple and orange. Once I poured one of my father's beers onto the drive, to watch it foam. My father spanked me when he got home from the hardware store where he worked and found the empty can.

"Don't need you pissing away my money," he yelled.

"You don't need help with that," my mother retorted, and ducked before he could slap her.

She stayed home with me and my two younger brothers, twins named Roy and Davis. My older brother, Robbie, had joined the army right out of high school, got stationed in Fort Bragg, and never looked back. This was before my mother took off. We never knew where she went, if she was still alive or dead. I found

some of her leftover makeup, Maybelline lipsticks and blue Yard-
ley eye shadow, and hoarded it along with the broken crayons
I hid in an old coffee can under the bed in the room I shared
with the twins. The room always smelled like pee, but I didn't
mind so much since it hid the smell of the tempera paints I stole
from school. At night when Roy and Davis were asleep, I'd crawl
under their bed with a flashlight and draw on sheets of paper
while lying on the floor. I'd invented a comic strip called *Danger
Dog*, filling the backs of my school notebooks with pencil drawings of Danger Dog and his sidekicks, Bad Kitty and Meezum.
On Sundays, while my father was at his second job, as a janitor at
the hospital, I'd paint the color edition of *Danger Dog*, then let the
twins read it at night. I saved brown paper bags, and sometimes
my father would bring home cardboard cartons that I'd cut apart
and draw on. Once he brought a huge refrigerator box. The twins
and I dragged it into the overgrown backyard and I painted a city
on it—skyscrapers on one panel, trees on another, a grocery on
the third. Sidewalks and trains. The only real city I'd ever visited
was Waynesboro, but I'd seen movies, and Metropolis on *Super-
man*. We played in the box until rain and hard use reduced it to a
brown slurry indistinguishable from the mud around it.

At school I didn't play much with other kids. All I wanted to
do was draw. I was scrawny and, until I had an eye operation,
cross-eyed. My father took me to the same barber shop where he
and the twins got their hair cut; people used to think I was a boy.
Kids picked on me but I fought back, until my tormentors were
distracted by the arrival of a new kid, a soft-spoken black boy

named Alan. I came to his defense once and got a bloody nose and detention. When my father found out, he slapped me and my nose bled again.

"You're like your mama with the niggers," he said.

Things got better in fifth grade.

"That's a really good horse, Merle." A smart, popular girl named Donna stared at a drawing I'd made on a blank page in my social studies workbook. "It looks real."

That became the pattern for the rest of my school career. People thought I was weird, but when they saw my sketchbooks they shut up. I was an okay student, not great but good enough. I was really good at lying, making excuses for not bringing in juice, or presents for Secret Santa; not because I forgot but because my father wouldn't give me money. "They get my goddamn taxes, that's enough."

I hated high school, except for art class, and even that was a fight. In freshman year our teacher, Mrs. Caldwell, showed us slides meant to encapsulate the history of art, from cave paintings to Norman Rockwell. I loved the cave paintings best: animals from a dream of steppes and ancient forests, loping across the rough walls of places so dark and hidden it made me dizzy to think of them.

"How did they do that?"

Mrs. Caldwell shook her head impatiently. "Hands, please."

My hand shot up. She was already on to the Sistine Chapel. "Those cave paintings—how did they do that? What did they make the paint out of? And how could they even see in the dark?"

"No one knows," Mrs. Caldwell snapped. "They were very crude attempts; it was thousands of years before people learned how to draw properly."

Van Gogh and Picasso passed in a flicker of blue and yellow, fractured faces and a whirling nightscape I recognized.

"That's from that song," I said to the girl beside me. "You know, 'Starry, starry night.'"

"Shhh," she whispered as Mrs. Caldwell glared at us.

A door opened for me that afternoon. For the first time I realized that paintings weren't just things in books or on posters— they had a life of their own. They mattered to other people. Real people, not like Mrs. Caldwell, but people like the man who sang that song; people who were famous.

I began experimenting with what I drew. Mrs. Caldwell hated that, though in spring of my junior year the new English teacher, Ms. Aronson, used to come into the art room sometimes, and she liked my stuff.

"You're a real original, Merle." She was staring at a self-portrait I'd done, me as Van Gogh, with a pack of Marlboros where my ear should have been.

"Thanks," I said.

She turned to me. "Are you applying to colleges next year?"

"Yeah, I guess." I wouldn't meet her eyes.

"When the time comes, I'll help you with the paperwork. Okay?"

I nodded, and she left.

That was the spring the seventeen-year locusts hatched. There were cicadas everywhere, literally millions of them in trees and bushes. The noise they made was deafening, a shrill siren you couldn't escape unless you were inside a fast-moving car with the windows rolled up. The split skins they left when they crawled out of the ground covered everything, crackling underfoot like dead leaves.

I thought the husks were incredible, amber and topaz like bits of broken jewelry. The living cicadas were even more beautiful, with huge golden eyes and iridescent green bodies and long translucent wings, pale gold and veined with black. Their wings were like tiny stained glass windows, and when the cicadas began to die, I gathered hundreds of them for my junior art project.

I found a broken pane of glass and trimmed the jagged edge with a razor blade, and made a frame of splints of wood and masking tape. I carefully removed the cicadas' wings, then glued them onto the glass in a spiral, layering it with their emerald carapaces to create a rosace window, green and gold and onyx.

"Is that some kind of joke?" Mrs. Caldwell said when I gave it to her. She was hanging everyone's paintings in the hall. "You know this is half of your final grade."

Before I could reply, Ms. Aronson came up behind me. "A mandala." She shook her head. "An insect mandala. That's a showstopper, Merle. Let's put it where it can catch the light."

She slid the glass from Mrs. Caldwell's hands and walked to the end of the corridor, positioning it so that morning sun spilled through the image like a radiant eye. All that day students wandered through the hall to look at the juniors' paintings. When they came to my insect mandala, they stopped dead.

"Wow! Stained glass."

"It's like a kaleidoscope."

"It's so cool!"

Then they'd fall quiet, until someone would finally pipe up.

"Is that a—are those *bugs*?"

When it was time to take everything down, I gave the insect mandala to Ms. Aronson.

"Don't you want to keep this for your portfolio?" she asked.

I shook my head. "It'll only get broken at my house."

"Well, thank you, Merle." She set it gingerly on her desk and stared at it. "This will be my pension when you become famous."

When I got my report card three weeks later, Mrs. Caldwell gave me a C, with a note beside it:

The F on your final art project brought your semester grade down. Next time follow instructions.

2

Charleville, France

AT THE END of August he ran away to Paris. He'd saved or stolen only enough to pay for a train ticket to Saint-Quentin, seventy-three miles away, but his friend Luc still owed him money for doing his Latin homework.

"Here." Luc dug into his pocket and produced a few grimy coins. He picked lint from one and handed them over.

Arthur scowled. "That's not going to get me to Paris."

"Sorry. It's all I've got. What about Ernest?"

"He's broke."

"I'm broke, too!"

"Yes, but I don't like you as much." Arthur pocketed the coins. "Thanks. I'll bring you back a souvenir. Some hashish."

"Bring me a Parisian girl. All the ones here are ugly."

Arthur nodded and left, swearing under his breath. He should have planned better—the school in Charleville had closed because of the war, which meant he wouldn't be able to shake down anyone else till it opened again.

But he wasn't going to wait around for the war to end. He hated Charleville, that suburban shithole, and spent as much time as he could walking, trying to convince himself that he'd left it behind, that he was on his way to Paris. He was always walking: from his house to school; from school to town, where he'd steal archaic volumes from the local bookshop, books on necromancy and obscure religious cults; from downtown Charleville to the surrounding woods and fields, where he'd plan his escape and write poems in his head. He chanted words beneath his breath as he strode beneath the beech trees, the thump of his heavy boots keeping time, like the ticking of the old captain's clock on the kitchen mantel at home.

On blue summer nights, I'll wander lost footpaths,
Stung by wheatstalks, trampling the tender grass:
Dreaming, that cool touch under my feet.
I'll let the wind bathe my bare head.

I won't speak; I'll think nothing.
But infinite love will fill my soul,
And I'll travel an impossible distance, a wanderer
In the great world—happy, as with a woman.

It was a form of incantation, a means of welding the world inside his head to the one that surrounded him, words the fiery chain that bound it all together. Sometimes he'd forget where he was, so entranced by the rush of images that the countryside became a blue-green blur, until he stumbled on a rock or tree root. If he'd managed to steal a bottle of brandy, he'd stumble more often, and swear, furiously, all the vile words he'd like to throw at his mother.

Bitch! Shit! Goddamned sow!

His father had decamped years before, leaving her with four small children and the grimly expectant face of someone first in line to watch a public burning. Steel-eyed, knife-tongued, parsimonious, she was ruthless in her dealings with tradesmen and the farmhands who worked the family's fields outside Charleville, sometimes withholding payment for a year or more. Teachers at the local school were known to bolt classroom doors when they saw her coming, and itinerants had learned to avoid the Rimbaud courtyard unless they wanted a bucket of boiling water thrown at them. Frédéric, Arthur's older brother, had recently joined the army to escape her nightly harangues.

Arthur called her the Mouth of Darkness (not within earshot). If Napoléon III had conscripted her, France would not have fallen to the Prussian army. Even Charleville's chief of police lived in terror of Madame Rimbaud.

"Your mother was born too late," he once confessed, when Arthur was (again) brought before him for pinching newspapers from the local stationer. "They could have used her during the storming of the Bastille. A formidable woman. I hesitate to take up her time over such a minor matter." He shuddered, and released Arthur without notifying Madame.

So Arthur walked. He was researching magic—not legerdemain

or conjuror's tricks but necromancy and alchemy, sorceries that could be mastered through knowledge and practice and technique, and ancient Egyptian magic. The eye of Horus was said to aid one through cycles of rebirth, and there were holy men in India who could travel through time and space by means of *perambulation*, an intensely focused kind of walking. Hashish was supposed to augment this effect. Arthur had already decided he would find some when he got to Paris.

He bought the cheapest ticket he could, for Saint-Quentin; after S-Q he hid under his seat, holding his breath when an immense man reeking of cow manure settled into the cushions Arthur had just vacated. Within a few minutes the train started up again, and the man was snoring. Arthur yawned and scrawled notes for a poem on a scrap of paper, trying to keep a safe distance from the man's filthy boots. After an hour he too dozed off. When they reached the Paris station, a conductor stepped on his hand.

"Ow—what the hell!" Arthur scrambled into the train's narrow aisle, where the conductor grabbed him by the hair and dragged him outside.

"Another shirker," the conductor yelled at the stationmaster.

"I'm not a shirker! I'm a journalist!"

The stationmaster snorted. "And I'm Emperor Napoléon. Let's go."

Arthur was hauled off to the police station.

"How old are you?"

Arthur glared at the chief of police. "Seventeen." A lie: he wouldn't be sixteen till mid-October.

"Seventeen?"

The man gazed at him dubiously. There was an ormolu mirror behind his desk, and in its clouded glass Arthur could see what the police chief saw: a round-faced boy who looked even younger than fifteen, with tousled straw-blond hair and a smudge of dirt on one cheek. Yet Arthur could also see the man's hesitation.

Because the boy's mouth was obdurate, even grim, and the eyes that stared unflinchingly at the policeman were the wintry gray-blue of frozen slate. It was an unsettling gaze, with the chilling self-containment of an anarchist moments before he hurls a bomb. The chief of police looked away.

"Seventeen," Arthur repeated. "Ask anyone."

That was his first mistake. Seventeen was old enough to be a soldier, or even a spy. The Prussians had invaded France a few weeks earlier, and now everyone was obsessed with spies.

His second mistake was not having any money for his train ticket. His third was not having any identification.

After that, the mistakes piled up so fast they buried him.

"You're a vagrant," the police chief finally announced with relief. He stamped a sheaf of papers, glanced at the guard standing by the station door. "Another for Mazas."

"Mazas Prison?" Arthur stared at him in disbelief. "Are you insane? You can't send me there!"

The guard dragged Arthur out of the station, toward a windowless black carriage rocking ominously behind two motionless horses.

"What the—shit!" Arthur kicked at him. "This is crazy, you can't—"

Another policeman grabbed him, unbolted the door to the

wagon, and watched impassively as the boy was thrown inside. The door slammed in Arthur's face. He clawed at the grille, shouting as unseen hands pulled him backward into a throng of drunken men as the carriage lurched off.

He never knew how much time passed before they reached the towering black fortress that was Mazas Prison; never knew how many men he fought off inside the wagon until, exhausted and beaten till his ears bled, he collapsed, and they tore at his clothes in the filthy darkness, searching for money, tobacco, anything of value.

"Leave him!"

Arthur moaned as someone pulled him from the floor. A man cursed angrily, grabbing at the boy's coat, then screamed in pain as a flash of quicksilver momentarily flared: a knife. The man fell back. Arthur found himself propped against the wall of the wagon.

"Are you all right?"

Arthur blinked, wiping tears and grime from his cheeks. A young man perhaps five years older than he crouched a few inches away. Deep-set eyes; a lean, slightly wolfish face; shaggy dark hair spilling to his shoulders. He set a hand on Arthur's knee, glancing at the subdued group behind them, then spoke in a low voice.

"Your first time?"

Arthur nodded.

"Do you have family here?"

"Not in Paris."

The young man shrugged. "Maybe for the best—these days,

they might hunt them down and throw them in with you. I'm Leo. What are you in for?"

"Vagrancy. Arthur."

"Vagrancy, that's not so bad. If you send for someone, they'll release you. Can you pay the fine? I've been here seven times—vagrancy, theft, collusion, you name it. This time it's for spying."

"They thought I was a spy. But I'm not."

"Well, I am. Or I was, anyway. Carried a few letters for a Prussian soldier—love letters to a girl here in Paris. She'll be crying her eyes out that she's never heard from him. That idiot police chief thought they were some kind of code."

"How do you know they weren't?"

"Because that Prussian was dumb as a plank, that's why—he could barely spell his own name. Serves me right for doing a favor for someone even stupider than I am." Leo grinned and settled beside Arthur. "But if you're going to prison, Mazas is the place. Relatively clean, and they let you outside for an hour every morning. Can you write?"

"Yes."

"Ask the guard to bring you paper and a pen; you can write a letter to ask for help. Make sure it doesn't look like it's in code. If you want to talk to other prisoners, do this"—Leo rapped on the floor—"once, that's A; twice, B; three times, C."

"And what? Twenty-six knocks for Z?"

"Try not to use Z. Actually, try not to use anything after I." Leo leaned against the wall and dug in his pocket for a pipe and a twist of tobacco. "You learn to be creative in Mazas. Also concise."

He lit his pipe, drew avidly on it, and passed it to Arthur. Exhausted as he was, after a few minutes Arthur fell asleep, his head pillowed against Leo's arm. When the wagon finally halted, Leo helped him to his feet, his hand lingering on Arthur's shoulder as he gazed into his face.

"Look for me when they let you go outside," he said softly, and squeezed his shoulder. "We can share another smoke."

Arthur joined the queue of men being pushed toward the entrance by guards armed with truncheons. Inside, they stripped him and searched his pockets, finding only a stub of pencil and the wad of poems he always carried. They shoved these back into his overcoat, then proceeded to shave his head against lice, pour disinfectant that burned like acid onto his bare skull, and finally toss him back his soiled clothes.

"'Raimbault,'" the registration clerk said, squinting to read a scrawled document. "'Vagrant.' This way."

He was marched down one cold, echoing corridor after another, past ironclad doors and ranks of silent, tight-mouthed warders. He looked in vain for Leo, avoiding the dispassionate gazes that followed him down the dim hallway as he passed each cell with its grated window.

"Here," the warder announced at last, opening a heavy door with an iron grille. "Good afternoon, Monsieur Raimbault."

The room was large and empty save for a wooden stool, a small oil lantern, and a tin ewer filled with water. After an hour, a warder returned with a tin plate of greasy potatoes and dense black bread.

"Do I sleep on the floor?" demanded Arthur.

The warder cocked a thumb at the ceiling, where an intricate array of ropes and canvas hung, like the rigging for a sailboat.

"There," the warder grunted, and left. Later, he came back to collect the empty plate, and used a long wooden pole to release and lower the ersatz sail, which after some untangling became a canvas hammock. "Voilà: your bed."

Then the warder was gone. For some minutes Arthur sat on the wooden stool and surveyed his bed, which in the flickering lamplight seemed at first a crumpled tent, then a fragile boat, and finally a stained bolt of unbleached canvas, suspended by ropes from a wooden block and tackle. He settled himself into it, gingerly, and was immediately dumped onto the floor.

"Goddamn it!" he shouted, and heard an echoing chorus of curses and laughter from the corridor.

"Need someone to tuck you in, sweetheart?" a voice called out, and was silenced by the warder.

Arthur swore again, but softly. He began to pace the cell, counting off the steps; walked the perimeter of the room, one hand on the wall as he shut his eyes. He tried to summon the city outside the prison walls, but saw only a courtyard, rainswept, the looming shadow of a gallows and a line of hollow-eyed figures that grinned as they reached for him with skeletal hands.

He took a deep breath, trying to calm himself, then pulled out his bundle of poems. He found a nearly blank sheet, blotched where he'd spilled something on it. He sharpened the tip of his

pencil with a fingernail, and scrawled a few lines across the crumpled page.

From the black gallows,
Obliging with its one arm,
The devil's emaciated warriors dance and dance,
The skeletons of Saladins.

My Lord Beelzebub yanks them by the neck
And his little black puppets grin at the sky.
He hits them upside the head,
Makes them dance and dance to an old Christmas song.

He had not in fact seen a gallows anywhere at Mazas, but that
didn't mean there wasn't one. And he was certain there were
hundreds, maybe thousands, of bodies buried on the premises.
He read over what he'd just written, skin creeping as he thought
of a body he and Ernest had once seen hanging from a tree outside Charleville. A deserter, or maybe a Prussian spy. Either way,
he was dead.

It was perhaps not the best thing to be thinking about, alone
in a prison cell.

Arthur hurriedly folded the paper and shoved it back into
his pocket. He pulled his coat tight around him and scrambled
closer to the lantern, warming his hands. After a few minutes
he stumbled to the door and shouted for the warder until he
was hoarse.

The man appeared at last. With his shaven head and patched uniform and bleary eyes, he seemed scarcely less miserable than Arthur.

"What is it?" he croaked.

"Can you bring me paper and a pen? I need to write a letter so I will be released. Please," Arthur added.

The guard peered through the grate in the door. "You can write?"

"Of course I can write," Arthur snapped, then poked a finger through the grate. "Listen, please—this is all a mistake, I swear, just let me write to my mother and I'll be out of here. The police chief in Charleville knows me, I'll make sure you get a promotion. Please?"

The guard stared at him, shook his head, and turned away. But some time later he returned and slid several sheets of coarse paper and some envelopes beneath the door, then passed a pen and bottle of ink through the grate.

"Don't forget about the promotion," he whispered.

Arthur sat on the floor of his cell, squinting in the feeble lantern light. First he wrote a brief letter to the police chief in Charleville, professing outrage at the inferior intelligence and standards of the Paris constabulary, especially compared to the superior intellects of their provincial counterparts, and promising to inform Madame Rimbaud of the exemplary behavior of Charleville's prefect in this irksome matter.

He then penned a briefer note to his mother, reminding her of the boundless love and deference he bore her, also noting the

grave disrespect shown to the Rimbaud family name by the inso-
lent behavior of local railway employees.

Finally he composed a longer missive to Georges Izambard,
his closest friend. Georges had been Arthur's teacher at the secondary school in Charleville; he was only six years older, amused
by Arthur's precocity and (though he could never admit it) hugely
entertained by his student's unrelenting rebellion against whatever authority happened to be in the room.

> *I know you told me not to, but I ran away to Paris. I
> didn't have enough for the ticket, so they threw me in
> Mazas Prison and now they're going to sentence me!
> Agh!*

Arthur paused. In the next cell, a man shouted and pounded at
the wall. Arthur winced and returned to his letter.

> *You always said you'd help me—if you don't hear from
> me by Wednesday, get on the train and COME GET
> ME!*

Arthur bit his lip. What if Georges didn't receive the letter
in time? What if he was finally so fed up that he decided to let
Arthur rot in prison or, worse, turned him over to his mother?
Georges was visiting his aunts in Douai. If he didn't get this letter
in the next two days . . .

Arthur frowned, licked his finger, and let a drop of saliva fall to the page, causing a small blot on the salutation. He gazed at the false teardrop, his eyes welling with real tears as he envisioned his own slight form dangling from the gallows: that poor, brave wanderer, hanged for lack of a third-class rail ticket to Paris!

Tell them I'm not a vagrant, pay the fine and I ORDER
YOU, write my mother and tell her I'm alive! Write me
too!

He stabbed the pen into the inkwell, and with a flourish signed his name.

Your poor Arthur Rimbaud

P.S. If you get me out of here, take me to Douai
with you.

He slept fitfully that night, wrapped in his canvas cocoon, and dreamed of being tossed in a small wicker boat plunging down a ravine choked with icemelt and biting stones. When the warder brought him breakfast (boiled onions, another chunk of black bread), Arthur handed him the three letters.

"You'll post them today?" he asked anxiously.

The warder shrugged. "I'll try. Mail doesn't get out so fast, because of the war."

At midday, the prisoners were permitted to go outside and mill around a courtyard of trampled grass and gravel, under the bored gaze of a half dozen warders. Most of the other prisoners ignored Arthur; a few leered at him and made rude remarks regarding his baby face and red-rimmed eyes.

"Good morning, Sleeping Beauty! Need a wake-up kiss?"

"Kiss *this*," yelled Arthur. He grabbed a handful of gravel and drew his arm back to hurl it when someone clasped his wrist.

"Save your kisses for me. That guy's much too old for you."

Arthur whirled to see Leo, his head now shorn, clad in a dark-blue prison uniform.

"I'm here for a longer visit this time," Leo went on, turning to walk toward a corner of the prison yard. "I gather you're not."

"No." Arthur followed him, casting a vicious backward glance at his tormentor. "I've already written to everyone back home; they'll get me soon. This is all a big mistake."

"Of course," said Leo. He stopped, leaned against the stone wall, and lit a clay pipe. "Smoke?"

Arthur nodded. "Thanks."

They passed the pipe back and forth, and watched as the other prisoners started up a ragtag game of keep-away involving someone's shirt. After a few minutes, Leo gestured at the wall beside him. "Why don't you come closer? It will be easier to talk."

Arthur handed back the pipe and joined him, the stone wall cool against his back. Leo edged closer, until their bodies touched, and slung an arm over Arthur's shoulder. "There. Now no one can hear us."

In fact they hardly spoke, not that day or the next, or the one following; only found their appointed spot each midday, the sun directly overhead and the smell of crushed grass sweet in Arthur's nostrils as they smoked and stood side by side, so close that he could feel Leo's skin burning through layers of rough cambric and linen, and, once, felt Leo's hand slip beneath his shirt to trace the contours of Arthur's shoulder blade as the older boy shut his eyes and sighed.

"I'll miss you," he murmured. "Here"—Leo opened his eyes; he dug into a pocket and withdrew his clay pipe, handed it to Arthur—"keep this. So you'll think of me sometimes, outside."

Arthur flushed. He said nothing, only nodded and, very carefully, wrapped the pipe in a bit of cloth and hid it inside his coat.

EARLY THE NEXT MORNING HE WAS SUMMONED TO THE REGISTRAR'S office. The warder held the door for him, then escorted him to the room where Arthur had first been admitted. The registrar glanced up from behind his desk, and held up an envelope.

"You've been released. Monsieur Izambard has very kindly agreed to pay for your ticket to Douai. A member of the constabulary will bring you to the station and accompany you there, so you will not forget to leave the train at your appointed destination."

"Can I—do I have to leave now?"

The registrar raised his eyebrows slightly. "Why? Do you wish to extend your visit here?"

"No, just . . ." Arthur hesitated, thinking of Leo, how there would be no chance now to say good-bye, or thank you. "No," he said at last, staring at the floor. "I'm ready."

Georges met him at the station in Douai. "Ah, the peripatetic

Arthur Rimbaud," he said drily. "Since my vacation here began, I have scarcely had the concentration to read an entire newspaper. Whereas in that same time, you have managed to steal an incunabulum from Monsieur DeVries's shop, run away from home, fail to purchase a train ticket, get arrested, and throw the entire Charleville police force into a state of heightened anxiety by suggesting to your mother that their neglect somehow precipitated your own little vacation in Mazas Prison." He glanced at the letter of release the registrar at Mazas had sent with Arthur. "'Vagrancy'—is that the best they could do? Another depressing failure of imagination on the part of Parisian law enforcement. Have you anything to say for yourself, 'Monsieur Raimbault'?"

"It was the *Collected Prophecies of Nostradamus*," said Arthur, and shot his teacher an airy look. "Not an incunabulum."

Georges snorted, and directed him toward the main street.

ARTHUR STAYED IN DOUAI FOR THREE WEEKS, CONVENIENTLY FORgetting to inform his mother. Georges had three maiden aunts who feigned horror as Arthur displayed his shorn head and told them dramatically embellished accounts of his time in Mazas. They baked him plum tarts and beignets dusted with sugar; the youngest, who had poignant memories of a lost love who had joined the priesthood, shared her hidden stock of Armagnac. Some evenings the two of them would sit together in an alcove overlooking the garden. The youngest aunt would stroke the soft stubble on his scalp as they sipped the Armagnac and listened to thrushes singing in the plum trees.

After a few days, Georges introduced Arthur to his friend Paul Demeny, a bad poet but a published one, who owned a stake in a bookstore in Paris.

"I'll let you publish my book when it's done," Arthur said as they shook hands.

Demeny regarded him, bemused. "Maybe when you're old enough to write one."

"I've just been released from prison. Mazas."

"For loitering," said Georges.

"With criminal intent," added Arthur.

Georges sighed. "All of Paris sleeps soundly tonight, because Arthur Rimbaud is in Douai."

The days passed in a luxurious dream of reading, sleeping, drinking. At lunch, the maiden aunts scolded him for belching at the table.

"I can't help it." Arthur smiled sweetly. "This goose is fantastic."

Georges rolled his eyes, but the aunts laughed. "Flattery will get you everywhere," the youngest said, and handed Arthur a full plate.

When he grew bored of reading, he composed complaining letters to the local newspaper and argued politics with Demeny and Izambard.

"What do you think of me becoming a war correspondent?" he asked one afternoon while they were drinking at the local café.

Demeny laughed. "What, you think Georges can bail you out of a combat zone?"

"It's not a bad idea," said Georges. "He's a good writer."

"Of course." Demeny finished his beer. "He can read his

poems to the enemy. It'll be a form of torture. They'll surrender, and Arthur'll be a hero. Hey!" He dodged as Arthur tossed his napkin at him.

Sadly, Arthur's journalism career was cut short when, after several weeks, an envelope arrived, addressed to Georges Izambard in small, tight letters.

"From your mother." With two fingers, Georges gingerly placed the sheet of paper on the floor, as though it might detonate. "She's accusing me of 'kidnapping, white slavery, contributing to the corruption of a minor.' Also"—he squinted at the letter—"'encouraging impiety and hylotheism.' I don't even know what that means."

"Equating God with the world around us." Arthur snatched up the page. "Did she really say that?"

"Yes. And she's summoned the Paris police to Charleville, and she says she's going to send them here unless I pack you back home." Georges sighed. "I'm sorry, Arthur, but you'd better go. I could spring you from Mazas, but your mother?" He shuddered. "She says if you don't come back, she's coming here to get you. I think the shock would kill my aunts."

"Shit." Arthur stared at the page, then at Georges. "Will you come with me?"

"Is that the prisoner's last wish?" Georges grasped his shoulder. "Come on. I'll break it to the aunts. God knows why, but they're going to miss you. Me, too."

That night Arthur copied all his poems into a notebook. In the morning, he handed it to Demeny.

"Thank you." Demeny flipped through the pages and shot Arthur a sideways grin. "These will come in handy for lighting the fire this winter."

"Maybe they'll light a fire under your ass." Arthur gave him a mocking bow. "I'll see you in Paris."

"Not in a prison cell, I hope."

Arthur and Georges took the midday train to Charleville. The teary-eyed aunts waved good-bye as Arthur leaned from the window, fighting tears himself. When they arrived in Charleville, a thin rain fell as Arthur and Georges walked from the station beneath rows of linden trees, leaves burnished by the early dusk.

"You look like you're facing the guillotine at Mazas," said Georges.

"That would be preferable." Arthur stopped and stared up at Georges, his pale eyes desperate. "I can't stand this. I mean it—I'll kill her, or she'll kill me, or—"

Georges shook his head. "It will be all right. You can write me. And Demeny has your poems, maybe something will happen with that. Just try to stay out of trouble, will you?"

Arthur's mother waited at the door, a vengeful raven in black, mouth tight and eyes aflame. Without a word she slapped him, pushed him inside, then whirled to face Georges.

"How dare you show up here? I'm filing a complaint with the police, also with the school. If they even *think* of hiring you back there I'm going to—"

She slammed the door in Izambard's face. Inside, she tried to grab a lock of Arthur's unruly hair. But the hair, of course, was gone.

"You and your father!" She slapped him again. Arthur turned and raced upstairs to his room. "You think this is some kind of joke, running away? Do you? *Do you?*"

"Why the hell do you think he left?" Arthur shouted back at her. "He hated you! Frédéric joined the army because he hates you! *Everybody* hates you!"

The entire house shook as she stormed outside. Arthur dived onto his bed and covered his head with a pillow. Moments later, someone knocked furtively at Arthur's door.

"What?" he demanded.

The door cracked open and his younger sisters came in.

"I thought she was going to kill you," said Vitalie as she settled on the bed. "What was Paris like?"

"A lot of dead people. A lot of soldiers. Everything was all bombed out."

Isabelle stood near him and sucked her hair ribbon. She was ten, but acted younger because she was the baby. "What happened to your head?"

"Don't touch," he warned. "They shaved it. I got lice."

Vitalie shrieked, but Isabelle only nodded solemnly. "Did you see Frédéric with the soldiers?"

"No." He hated his older brother. "Frédéric's hiding under a log somewhere. Go away, I need to sleep. Wait, here"—he pulled two lumpy packages from his pocket, each wrapped in a linen tea towel—"apple tarts, from Georges's aunts. I saved them for you. Don't let the Mouth of Darkness see them."

"We won't." Vitalie handed one to Isabelle, turned to pat her brother on the forehead. "I'll bring you supper later."

When his sisters left, he pulled out the wad of pages he'd been carrying since he first left Charleville, almost a month ago. Notes, some antiwar cartoons he had tried to sell to the newspaper in Douai, the poems he'd copied into the notebook he'd given to Demeny. After a few minutes he shoved them under the bed. He shouted a curse and punched the wall, leaving a dent in the plaster.

Prison would have been better.

Two weeks later, he ran away again. Before leaving, he tracked down his friend Ernest, telling him outrageous lies about a girl who was waiting for him in Douai.

"Beautiful. She has a friend, too; I'll get her to introduce you. I said I'd go back and meet her for dinner, only I need the train fare. Maybe you can set me up, and I'll pay you back when we all get together, how's that?"

Ernest gave him a few francs. Not enough for the train to Douai, but Arthur wasn't headed to Douai—he was on his way to Belgium.

He left shortly after breakfast. That afternoon he stopped for supper at a place called the Green Tavern, where he had a rush of pure happiness: a beer on the table before him, sun slanting through the windows, a buxom blond waitress who flirted with him and laughed when he asked if she had a friend.

"What, I'm not enough for you?" she said, tweaking his ear.

After she brought his food, he sat and wrote, and it was as if the words on the page and the words in his head and the room around him all became one thing, a dazzling light that spilled from his eyes onto the creased notepaper.

> *Eight days, I'd worn my boots to shreds*
> *On the stony road. I got to Charleroi.*
> *"The Green Tavern": I ordered bread and butter,*
> *A slab of warm ham.*
>
> *Feeling good, I stretched my legs under the green table,*
> *Checked out the graffiti on the wallpaper—*
> *And what could be better than when the laughing girl*
> *With the "I'm available" eyes—*
>
> *A kiss wouldn't scare that girl!—*
> *Brings me bread and butter,*
> *Lukewarm ham on a bright-colored platter—*
>
> *The ham pink and white, perfumed with garlic—*
> *And fills a huge beer mug, its foaming head*
> *Gilded by a ray of dying sun.*

Remembering it long afterward, he could have kicked himself for not getting her name.

3

Washington, D.C.

APRIL 1978

THE FALL SEMESTER ended. I went home for a few days, then returned to D.C. to wait out the weeks until the January term began. Winter melted into an early spring. Clea and I would meet in the afternoons, after my life-drawing class; sometimes in the evening, if her husband was studying late. We never returned to the Blue Mirror or anywhere else near the Corcoran; not to eat, anyway. Instead she took me to rib joints, an Ethiopian place in a storefront out on Georgia Avenue, a Japanese place where I ate sushi for the first time. Occasionally I'd hang out with people from school: another painter named David Fletcher; Tiny, a heavyset red-haired girl a year older than me who partied with a local band called the Bad Brains.

"So you got some kind of thing going with Clea Anersson, or what?" Tiny asked me once in the Corcoran's lobby. "I thought she was married."

"We just hang out," I said. "I like to draw her."

Tiny squatted on the floor beside me. She poked her hand into my bag and withdrew my makeshift portfolio, two pieces of cardboard tied together with a typewriter ribbon I'd found on the street. She undid the grimy ribbon and began to examine the scraps of paper and brown paper bags inside.

"These are all yours?" Her brow furrowed as she gazed at a portrait of Clea, naked, her body striated like a zebra's. "They're really good. They're like—I don't know what they're like. This thing you always do—"

She pointed from one torn sheet of paper to the next. On each I'd superimposed a blurred charcoal image over the original pastel drawing, so it looked like a double exposure, or as though the page had gotten wet. "That's really cool. Like a broken mirror or something."

"When I was little I had a bad astigmatism. Seeing double. I had my eyes operated on but I can still see things that way. Like this—"

I let my eyes go out of focus so that the world shimmered and split, Tiny's face superimposed upon the wall behind her even as she laughed and raised her hands.

"Stop, stop! You're crossing your eyes!"

"I know." I grinned and let my vision snap back into focus. "I used to think I could do magic like that. Like curse people. The evil eye."

Tiny laughed again, then looked over at me, puzzled. "Why aren't you ever in class? I thought maybe you just didn't have the chops for what we're doing, but . . ."

Her voice trailed off. She stared at the sketches in her hand, finally slid them back between the cardboard covers, returned the bundle to me, and stood. "You should be teaching that life class. Not her."

Week after week, Clea and I looked at paintings, not just at the National Gallery but also the Washington Project for the Arts and d.c. space. Divey places where we could drink and where I ate more stuff I'd never heard of: hummus and spring rolls, mussels in garlic and white wine.

"What, did you live on Fritos back in Norville?" Clea shook her head, sipping her wine while I scarfed down papadums and vindaloo at the Taj Mahal.

"Pretty much. Pancakes and Karo syrup—my mom used to make that for dinner a lot."

"What's Karo syrup?"

"And fried potatoes. I dunno what Karo's made of. Sugar? And potato chips smashed up in cottage cheese. That's really good."

"White trash food." Clea laughed. She leaned across the table, close enough that I could smell her, jasmine and cigarette smoke. "Right? You little white trash wild girl. Give me some of that vindaloo."

She paid for everything. Afterward we'd lie in my squalid room on Perry Street, the window open to let in the scents of car exhaust and honeysuckle, kids from the nearby projects carrying boom boxes that trailed funk and go-go, a bass pulse that kept time with the beat of my blood. The truth is, I didn't care much one way or the other about sleeping with Clea; what I wanted was to capture that sleek, detached beauty on a wall or page or fold of canvas. I thought of my father deer hunting back home, before my mother left: how he'd be gone for a day, sometimes an entire weekend, only to return empty-handed, his old Remington cradled in his arm like a puppy. He never bagged anything, but he never looked happier than when he'd seen a buck in the woods, or spied on a feeding doe beneath his tree stand.

"You never saw anything so beautiful, Merle," he told me once, popping a beer. "That doe just came right up and browsed, so close I could've done like that—"

He let his hand rest gently on my head, just for an instant. "That's how close she was. I could smell her breath. Like sweet fern."

"How come you didn't shoot?" I asked.

He sipped his beer. "I could have," he said after a minute. "Easy. But then I wouldn't have been able to watch her. I decided I'd rather just look."

That's how I felt about Clea. She knew a lot about artists, and I liked going with her to the Hirshhorn Museum, and listening to her talk about people I'd never heard of—weird names, Rothko, Ruscha, Miró—and some I did recognize, like Andy Warhol and Picasso. And I liked that she liked my work, though it soon got uncomfortable in my life-drawing class, where I knew some of the other students were aware of our relationship.

Mostly I just loved drawing her obsessively, stretched across the mattress, her hair silvered with cigarette ash, sweat pooling in the declivity around her navel. She was so beautiful, and I loved it when she was asleep and didn't even know what I was doing. It was like sketching the ocean then, or clouds, something unfathomable that momentarily could be seen through the haze of smoke and dust in my bombed-out room. I painted the walls with acrylics I stole, painted the door. Once I painted the floor around the mattress while she slept. She woke, panicked—she was late to meet Marc—and threw a fit because the paint hadn't dried yet.

"Goddamn it, Merle, I have to go!"

"So wait five minutes, it'll be dry."

She swore furiously, grabbed her bag, and tried to jump over the wet spots. She didn't make it.

"You stupid, *selfish*—" She staggered to her feet, a grid of gamboge and black across one leg of her designer jeans. "You and your redneck shit."

What Clea really hated was that she couldn't take along the floor. Whenever she left my room, whatever I'd drawn that afternoon went with her—paintings, sketches, portraits done hastily on wadded-up paper bags, torn cardboard. I don't know what she did with them. She lived in Potomac, a ritzy suburb. In all the months we were together I never saw her house, never met her husband.

I didn't complain, not about her taking my sketches, anyway. It seemed like a fair shake. She picked up the tab, bought my dinner at places where we wouldn't run into anyone she knew; paid for my cigarettes and gallons of cheap bourbon from Central

Liquor, pastel pencils and drawing paper, charcoal, oil pencils, tubes of paint and brushes, Magic Markers.

And in April, she took me to New York City for a long weekend.

"Marc's got a bunch of interviews in Chicago. Get your stuff, meet me at Union Station. A friend of mine's got a fellowship at Berkeley this semester; we can crash at her place in the Village. There's a train at five. I'll meet you after I get done with my Wednesday seminar."

We arrived in a downpour. There was trash in the streets, rats humping along the curb outside Grand Central while a scummy little river rushed past, filthy water carrying cigarette butts, wads of newsprint, a child's sneaker. The air smelled of roasted chestnuts and hot dogs, marijuana smoke drifting from a darkened doorway, the wet-laundry reek of steam hissing from manhole covers. I huddled beneath an overhang while Clea snagged a cab, ignoring the shouts of a businessman running up behind us.

"Hey, that's *mine*—"

We piled inside, and she slammed the door in the man's face.

Clea's friend had a loft downtown, in an abandoned warehouse turned into studio space for artists, spare steel-and-brick cages crosshatched with rooms and tunnels assembled from plywood, cardboard, rusted metal culverts, chain-link fences, all of it ringing with music pumped from dozens of boom boxes and turntables. A different beat from D.C.'s bass-heavy go-go: faster, louder, metallic—voices synthesized so you couldn't tell if it was a man or woman singing, human or robot. It was the sound of things falling apart overlaid with the shriek of things being put together—welding torches, canvases hammered out of scrap wood and torn clothing, old TVs and Bakelite radios cannibalized for machines designed not to move but to explode.

The Corcoran's studios and classrooms had been a monastery, muted and orderly. This was a madhouse forge, sparks flying everywhere and everyone dressed for some crazed masquerade in tatty crinolines, neon-yellow jumpsuits, uniform jackets covered with plastic flowers, leather loincloths, corsets and bondage pants and Lycra tube tops. A girl wearing a dress made from an American flag handed me a mirror with some white powder on it and a straw.

"We're going to Hurrah later, if you wanna come."

Clea seemed nonplussed by it all. "I liked her old place better," she said, surveying our sleeping arrangements: a car's passenger seat atop a mound of unwashed clothing, surrounded by chicken wire.

"Makes my place look pretty good," I said.

"No kidding," she said, and pulled me onto the makeshift bed.

Those were radiant days, sun streaming through the scrim of new leaves on the ailanthus outside and igniting dust in the air once the rain stopped. I thought we'd go to the Museum of Modern Art and the Metropolitan. Instead Clea took me to a bunch of galleries downtown, which were less like galleries than squats with an open-door policy. Tattered sofas and chairs, overflowing wastebaskets, skinny guys and girls hanging around in a haze of cigarette and pot smoke. There was stuff on the walls, sometimes in frames, usually not: penciled scrawls, blobs of viridian and cadmium-yellow acrylic. Once Clea sank into an armchair leaking foam stuffing and with a curse leaped up, the seat of her jeans torn by a spring poking from the upholstery.

Some places were like the insides of people's apartments, scabbed kitchen counters overlaid with clay or multicolored layers of paint that had dried like dripping candle wax, refrigerators and stereo speakers kitted out with knitting needles, animals twisted of coat hangers and mesh. After I'd seen two or three, I realized they *were* apartments. Saturday night we attended an opening where a guy wearing a kilt made of aluminum foil served drinks in laboratory equipment—test tubes, beakers, stuff like that. In the middle of the room a toilet had been filled with chocolate mousse. There were no paintings, only hundreds of columns of text painstakingly written on the walls in colored pencil and Magic Marker. When I tried to read them, I found they were in an invented language of symbols and ideograms, tiny characters that spelled out some arcane history that would never be deciphered and, according to a xeroxed press release, would be painted over the next day.

It reminded me of the D.C. Metro, where I'd gaze out the window of some nondescript train car and see another world rushing past. I loved that feeling. In New York, Clea wanted to take cabs everywhere. But there were some places where cabs refused to go, so we took the subway.

And I discovered graffiti.

I'd seen it before, of course, in D.C., painted on the sides of housing projects and beneath underpasses, on crumbling walls in decaying neighborhoods like Shaw and on bridges, like that Beltway overpass near the white spires of the Mormon temple where someone had spray-painted SURRENDER DOROTHY. The D.C. Metro had opened two years before; the trains only ran until midnight, and a round-the-clock cleaning crew washed down the subway cars each night, inside and out, erasing every trace of graffiti: every tag, crew name, aerosol blip, and penciled phone number.

Here in New York, though, that chemical army had not yet been successfully deployed against the battalions who bombed subway cars in rail yards and lightless tunnels.

"Holy shit," I breathed as we stepped onto a stinking subway platform. A group of boys carrying boom boxes loped past, weaving between concrete pillars and a broken pay phone. From the tunnel's black mouth echoed a grating shriek that grew deafening, a relentless hot blast that flattened my hair and sent a whirlwind of newspapers and grit flying into my face.

I rubbed my eyes and shrank from the platform's edge. On the opposite side of the tracks, a train abruptly ground to a halt in an ear-popping frenzy of brakes. Grimy windows gave a glimpse of the crowd of people inside, thronging toward doors that opened onto the platform opposite.

But all I could see were the outer walls of the cars that faced me, gray sheet metal lost beneath a hallucinatory whorl and splatter of bubble-painted images—names, cartoon faces, numerals, clouds, lightning bolts, arrows—in an explosion of fuchsia, cerulean, acid green, black, barn red, turquoise, sunflower yellow.

Before I could even register what I was seeing, the train ground back into the tunnel. Minutes later another thundered past without stopping, a bright blur like those luminous spots you get when you press your knuckles against your eyes. Glowing letters erupted in the air and faded as the train roared into the darkness. When our train finally arrived, Clea and I elbowed our way into the car and sat. I looked around eagerly.

I was disappointed: here the walls and seats were covered with crude scrawls in Magic Marker and black ballpoint. Obscenities, names, phone numbers, and addresses covered advertising posters whose logos had been defaced with childish renditions of genitalia. It was grim and dispiriting, like a noisy, moving high school bathroom, and I quickly hurried after Clea when we reached our stop.

Outside a warm wind scattered white petals. A faint smell of the sea mingled with diesel exhaust and cigarette smoke. The sky was a brittle, lacquered blue, and you could see more of it. There weren't as many tall buildings here, though in the distance I could see the twin monoliths of the World Trade Center. The streets were wider, the sidewalks littered with broken bottles and burst trash bags. There were no taxis but a lot of trucks and, surprisingly, limousines. Old men were passed out in doorways; young guys, too. A swaybacked mongrel nosed at the hand of a girl my age with tangled platinum-blond hair. She leaned against a shuttered storefront and stared at us with glassy blue eyes, a life-size Barbie doll in a ripped fifties cocktail dress and one high-heeled shoe.

"The drugs here are so bad." Clea pulled me close to her. "It's like a goddamned war zone."

We walked past vacant lots and blocks where buildings had collapsed into piles of broken brick and plaster. Ragged figures huddled around a pile of smoldering mattresses, passing a brown bag between them. The graffiti here seemed less defiant than desperate, illegible zigzags or black starbursts on crumbling walls and sidewalks.

Then I began to see the messages.

SAMO© AS AN ESCAPE CLAUSE

That was the first one. On the next block I saw another.

SAMO© AS AN END 2
VINYL
PUNKERY

And then a third:

SAMO© SAVES IDIOTS AND GONZOIDS

I stopped and gazed at dripping red letters on a plywood wall. I realized I'd seen the same name near the warehouse where we were staying, painted on a bench, trash cans, the door to a street church.

"Who is SAMO?"

Clea shook her head. "No one knows. Some graffiti guy. It's *Same*-o, not *Sam*-o."

"What does it mean?"

"You know. 'Same-o, same-o.' Same old shit."

"SAMO." The name felt like an incantation. I traced the

letters slowly, the splintered wood rough beneath my fingertips. "So it's a person?"

"Like I told you, no one knows. But yeah, it's some guy with nothing else to do. Come on, we're almost there."

"There" turned out to be the corner of a long, low building of gray stone. Its windows had been covered with huge rolls of white paper on which someone had printed NEMO GALLERY in big red letters. The door was propped open with a headless mannequin, also painted red, wearing a red T-shirt with the gallery name on it.

Inside smelled of fresh paint. About a dozen people stood talking and staring at a series of sheets of plywood covered with broken glass—wine bottles, liquor bottles, shards of plate glass, pressed glass, jagged bits of cut crystal.

It was like staring into a landfill. I wondered how the glass stayed on the plywood—Krazy Glue? Bondo? Whatever it was didn't hold all that well: a woman shrieked as a wedge of green glass fell at her feet and shattered.

A dreadlocked man in his twenties ran out with a push broom and began sweeping up the glass. I picked up a pebble-size chunk that landed near my foot. The bottom of a beer bottle—Rolling Rock.

"That'll cost you two grand." I turned to see a slight woman dressed in black. "Kidding!" she said.

She plucked the broken glass from my fingers and pocketed it, looked up to see Clea beside me, and squealed. "Clea! My God, you've left the provinces!"

Clea laughed as they hugged. The guy shook his head, gave me a sympathetic grin, and went to empty a dustpan full of glass.

"Anna, this is Merle Tappitt. Merle, Anna Greenhouse." Clea took my shoulder and pushed me forward. "Merle's one of my BFA students. She is *amazingly* talented," she added. "Right up your alley, I think. Very . . . unspoiled."

I stood as Anna Greenhouse gazed at me, her head cocked as though she surveyed a puzzling canvas. She was tiny, smaller even than I was; fine-boned, with pale skin and a small mouth lipsticked in deep mauve, and glittering eyes fringed by spidery lashes. The sort of woman people often describe as birdlike, only she reminded me not of a sparrow or wren but of a shrike, which farmers call the butcher-bird, because it impales lizards and grasshoppers on barbed-wire fences. She wore a very short, black silk sheath, sheer black stockings, and high-heeled alligator shoes of glossy emerald green. Her only jewelry was a pair of emerald earrings, each faceted stone the size and shape of a gecko's eye.

"She's so young," she said, and gave me a tight smile.

I shrugged. I knew what she saw: a slight, boyish girl with cropped black hair and a freckled face—no makeup—my hands jammed into the pockets of an ink-spattered pair of white paint-er's pants, wearing a kid's *Star Wars* T-shirt I'd found on the street and red Keds repaired with electrical tape.

"And when is young a bad thing?" retorted Clea. "Especially with you?"

Anna's tight smile turned into a humorless laugh. "What kind of work do you do, Merle?"

"I dunno. Paintings and stuff."

Anna glanced impatiently at the door, gestured at two director's chairs beside it. "Okay. Let's see what you've got."

"I don't have anything—" I began, but Clea cut me off.

"Here." She pushed me toward the chairs, opened an Etienne Aigner satchel that resembled a doctor's bag, and pulled out a leather portfolio. She thrust it at Anna, who perched delicately at the edge of the chair, her pointy green shoes tapping at the floor.

"Hmmm." She unzipped the portfolio and flipped through the pages inside. "Hmmm. Hmmm. Hmmm. Hmmm."

I shot Clea a dirty look. "Those are my drawings."

"Of course they're your drawings." She pointed at a close-up of her own sleeping face, lips parted to show a single eyetooth, needle-thin as a cobra's fang. "That's me. Good, no?"

"Very good." Anna's voice was without expression. "Very—hmmm. Sort of Southern gothic, don't you think? You're from the South, right? That accent."

"I live in D.C."

"Yes, but your accent—Alabama? Mississippi?"

"She's from the Shenandoah Valley," said Clea. "Virginia."

"Oh. Appalachia." Anna held a drawing in each hand, as though weighing them. One was a whirlpool of tiny print, words I'd copied painstakingly from an automobile-repair manual; the other was a series of concentric circles done in colored pencil and ballpoint, sketches of microscopic eyes so small you'd need a magnifying glass to see them. "I like these. Kind of a rural tantric,

Antonioni feel. But nice draftsmanship. I'll take these two." She hopped to her feet, green shoes clattering.

"They're not for sale."

Both Anna and Clea stared at me as though I'd spit on the floor.

"None of them's for sale."

Anna regarded me coolly. "I only want these two."

"They're mine," I said as Clea glared.

Anna looked from one of us to the other, and gave me an icy smile. "Of course they are," she said, handed them to me, and turned to Clea. "Don't bring any more hicks here, okay? And buy her some clothes. She looks like a refugee."

She strode across the room to greet someone. I grabbed the leather portfolio from the floor and stormed outside, giving the headless mannequin a shove. It fell with a hollow bang, so that Clea had to step over it to chase after me.

"What the hell was that?" she yelled, grabbing my arm.

"What the hell were *you* doing, trying to sell my stuff?"

"I was doing you a favor! And she's right"—she snatched the portfolio from my hand and stuffed it into her satchel—"you *are* a hick. Stupid little white trash kid who isn't even smart enough to know she's getting a break. People would kill for that, you know? Anna Greenhouse wanting their work—"

"Give it to me." I tried to grab the portfolio. "It's mine, give it—"

I knew I sounded ridiculous, screaming in the middle of the

sidewalk like a three-year-old, but I didn't care. Clea stared at me, flushed. One of her combs had fallen so her hair sprang around her face in snaky coils. She pushed it from her forehead, sighed, and withdrew the portfolio again.

"Here. Put the others in there before they get damaged. She's right, those are the strongest."

I shoved the drawings into the leather folder and stuck it into my bag.

"Come on," said Clea. "We need to get ready for the train."

We walked for several blocks without speaking. More messages floated across burned-out buildings:

SAMO© 4 U
SAMO© ANTI-ART!
SAMO© DO I HAVE TO SPELL IT OUT!!

On the next block, I froze, staring at a painted window.

SAMO©
FOR THE
URBAN RED-
NECK!!!

I turned and raced back down the street to where I'd seen a hardware store. Clea gave chase and caught up with me as I hurried back out.

"What are you doing?" she demanded. I pulled an aerosol can

from the side pocket of my painter's pants and retraced my steps to the corner. "Oh my God. Did you *steal* that paint?"

SAMO©
FOR THE
URBAN RED-
NECK!!!

"I don't believe in this." I yanked the top from the spray can.

"What are you talking about? Why did you steal that—I have money! Are you out of your mind?"

"'Same old, same old.' That's bullshit. No 'SAMO.' Everything is new."

I shook the aerosol can, then sprayed a daffodil-yellow arc across SAMO's tag, and a sun like a rayed eye surmounted by swooping letters as long as my arm.

RADIANT DAYS

"You're never supposed to do that, you know—paint over someone else's graffiti. 'Radiant days'?" Clea wrinkled her nose at the smell of paint. "What does that mean?"

"Rural tantric," I said, and started laughing. "I'll explain it later."

I turned and ran toward the subway entrance.

4

Near the Brussels–Charleroi Canal

OCTOBER 7, 1870

IT WAS LATE afternoon by the time he left the Green Tavern, still intoxicated by the sunlit joy of an afternoon all to himself, poems in his pocket and the memory of the blond waitress's sly smile as she waved good-bye. On the outskirts of town he found a path that led across fallow wheat fields. He followed this until it faded into the encroaching beech woods. Beer and a full stomach made him drowsy; after an hour or so he made a bed from the spicy fronds of sweet fern, threw himself across the fragrant greenery, and within minutes was asleep.

When he awoke it was dark. He rubbed his eyes, trying to remember where he was, stumbled to his feet, and carefully picked his way through the trees, until he emerged onto a long sward that gave way to a well-trodden trail—the towpath that ran alongside the Brussels–Charleroi Canal.

Overhead a moon nearly full shone in a sky the deep lacquered blue of an apothecary jar. Owls hooted in the woods. He heard a nightjar's twanging cry, the sharp bark of a fox. The air smelled of distant woodsmoke, crushed acorns, and wild grapes. Above the canal, skeins of mist gleamed like milk in the moonlight.

He headed to the canal's edge and stared into the dark water. His reflection gazed back, face pale as the moon, his eyes ice-bright. He rummaged in his coat pocket and pulled out a small bundle. With great care he removed its flannel wrapping, until at last he revealed the clay pipe Leo had given him in Mazas, along with a small tin of matches and a handful of tobacco leaves he'd pinched from the tobacconist in Charleville.

He lit up, sucking at the pipe as he began to walk along the tow-path with a trail of smoke behind him. The canal wound beneath the trees, the stones alongside it slick with moss and fallen leaves. After a few minutes, Arthur knocked the ashes from the pipe, and stuck it back into his coat pocket.

"Got any more smoke?"

He looked up, startled. An old man stood at the edge of the canal. A *clochard*—a tramp. He held a fishing pole above the sil-very water.

Arthur nodded. "Sorry—I didn't see you there. Here." He dug back into his pocket for the tobacco. "You're lucky, I just got some on my way out of town."

The old man handed his fishing pole to Arthur. "Hold this." He withdrew an ancient, wood-stemmed pipe from a pocket of a coat as ragged as it was voluminous, patched with leather and stained cloth and what looked like fish skin. He took a twist of tobacco from Arthur's pouch and poked it into the bowl with a blackened thumb missing most of the nail.

"You need a light?" Arthur fumbled in his own pocket, but the man only grunted. One finger moved swiftly in the moonlight; there was a blue flare, and the tramp inhaled greedily as he passed the pouch back to Arthur and took the fishing pole. Arthur stared at the glowing ember in the pipe's bowl and frowned.

"How'd you do that?"

"Practice. Where you going?"

"Belgium. Charleroi."

"Belgium?" The tramp snorted. "Well, better than Paris. Everyone's leaving Paris because of the war."

"That's why I'm going. I'm a writer."

"That's good." The tramp coughed, then spit. "Writers need lots of practice at starving."

He flicked the tip of the fishing rod, watched the line sail above the canal then land with a soft *plop* near the far shore.

Arthur bent to pick up a chestnut, smooth beneath his calloused thumb, and stuck it in his pocket. "Why are you fishing in the dark?"

"Full moon's good for carp. Three days before, three days after." With one hand the tramp dug into the folds of his coat and produced a leather bottle, scabbed and filthy as his hand. He prized the cork from it and took a swig, handed it to Arthur.

"Don't drop it, boy."

The fiery liquor burned through him, harsh and resinous and so strong that Arthur choked. Still, when the tramp passed the bottle a second time, he took a longer pull before returning it.

"Hush!" the tramp exclaimed, though Arthur hadn't spoken. The fishing pole arced toward the water like a diviner's wand. The man hopped away from the bank, grasping the pole with both hands, and with one quick motion yanked it upward. A silver-gold comet trailed after it, sending out sparks that spattered Arthur's face. The tramp dropped the pole and caught the comet before it struck the ground: a flopping carp the size of a small cat.

"Hand me the pail, boy."

Arthur picked up a battered tin bucket filled with water. The tramp dropped the carp into it. The fish twisted and turned upon itself, flashing goggle eyes and scales large and thick as fingernails before settling into a sullen coil at the pail's bottom. Arthur stared at it, fascinated.

"Do you eat it?"

The tramp made a noncommittal gesture. "I tend them."

He picked up the bucket, slung the pole over his shoulder, and began to walk toward the woods. After a few steps he glanced over his shoulder.

"There's a lockhouse." He cocked a thumb in the direction Arthur had been headed, spit, and continued on his way.

Arthur nodded thanks and walked on. Repulsive as the carp had been, it made him think of food, and the fact that he'd had nothing to eat since early evening. He wandered from the canal path and kicked through fallen leaves, looking for chanterelle mushrooms, and gathered a few orange trumpets that gave off a musky smell when he picked them. He ate them, searched until he found a handful of beechnuts, peeled away the spiny shells, and chewed the bitter kernels. He wished he had more of the tramp's liquor to wash them down.

He yawned, shivering, and wondered where to sleep. He hadn't seen a farmhouse or barn for hours. The tramp had said something about a lockhouse, but he saw no sign of it, and he was too tired to go on. He found a hollow between some beeches not far from the canal, gathered a heap of dead leaves, and covered these with armfuls of dried ferns. He lay down and breathed in the sweet scents of bracken and beech mast, ink beneath his fingernails, tobacco.

Branches moved against the face of the moon as it slid toward the rim of the world. Something splashed—feeding carp lured by the moonlight, or perhaps a hunting mink. A fox barked, its fitful cry wound about a memory of the tramp's voice—*I tend them*—and the rustle of the chill night wind in the trees. Arthur dug his hand into a pocket and found the chestnut, closed his fist around it as he fell asleep.

> *I journeyed beneath the stars, my faithful Muse,*
> *And oh, what marvelous loves I dreamed!*
>
> *. . . My inn was the Great Bear;*
> *I heard the sweet rustling of stars and sky*
>
> *There on the roadside,*
> *Those sweet September nights where I felt*

The dew on my face like strong wine
And composed poems among eerie shadows,
My weathered bootlaces for harp strings,
One foot beside my heart.

Another hand seemed to move beside his own; the tramp's eyes flickered into those of the girl at the Green Tavern, now a man, now a woman, now a carp that wriggled into a boy as Arthur cried out in his sleep and vainly sought to clasp it to his chest.

5

Washington, D.C.

APRIL—OCTOBER 1978

EVERYTHING PRETTY MUCH went to hell after the trip to New York. Clea was pissed I'd screwed things up with Anna's gallery. I was pissed she'd shown my pictures without asking me first. Three months later, we were still fighting over it.

"What'd you think, you were going to take your trained redneck to the big city and make a million dollars?"

"Don't be an idiot. That could have been your ticket out, Merle."

"Out of where? I like it here."

"You would."

I ignored her and squatted on the floor of my room, cleaning the nozzle of a can of yellow spray paint with a safety pin. I'd stopped drawing much, stopped going to classes, the end result being I got bounced from the Corcoran even before the semester ended. I still hadn't told my father, not that I'd spoken to him since Christmas. Clea looked tight-lipped when I broke the news to her.

"Maybe you're next," I said, staring at the dismissal notice I'd received from the Dean of Students.

"You think that's funny? You'd like that, wouldn't you?"

"No. I just thought, you know, probably they're gunning for you and maybe you should be careful."

"God, I hope not. Marc would kill me. What a mess."

Still, she wouldn't stop seeing me. Less often now, as the summer passed, and we didn't go out to eat as much. I still didn't have a job; fortunately, by now I'd paid off my share of the Perry Street rent. To get by I scrounged change from D.C.'s myriad fountains, wading in after dark and pocketing handfuls of wet quarters and dimes. I quit smoking. Most of my meals came from the roach coaches outside the National Gallery, hot dogs with sauerkraut and a Snickers bar. Painting supplies I stole from hardware stores or auto-supply shops, though after a while I got paranoid. People were starting to recognize me. Once I had to dump a bunch of brushes and leave when I noticed a guy following me through the aisles. I started taking the 80 Metrobus over the District line to Maryland, and hit places in Mount Rainier and Hyattsville. Sometimes I'd bomb the Dumpsters behind Giant Food or Peoples Drug, and once I bombed the wall of a seedy apartment building in Queenstown frequented by biker drug dealers and students from the University of Maryland.

But most of my time I spent in Northeast D.C., where I'd paint my tag along the plywood barriers that surrounded the construction sites for new Metro stops. I tried to hit places that could be seen from a moving train, or near the bus routes shuttling people to and from work in parts of the city where the subway didn't run yet—Anacostia, Shaw, Georgia Avenue. These were sketchy parts of town back then, just as Perry Street was. The gentrification that would overtake the city was just beginning to creep toward the old riot corridor along H Street, and even Capitol Hill could be a dicey place after dark.

That's what I loved about the city, though, and that's what I loved about tagging: not just the rush of danger and hide-and-seek with the cops, but people living their lives where you could see them, the way you could back in Norville, sitting on their front stoops smoking and talking, the tropical explosion of pink and orange geraniums in window boxes in Anacostia; old men drinking on the street corners, and kids dancing to the boom and talk-back of go-go at the Washington Coliseum. I wasn't stupid; I knew I was a skinny white girl in parts of the city where white girls didn't go, especially if they had a Greene County accent; but I knew when to keep my head down and when to meet a gaze head-on, nod, and keep on going. I wore my baggy painter's pants with the deep, saggy pockets, where I hid cans of spray paint and fistfuls of change. After I bombed a place I'd hightail it to the nearest Metro station and hop on the first train back downtown, so I could stare out the window and see my tag rising from rusted sheet metal or broken brick, a rayed sunburst and goldenrod letters: RADIANT DAYS.

It's impossible to imagine now, but back then almost no one was doing graffiti in D.C. You'd see half-assed scrawls under bridges and around the projects, but they were mostly locker room stuff. So when RADIANT DAYS started showing up everywhere in OSHA yellow and orange and gold, it was like the way the desert blooms after a year without rain: improbable, garish, miraculous. The *Georgetown Voice* even did a feature, called "Radiant Daze," wondering about the guy who left his mark throughout the city. People wrote letters after that, some of them complaining about the rampant vandalism, others defending the work because it was "raw" and "primitive" and "vital." Nearly everyone offered suggestions as to who the artist/vandal was— someone recently sprung from prison, or a group of streets artists from New York, or a disgruntled federal employee from the Department of Transportation.

No one thought it might be a skinny white girl from Greene County, Virginia.

Still, after a while I had company. I started to see other tags—cool "disco" dan; Snoop, whose double *O*s became eyes in a Kilroy-type face; gagc, the Georgia Avenue Go-Go Crew.

I never ran into any of them, and I was always respectful of their work. I never again bombed over another artist's tag the way I had SAMO's, though sometimes I'd see a big black *V* painted over a tag, the mark of vandal squads from the DCPD or Amtrak. This meant the cops knew who you were, and a later *Voice* story talked about raids on people's homes, cops busting in to confront parents over their kids' hooliganism.

But it was too late by then to stop the flow of words and images on the streets and buildings. You might as easily try to recapture all the tiny seeds from a windblown dandelion, before they fell into cracks in the asphalt and gave birth to a thousand miniature suns.

I'd just started cleaning another can of spray paint when

Jasper, one of my roommates, stuck his head in the door.

"Oops, sorry," he said when he saw Clea. No one knew what to make of her, with her expensive clothes and gold hoop earrings. Everyone had heard about the husband. "Just wanted you to know that Kosowski came by and said the place got sold. So we're now officially evicted."

"Shit." Kosowski was our landlord. He'd warned us that a developer was interested in buying the Perry Street house; they wanted to tear it down to make way for condos. "So now what happens?"

"Nothing." Jasper lit a cigarette. "We can pretty much squat here as long as we want without paying rent."

"Until they turn the electricity off," said Clea.

Jasper shrugged. "We can use candles."

"And the water."

"That would be tough," Jasper said.

Sure enough, at the end of August the electricity was shut off. Jasper and his girlfriend moved out, and over the next few weeks so did everyone else, as they found new apartments and headed back to school. Those last weeks were a long, drawn-out party, with people smashing empty bottles in the living room fireplace and doing lines off the kitchen counter. I didn't indulge much in either. I'd seen what drinking did to my father back home, and while I'd liked being up for forty-eight hours in New York City, the notion of being sleepless in an increasingly disintegrating D.C. frame house with no running water wasn't as appealing.

After the fall semester began, Clea rarely came by Perry Street anymore. Instead we'd meet at the east wing of the National Gallery, beneath its huge Calder mobile. I loved it there. Even on rainy days, the east wing was filled with light: with its vast windows, angled walls, and glass ceiling, it was like being inside an enormous prism, a kaleidoscope filled with people rather than colored glass. I wanted to look at this painting by Jackson Pollock called *Number 7*. It reminded me of the graffiti I'd seen in the New York subway, seemingly random loops and whorls of spattered black.

I stuck my face as close to the canvas as I could and caught a whiff of the pigment he'd used, more than twenty-five years before.

"Why do you think he called it *Number Seven*? Was there a *Number Six*?"

"I don't know. Maybe." Clea glanced around impatiently. "Look, do you want to get something to eat? I need to talk to you, and I have to meet Marc at one."

We went downstairs to the cafeteria and got lunch, sitting at a table in the corner.

"Look. This is really hard for me, but . . ." Clea sucked the last of her cheesecake from a fork and sighed. "I have to end this."

"The cheesecake?"

"Don't be obtuse, Merle. It's not funny. I can't see you anymore. I have to—Marc's been offered a job out in Chicago, and we're moving. Not till December, but I've got to start getting things organized to go, plus I have my class and . . ."

She stared at her plate; gave me an odd, almost furtive look; and smiled. "I'm pregnant."

"What?"

"I'm pregnant. We've been trying for a long time, and to be honest, maybe the timing isn't perfect with the move, but, well, I'm really happy."

I stared at her, too stunned to say anything. The furtive smile grew smug. She tucked a curling strand of hair behind one of her feathered combs, and added, "I know—I don't look it, but I'm eating like a pig. I've gained seven pounds."

"I don't get it. You're—you said you hated him. And now you're—"

I shoved my chair back. People turned to stare at us.

"Stop," hissed Clea. "Don't make a scene, okay?"

"A scene? You don't want a scene?" I grabbed a plate, saw a security guard observing me from the other side of the room. I set the plate down. "I want my pictures. All of them, whatever you hid away. Get them."

Clea laughed. "What, you think they're in my bag?"

"I don't care where they are. I know you kept some hidden away someplace. I want them."

"I really don't think I have anything, Merle, but if they turn up while I'm packing, I'll mail them to you." Her voice sounded prim and high-pitched. "I mean, if I can even find you. I guess I can always send them to your father back in Dogpatch."

From the corner of my eye I could see the security guard heading toward us. For a moment I stood there, trying to summon a devastating comeback that would make Clea swallow that simpering smile and tell me it was all a joke.

I knew it wasn't. Clea had used me, just as I'd used her. The last year had been like some prolonged game of chicken. Somewhere in the back of my head, I always thought that I'd pull away first, and that would somehow make me the winner.

Instead I'd lost my scholarship, my squat, most of my work, and now Clea. And at that moment I realized what had mattered most.

"You should get a job, Merle. Get a decent haircut and some clothes, go home to Norville. There must be an art store or someplace like that. Maybe in a year you could enroll in community college."

"I have a job."

"Vandalizing vacant lots isn't a job, Merle. Drawing on walls isn't a job. Teaching is a job. Washing dishes is a job. You don't need a BFA for that."

"Bring my drawings to the house." I was so angry my voice shook; it was an effort to keep from throwing my coffee in her face. "They're mine and I want them back."

I turned and walked out of the cafeteria. Janis, the last of my roommates, had taken off that morning, having finally convinced her boyfriend to let her live with him in Adams Morgan. I'd left my bag back at Perry Street; the drawings I'd done most recently were in it, some sketches of Clea along with a few detailed, mandala-like images, eerily beautiful refinements of the rayed eye I used as my graffiti tag.

But I was too upset to return there right away and face an abandoned house. I could admit that most of my passion for Clea had been fueled by my obsessive desire to paint her. What was harder to accept was that I had cared for her, too: her knowledge of painting and sculpture, the way she'd laugh and gently correct my mispronunciation of words I'd only ever seen on the page; her generosity in sharing the cultured world she'd had access to for her entire life, with its foreign films and exotic food, the sinuous music I had no name for but learned was Miles Davis.

Most of all, the fact that she alone in the entire world had seen my work and understood it in a flash, without needing any explanation or excuse for what was on the page before her. She thought my paintings and drawings were not just beautiful but important, enough so that she was still trying to keep them.

In some way that I could neither wholly understand nor articulate, I believed that was a far more powerful bond than mere love. And yet it was a betrayal as well, because we both loved my paintings and drawings more than we ever cared for each other—a perverse love triangle: Clea, me, and my work.

I didn't understand yet that it was possible to love someone *through* art. I only knew that I was alone, even if it was my own choice; and the one person I had believed could see me through the wall of pigments and pens and paint that I had constructed around myself was gone.

6

Near dawn, Brussels–Charleroi Canal

OCTOBER 8, 1870

IT TOOK HIM a long time to fall asleep, between the sound of wind and the steady purl of water in the canal, twigs poking his stomach and the bristly touch of dried bracken like an unshaven cheek against his own. When he finally dozed, he dreamed of a silent bombardment along the ramparts of the Place Ducale back home in Charleville. His sisters ran toward him with their mouths open, screaming soundlessly.

Arthur! Arthur!

He jolted awake and lay frozen with terror.

A rippling curtain of green and azure split the sky, rent by crimson flares that streamed from horizon to horizon. Gold sparks leaped above the trees, darkened to scarlet then violet then deepest indigo, a blazing veil that consumed itself only to spiral up from its own embers in plumes of emerald and black.

The Prussians!

It was the only thing he could imagine: that Prussian soldiers had burned Charleroi and were now marching through the forest. He sat up, heart pounding, and heard a strange crackling noise all around him—a horrible sound, as though the surrounding trees were made of ice and had been struck and shattered.

But the noise didn't come from the trees.

And it wasn't cannon fire. It came from the sky, from the sheets of green and violet snapping and lashing across the heavens, driven by a wind that roared from someplace behind the stars.

He stumbled to his feet. Above him a celestial river spewed flames of yellow and violet. He shook uncontrollably, overcome by an emotion beyond terror or astonishment, something that hardly seemed a feeling at all, but a new color or smell. He gasped and shut his eyes—the fire still blazed—opened them to gaze into a sky that mirrored the inside of his skull.

The veil between himself and the world had been ripped away. He was everything, nothing. He was someone else.

He threw his head back. The crackling noise faded, but the iridescent storm raged on.

Aurore boréale, he thought. The northern lights.

He stood enthralled. When a shrike called hoarsely he started, and realized that the greening on the horizon wasn't spectral flame but dawn. Slivers of gold flickered above the canal, like a cloud of minnows darting through the sky, and were gone.

Cold wind dried his cheeks. A cock crowed. He rubbed his eyes and brushed dried leaves and dirt from his clothes, and walked unsteadily toward the canal, where he knelt and splashed water onto his face. When he straightened, he looked around and glimpsed something that loomed from the shadows a few yards off, tucked into the trees near where he'd seen the tramp.

A lockhouse.

He frowned. He couldn't imagine why he hadn't seen it the night before. He walked to the heavy oaken door, knocked tentatively, then yelled a greeting. When there was no reply, he shoved the door open and went inside.

The single small room held a cot, a chair, a table with the keeper's logbook on it. An oilcloth coat dangled from a peg. The cast-iron stove was cold. Above the bed hung a plaque with a simple motto carved into the wood: *Dieu me conduisse*. God guide me.

He searched but found no sign of food. With a yawn he flung himself onto the cot and pulled the thin blanket around his shoulders. He didn't bother to remove his boots.

Filaments of azure and gold continued to flash at the corners of his vision. His ears buzzed, as though he'd stood too close as the lock's mechanisms were engaged, with their roar of gears and water sluicing through the gate. He stared at the plaque above his head, after a minute withdrew a stub of chalk from his pocket, and wrote on the wall: *Merde à Dieu*, his customary obscene scrawl. Beneath that he drew a crude sun with an eye in its center. He burrowed his face into his sleeve, and slept.

7

Washington, D.C.

OCTOBER 8, 1978

I ENTERED THE underground passage that connected the National Gallery's east and west wings. Clea didn't follow me. Neither did the security guard. I stepped onto the moving sidewalk, still a novelty in those days, closed my eyes, and imagined traveling from one world to another. Not as stupid a notion as it sounds: the east wing contains mostly twentieth-century art, whereas the older west wing is all the stuff that put me to sleep when Mrs. Caldwell showed us slides back in high school. Landscape paintings, still lifes, gloomy portraits of people in clothing so uncomfortable-looking that the dejected subjects appeared to be facing a firing squad. There were almost no woman artists other than Mary Cassatt and Grandma Moses.

When the moving sidewalk came to an end, I trudged upstairs and began to wander through the galleries. I didn't glance at the paintings on the walls, though I did a quick surveillance of one of the fountains and when no one was around scooped up some change, which I shoved, dripping, into my pocket. A noisy group of schoolkids clattered into one of the corridors, and to avoid them I ducked into first one room and then another, until I finally reached a room that had no one in it, not even a guard. I sank onto the wooden bench in its center and for a long time stared at the floor. Finally I stood. I started to retrace my steps back into the corridor, then stopped.

On the wall hung a painting. Small, about two feet wide, oil on wood. At first it seemed like an ordinary landscape—blue sky and clouds and trees, a little hut with people sitting or walking outside it, also a tepee. In the distance loomed a castle and, even farther away, a city encircled by a winding river or canal. There might even have been more cities—I couldn't be sure.

Because when I really started to examine the painting, I saw that nothing in it was ordinary. A pair of legs protruded from the roof of the hut. On the ground, a group of people appeared to be carrying a giant fish—only the fish had legs. There was a wingless bird like a kiwi, and tiny, goblin-like people hiding in the hut's roof, and other people who were all legs. What I had at first thought to be a tepee was really an immense man—a giant—with a jug on his head. Another jug hung from a tree, although closer perusal made me wonder if it wasn't a jug but a birdhouse.

And the trees! They were amazing—at once beautiful and mysterious, and so realistic that I drew my head beside the panel and held my breath, listening, as though I might hear them stir in the wind.

"No touching, please."

I jumped as a guard called to me from the doorway. "Sorry," I murmured, and reluctantly took a step back.

I didn't want to touch that painting. I wanted to be *in* it. The panel was like a door in the wall, or a window, opening into that strange other place.

And it *was* strange. Things floated in the air above the canal, people and creatures like spiders, only too big and with the wrong number of legs. A boat sailed through the clouds with a man in it. He wore a pointed cap and waved at someone else, who rode a seal through the air.

I couldn't stop staring at it, this surreal world within a world, familiar objects out of scale or utterly out of place. A flying seal? Who the hell would have painted *that*? The painting's label said only that it was done by a follower of Pieter Bruegel, the famous Flemish painter from the mid-1500s. The title was *The Temptation of Saint Anthony*, but even that made no sense—there was no one who looked remotely like a saint, and nothing that seemed in the slightest bit tempting, unless you had a taste for hallucinogens.

I wandered around the rest of the room, but there wasn't much else to see. A single Hieronymus Bosch, a few musty-looking old saints and madonnas. I returned to the panel, stood as close to it as I could, and just stared. When the guard stepped momentarily out of the room, I ran my finger across the painted wood. I traced the line of the canal with its glinting pewter surface, a pale glaucous sky that resembled the sky outside. Even though the painted trees were green, their canopies summer-full, the scene had a charged, autumnal feel: an October sense of the world spinning too fast for me to catch it, before leaves and clouds and canal and sky were all snatched away.

The guard stepped back into the room. I moved away from the painting, but stopped when I noticed something I hadn't seen before.

A man stood in a hole in one of the trees. An old man, dressed in gray, his head surrounded by a gray hood. He was smiling, hand outstretched to touch a bucket with a knife balanced on it. The bucket appeared to be floating in the air, and something dangled from the hole in the branch—a large key, suspended from a chain or thread.

"Don't touch the paintings!"

I backed away. Behind me a group of tourists paraded in, led by a docent who stared at me pointedly until I moved aside.

"Dutch and Flemish paintings from the sixteenth and seventeenth centuries," she announced, and I left.

I went back to the place on Perry Street. Now that I no longer had the distraction of that strange painting, the final rupture with Clea hit me hard. I walked slowly from the Brookland Metro station, dreading the moment when I'd turn the corner and see the abandoned house.

Yellowing ginkgo leaves drifted against the front steps like hundreds of tiny, discarded paper fans. A stray cat dozed in the sun, stared at me through slitted eyes before crawling through a gap in the concrete foundation. There was an acrid smell from where guys had been pissing outside after the water was shut off.

I fumbled in my pocket for the key, but when I reached the top step, I saw that the door was ajar.

"Hello?" I stopped myself from calling Clea's name, instead made my voice sound as loud and confident as possible. "Jasper, that you?"

Inside was dark. Chilly afternoon light spilled through the filthy windows. I stepped over empty beer bottles, a stained pair of drawstring pants I recognized as my own. It was colder than outside and stank of wet cigarette butts, with an underlying reek of sour beer and sewage. Someone, presumably Janis, had written BYE MERLE across a wall pleached with mildew.

For the first time, I felt a stab of fear. I couldn't stay here alone, in the dark and cold, with police sirens going off all night and the ceaseless throb of traffic outside. There was no telephone, no electricity; nothing but the rustling of feral cats in the basement, hunting the rats that had taken over once the power was shut off.

But I had nowhere to go. Even if I'd wanted to return to Greene County, I didn't have money for the train or bus. I drew a shaking breath and headed for the steps to my upstairs room.

Someone was there. I gasped, too shocked to scream, as a slight figure flung himself down the steps, knocking me against the wall as he fled. Before I could straighten, a second figure barreled past me.

"*Run!*" he shouted, and I recognized him—Errol, a boy of twelve or thirteen who lived at Edgewood Terrace, the projects a few blocks away. He hung around the 7-Eleven, and I used to say hi to him and his friends when I'd go there to buy Snickers bars.

"Errol!" I yelled.

He paused in the doorway and stared straight back at me with his head cocked. Something dangled from his hand. I pointed at it, then lunged at him.

"That's my bag!"

The boys turned and clattered down the steps. I chased after them, and almost fell as I skidded down the steps to the sidewalk. The boys were already at the end of the block, racing across Michigan Avenue and laughing as they looked over their shoulders. A bus pulled over at the corner. I started to dash across the street, halted, breathless, as the light changed and traffic roared toward me.

By the time I finally reached the other side of Michigan, the bus, and the boys, and my bag, were gone.

"Bring it back!" I screamed.

Everything was in there—everything that Clea hadn't taken, anyway. Sketches, a book filled with drawings, wads of paper where I'd drawn bleary-eyed passengers on the Metro, homeless people on park benches, rough sketches for new tags.

But no wallet, no money, no credit cards or checkbook or ID: nothing that would have made the old canvas bag valuable to anyone but me.

I swore and began to cry, but there was no point. The bus was long out of sight. My only hope was that the boys might leave it on the seat or dump it wherever they got off. I wiped my eyes and ran back across the street, up the steps of the house, and on up to my room.

The place looked ransacked, but it had looked that way forever. As far as I could tell, nothing had been taken except my
bag, not that there was anything to take. Some T-shirts and flannel shirts, dirty sheets and pillows, a mattress on the floor, cans
of spray paint. I picked among these, shaking each can until I
found one that was mostly full. I set it aside and kicked at the pile
of clothes until I found a pair of painter's pants, a long-sleeved
T-shirt, the old leather bomber jacket I'd bought at a thrift shop
months ago but never worn.

I pushed a broken chair against the door and changed. Then I
crossed to the windowsill and gingerly felt around inside the fist-
sized hole in the wall beneath it, until my fingers closed around
the plastic change purse wedged inside. I removed it, dumped the
coins on the floor, and counted them: thirteen dollars and twenty-
seven cents. I put the money back into the change purse and
shoved it into a pocket, went to the ancient tackle box that held
my art supplies, sat cross-legged on the floor, and pored over them.

I finally chose a few oil pencils: jade green and viridian and
Moorish red; a cobalt that, when mixed with Moorish red, turned
a startling violet; Alizarin crimson; coal black and narcissus yellow. I took some charcoal pencils and an orange marker; some
expensive brushes I'd stolen. A sketchbook the size of my hand,
its first few pages covered with rough drawings of eyes but otherwise blank. I tore a piece of flannel from a gray plaid shirt and
rolled the oil and charcoal pencils inside it; tore the sleeve from
the shirt and slid everything else into it, tied off the ends, and
stuffed it into the deep pocket of my pants. The sketchbook went

into another pocket, along with the nearly full can of yellow spray paint.

I stood and surveyed the room. Light sifted through the windows, amber deepening to russet in the corners. Across the walls and ceiling, Clea's painted image slept and laughed and danced, her long eyes fixed on mine, her mouth parted to murmur a secret no one would ever hear. Like the leaping forms of ibex and bison and mammoths, flowing across the walls of an undiscovered cavern: a lost world that no one but me would ever know had once been real. I pressed my hand against the wall, for an instant let my cheek rest upon Clea's profile, those lovely, empty eyes that stared into the darkening room.

Then I split. I took the stairs two at a time, and left all the doors open behind me. When I reached the sidewalk I stopped and turned, with all my strength hurled the key at the vacant house, and raced across the street to catch the 80 Metrobus, the same one the boys had taken.

I grabbed a window seat near the door and pressed my face against the glass, scanning streets and sidewalk. I didn't see anything that resembled my bag, or anyone who looked like Errol. The bus rumbled down North Capitol Street, past the old post office and the sandblasted hulk of Union Station, cut alongside the Mall, and headed toward Northwest. The seats and aisles grew crowded with people, carrying briefcases, Sunday newspapers, shopping bags from Hecht's and Woody's. A skinny guy with a Mohawk shambled on board, pushed his way to the back of the bus, asking for change.

"Get a job," I said.

He looked at me and laughed. "Sure. You hiring?"

He jumped out at the next stop. I watched him go and thought, *My bag is gone, and I'm never getting it back again.*

At the next stop, an old woman pushing one of those little foldable grocery carts struggled to get into the aisle. I stood quickly.

"You can have my seat. I'm getting off here."

I didn't look to see what stop it was; just hopped out, elbowing past a line of people waiting to get on. I walked with my head down, paused at the corner while the light changed, and hurried across. When I got to the other side, I glanced at a street sign.

I was in Foggy Bottom. I stomped through a flurry of pigeons picking at a hamburger roll and climbed onto an empty park bench. My heart jounced as a woman who looked like Clea walked toward me, face down so I could see only her corkscrew hair; she lifted her head to gaze at me with incurious blue eyes in a bland freckled face. I turned away.

Crowds straggled onto the sidewalk, people emerging from fast food joints and the hushed restaurants where politicians and lobbyists met to shake one another down for favors. Traffic clogged the streets, Yellow Cabs and buses and cars that inched toward the suburbs, spilling snatches of music: "Bootzilla," "Le Freak." A blue Impala stopped in front of the bench, windows open so I could see a red-haired girl behind the wheel, singing along with a tune blasting from WGTB.

". . . fallen in love with someone, fallen in love with someone, ever fallen in love with someone . . ."

Traffic surged forward, and she was gone.

I stepped down from the bench, staring into a sea of taillights. On the near horizon, I could just make out the yellowing tops of trees beyond the K Street corridor. The wind shifted, and for an instant the stink of exhaust and grease mingled with a green cool smell, the scent of damp stone and moss: the Chesapeake and Ohio Canal. Clea and I went there sometimes to walk. Once we'd come across an overgrown culvert, on the far side of Georgetown, near Key Bridge and shaded by maple trees and sumac.

"Check that out," I'd said, and peered inside. It was bricked up about ten feet from the entrance. There was no sign of anyone living in it, which struck me as strange, considering all the home-less people in D.C. But then, some Vietnamese guy came here after the war and lived for years in Rock Creek Park near the zoo without anyone knowing.

It was a long shot that the culvert would be unoccupied. Still, if it was, it would be a good place to crash. The traffic stalled again, and I threaded my way through buses and cars, heading toward the C&O. The canal begins in Georgetown and goes on to Harpers Ferry and Cumberland, miles away. In the District, it runs parallel to the Potomac River, with a towpath behind shops and restaurants and old warehouses. You see a lot of jog-gers there, and sometimes old men fishing. The canal is full of carp—gigantic goldfish, actually; for some reason, people like to toss goldfish into the canal. They get fed along with the ducks and pigeons, and the carp just keep growing. Once I saw one as big as a cat.

I walked to where M Street narrows. Not as narrow as the cobblestone alleys in upper Georgetown, where you can imagine what the city looked like a hundred years ago; but it still always feels like you're entering a different place, a city inside the city. Part of this is because there's no Metro station in Georgetown— the rich residents never wanted anyone from the rest of the city having easy access to their little golden world. I despised those people, which made Georgetown a prime place for me to leave my tag—the *Voice* article interviewed a bunch of folks who were totally apeshit over the fact that someone was leaving graffiti on their nice brick walls.

On my left, side streets sloped toward the Potomac, on the other side of K Street where it runs beneath the elevated White-hurst Freeway. Its green river smell wafted up to me: even now, in the fall, it smelled a bit like spring. I turned and headed for the river.

Steel girders arched overhead, echoing with the steady roar of the freeway, and traffic flowed smoothly along K Street. It was dim, with a crumbling sidewalk and an old warehouse that took up most of a block, its brick face broken by garage bays and delivery entrances.

That wall was a blank canvas waiting to be bombed with an aerosol can. Behind me, K Street traffic continued to move quickly. No one would have more than a few seconds to catch a glimpse of me throwing up my tag. I chose a spot near the corner, so I could make a dash if I had to; grabbed the spray can from my pocket, shaking it and removing the cap in one swift motion;

pointed the nozzle at the wall; and in a few deft motions drew Day-Glo yellow waves, a fiery eye rising from a golden sea.

RADIANT DAYS

I capped the spray can, shoved it into my pocket, and danced back a step to get a better look. My sun blazed from the brick like a neon sign. I covered the image with my palm, fingers splayed to fit inside the sun's rays.

Directly behind me someone honked. I whipped around and saw an old Imperial cruising past, its driver craning his neck to observe my work. He gave me a thumbs-up, then gestured to a police cruiser a few cars back, shouting, "Better move your butt!"

The Imperial stopped, leaving enough space for me to dart in front and weave through traffic. Horns blared as I jumped onto the curb. I glanced over my shoulder to see the Imperial already out of sight and the cruiser's cherry top flashing.

I turned and fled, head down, praying the cop had lost sight of me. I'd never been so brazen before—tagging a wall in George-town in broad daylight was heady stuff, and the rush of adrena-line spiked into exhilaration that I'd gotten away with it.

I saw no more sign of the cop, and after a few minutes I slowed and tried to catch my breath. In front of me was the Potomac, its oak-brown water flecked with sunset confetti, crimson and glittering gold. A narrow strip of scrubby park ran alongside the water, a tangle of sweetgum and ash trees, sumac and goldenrod still heavy with dusty yellow blossoms. Knotweed and spiky grass grew to the river's edge.

Clea had told me the city wanted to sell this land to developers and put up buildings or a parking lot, but they never did. Overgrown and neglected as it was, the place had a strange, expectant feeling to it—an islet unmoored from some far-off place that floated downstream until it fetched up here. There was a single bench, and an old sign telling you not to swim. It seemed as desolate a spot as I could imagine without returning to Greene County.

But I wasn't alone.

At the water's edge, about fifteen feet from where I stood, a solitary figure sat on a large, upside-down bucket, a cigarette in one hand and a fishing rod in the other. A brown paper bag leaned against his leg, a small plastic container beside it, along with a plaid flannel shirt and a second bucket. Even with his back to me, I recognized Ted Kampfert.

I'd never heard of Ted until I started at the Corcoran, where my friend David Fletcher used to bring his boom box to life-drawing class, before he dropped out to become an actor.

"Who the hell is that?" I demanded one morning, as a gravelly voice intoned the same song for the fourth time.

Several people looked up as David said, "That's Ted Kampfert."

"Who the hell is he?"

According to David, he was the biggest, most brilliant burnout who'd ever staggered along the streets of D.C., or anywhere. Years before, he'd been in a legendary band called the Deadly

Rays. At least David said they were famous, though mostly they seemed to be famous for *not* being famous.

"Yeah," broke in Tiny. "Everyone loved the Raisins."

"The Raisins?"

"It's a joke," explained David. "The Rays were supposed to do a gig once, but whoever made the flyers got their name wrong and printed it as the Deadly Raisins. So, like, their really tight fans call them the Raisins. Ted was so incredibly brilliant, you wouldn't believe it. I saw them once and I'm not kidding, he was better than Hendrix."

"Like *you* saw Hendrix," said Tiny.

"I saw that Woodstock movie. Believe me, Ted was better."

Everything I ever heard about Ted was pretty much the same story—that the Rays were a great band but they never made it, mostly because they were a bunch of drunks who would screw up anytime they played, usually on purpose. The band was Ted and his brother and two of their friends from a Catholic high school out in PG County; they'd wear dresses onstage, or perform naked, or dress up as priests. Sometimes Ted would play guitar with a pork chop taped to his leg. David said that after they recorded their most famous album, they got royally pissed at somebody, stole the master tapes, and threw them into the Potomac at Great Falls. The album was never released.

I pointed at David's boom box. "So how come you've got all those tapes?"

"Because Ted recorded all the songs on a little bitty tape player and sold the tape to Marginal Records, and they released it. The rest of the band completely freaked. That's when they threw him out. Some of them still live around here, but they won't even talk to him. Poor Ted."

"So were they, like, punk?" I asked.

David shook his head sadly. "They were everything."

I'd seen Ted a few times since then, always in Georgetown, where he'd shamble along M Street bumming smokes. I'd heard he liked to fish, also that he'd sometimes play his guitar on the street for spare change, but I'd never heard him play.

Now I stood and watched him, wondering if he'd get pissed off if I tried to sketch him. Probably. After a while he took a long drag from his cigarette, leaned forward to toss it into the river, reeled his line back in, and reached for the paper bag. He pulled out a bottle and turned to look at me.

"Huh." He grunted and spit on the ground, took a swallow. His eyes were pale amber, clouded like an old beer bottle. "Is it Tuesday?"

"No. It's Sunday."

"Good. If it's Tuesday, it must be Bellevue. Lookit that."

He tipped his head toward the water. A heron flew past, long legs trailing so they almost touched the surface, like a gigantic mayfly. We watched it disappear in the haze of trees on the far side of the river. Ted took another swig from the bottle and held it out.

"Want a taste?"

I hesitated, then took the bottle, which wasn't a bottle at all but some kind of old leather canteen. Not very hygienic-looking, but seeing as how I'd spent the last few weeks living without running water, I wasn't going to complain. I took a big swallow, immediately choked and doubled over, fighting to catch my breath. Whatever I'd drunk was slightly viscous, and so strong I felt like I'd gulped down butane that had been set alight.

Ted grabbed the canteen from me. "Jesus Q. Murphy, you're a flyweight." He popped the cork back in, shoved it into the paper bag, and lit another cigarette.

"Smoke?" He squinted at me and scowled. "Nah, I forgot. Flyweight."

He was unshaven, his face grizzled gray, his eyes so bloodshot there seemed to be no white surrounding the topaz iris, only red.

"I'm Ted Kampfert from the Deadly Rays." He said it all in a rush, as though that was his entire name.

"Yeah, I know." I spit to get the bad taste from my mouth. "Can I have a cigarette?"

He closed one eye, staring at me like I was the bull's-eye in a target, finally held out his pack. His fingers were cracked, the fingertips scarred and calloused. Some of the nails were black; not with dirt, but as though they'd been slammed with a hammer.

I took a cigarette. Ted drew his scarred fingers together and made a quick motion as though flicking water; held a scant, gas-blue flame to the cigarette's tip, then slapped his palm against his jeans.

"How'd you do that?" I'd seen no sign of a match or lighter.

"Get to be my age, you learn some shit. You cutting high school?"

"No. I'm in college. Was. I got kicked out."

"College? You don't look like a college girl." He shot me that one-eyed marksman's gaze and shook his head. "I woulda pegged you for, what, sixteen? Actually, I might not've pegged you for a girl at all—that hair."

He settled back onto the bucket, picked up the plastic container and popped the lid. He stuck in a finger and poked around, held up a worm as long as a shoelace. "Hungry?"

"No thanks."

I peered into the second bucket. It was half full of water, and in it was a single carp, its scales shimmering from dull gold to gray to bloodred. Its fins fanned slowly as its head broke the surface.

I stepped back, startled. Its eyes were a liquid black and gazed at me with a skin-crawling intensity, utterly unlike the eyes of any fish I'd ever seen. I looked away quickly, trying to regain my composure. "Do you—do you eat them?"

"Eat them?" Ted snorted, amused. "Nah. Too many bones."

"What will you do with it?"

"I don't know yet. I'm still thinking."

The wind blew off the water, the sun obscured by cindery clouds. I shivered. Even in my bomber jacket I felt cold.

"Getting nippy." Ted finished baiting his hook. He glanced at me and held the rod out. "Here, hang on to this." I took it while he pulled on his flannel shirt, then handed back the rod. "Where you from? Charlottesville?"

"No. Greene County, not too far from there."

"Bob Dylan lived in a group house in Charlottesville, you

know that? I lived there with him, same house, this was in the early sixties. Taught him everything he knows. How come you got booted from college?"

"I was in art school. They didn't like what I do."

"Yeah?" He cast a long way out. The worm sailed through the air, then sank beneath dark water. "So what do you do?"

"Different stuff. A lot of graffiti."

I stubbed out my cigarette and pulled the spray can from my pocket, walked to the weathered bench a few feet away. I squatted in front of it and shook the can, carefully began to paint on the slats: a sun glimpsed through Venetian blinds, the pupil of the rayed eye exploding in the middle of one narrow plank, all of it surmounted by my tag. Ted turned to watch me, the pole loose in one hand.

"'Radiant Days,'" he read when I was done. "Hey, I've seen that around. That's you?"

I capped the spray can and scrutinized my work. A shaft of sunlight burst through the clouds, momentarily igniting the bench, and the still-damp paint shone as though molten. I walked to the other side of the bench, stooped, and left my tag there as well, making the letters as big as I could, so they'd be visible from the road. When I was finished, I dropped the spray can into my pocket and walked back over to Ted.

"That's me," I said.

"It's good. Is all your stuff like that?"

"Not all. Some. I like to try different things."

"Got anything I can see?"

"No." I sank onto the brittle grass. A desolate wave overtook me as I remembered my stolen bag, the pictures that Clea had taken. "Someone ripped me off just a couple hours ago. I was squatting at this house in Northeast, there was nothing in it, but these kids broke in and stole my bag. There was no money or anything—all it had was my sketchbooks, a bunch of drawings, stuff like that. Everything else, my girlfriend took."

"Friend girlfriend or girlfriend girlfriend?"

"Girlfriend girlfriend. Well, ex-girlfriend. We just broke up this afternoon."

"Man, you had a worse day than I did, Little Fly." He reeled in his line, grimacing at the empty hook, opened his bait container, and picked through the worms until he found one he liked. After baiting the hook he removed the cork from his canteen and took another swig, then passed it to me. "Here. You could probably use that."

I took a more careful mouthful this time, swallowing it slowly. "What *is* this stuff?"

"Secret recipe. What, you don't like it?"

"No, it's okay. It's just . . . weird."

Ted shrugged. "Tastes fine to me." He took a long pull and handed it to me again. "How come you're squatting?"

I told him about the Perry Street house, and meeting Clea, about going to New York and discovering SAMO and everything that came after: my "Radiant Days" tag, getting kicked out of school, the fights with Clea, and then the final scene at the National Gallery cafeteria.

And maybe it was whatever came out of that canteen, but I

also ended up telling him about growing up in Greene County, my parents screaming at each other while I drew on the floor beneath my brothers' bunk bed, how pissed my father would be if he ever found out I'd dropped out of school—everything. I even told him about the bizarre painting I'd seen before I returned to Perry Street, just in time to watch Errol and his friend run out the door with my satchel.

"That painting was, I dunno." I stared at the river, trying to describe how the image had made me feel. "Spooky. Because it was so old but it also looked kind of like it could have been painted now. Like those prehistoric cave paintings, have you ever seen those? In a weird way they don't seem that old to me."

"That's because you're doing the same thing." Ted cast out, watched the bait plonk into the water, and tugged gently at his rod. "Right? Painting on walls in the dark."

I'd never thought of that. "Yeah, I guess you're right. Huh."

Ted continued to reel his line in and cast out, pausing to light a cigarette from that same odd flicker of blue flame. I stared at inky gray water, the unsettled October sky. Now and then he'd thrust his leather canteen at me and I'd drink and hand it back. The taste never got better—it was like drinking something that had dirt and leaves mixed into it, with a fierce burn like cheap brandy—but I got used to it.

I don't know how long I sat there. An hour, maybe. The memory of the day's events blurred into the image of that strange painting, overlaid upon the scene in front of me: the ragged old man fishing, the twilit river, gold-threaded clouds above the spires and towers of Rosslyn on the other side of the Potomac.

After a while Ted glanced at me and said, "You still here?"

I smiled woozily. "Yeah. Is that okay?"

"Quiet company's good company."

He tied off a new hook and bit the line, spit a curl of monofila-ment onto the grass. "You thinking about your girlfriend?"

"A little."

He shook his head. "You can't look back, Little Fly. You lose everything if you look back."

"I'm not looking back."

"Yeah, well, that's good. Because it's fucking deadly. Trust me, Little Fly. Hand me that bottle, would you?" He glanced over his shoulder at K Street. "Uh-oh."

A police car was in the outbound lane. As we watched, it slowed, then did a quick U-turn.

"Whaddya know," said Ted. "Company. Officer Friendly don't like me drinking with kids."

I lurched to my feet. For the first time I felt really drunk, and Ted grabbed my arm to steady me.

"Okay, listen." He fixed me with that topaz stare. "You know where the canal is?"

I nodded, and he dug into his pocket. "Here. Don't say I never gave you nothing. Look for the lockhouse."

He tossed me something. I caught it and he pushed me away. "G'wan, Little Fly! And don't lose that—it's the only one."

I glanced over and saw the police car stuck behind an eighteen-wheeler.

"Thanks!" I gasped, and took off.

I sprinted across K Street and raced up the side road. When I reached a spot where a mulberry tree hung over the sidewalk, I pushed my way through tangled limbs until I was safely out of sight, and peered out toward the river.

The police car had stopped at the pull-off beside the abandoned park. I watched the cop step out and walk to where Ted stood with his back to the world, fishing rod in hand. He turned as the cop strode over, and the two of them began talking. I waited a minute, extricated myself from the mulberry's branches, and began to walk. When I reached the canal path, I opened my hand to see what Ted had tossed to me.

It was a key. Not an ordinary door key but an ornate, old-fashioned skeleton key. The metal prongs were grimy and nearly black with tarnish, surprisingly heavy for something so small, and extremely sharp. I wondered if they could be silver. The rest of the key was a dull mottled brown, so that at first I thought it was carved from wood. When I held it up to the light, I saw it was a bone. Not a human bone; a fish bone.

I glanced around for a lockhouse. All I saw from the towpath were the backs of brick houses and older, wood-framed buildings, all well-tended: typical Georgetown. None of them seemed remotely like a place where Ted might live.

I kept going, passing a jogger and a group of girls from Sidwell Friends School. After several minutes I stopped to get my bearings.

There was still no sign of a lockhouse. A tall stone wall, overgrown with moss and ferns, hid the streets and buildings of

Georgetown. The land beside the towpath dropped down to a grove of birches. I edged down the slope, my feet sliding on loose gravel and dead leaves, until I reached the bottom.

The air smelled fresher here, wet stone and the spicy scent of bracken. The ground felt springy, the way it does in deep woods. Something brushed my cheek, and for a second I thought it was raining.

It wasn't rain: I'd walked beneath a weeping willow. Branches drooped around me, silver and gold and green in the waning light, so that it seemed as though I stood within a waterfall. The ground sucked at my sneakers, and clear water puddled up out of the moss underfoot.

Next thing I knew, I almost walked into the canal. I swore and staggered back. My sneaker was soaked. I shook my foot, then stopped.

Around me the air grew dark. Leaves faded into a haze like black smoke, but there was no smell of burning. Then, as quickly as the darkness appeared, sunset streaked the willow leaves. Yet something was still wrong.

The canal was in the wrong place.

I turned, frowning. East was where the canal should be, thirty feet from where I stood. And it wasn't just that the canal wasn't where it should have been. Normally the grass around it was neatly trimmed, the banks clear. There might be tossed bottles or trash, fallen leaves and dead weeds; but none of it would build up. The C&O is part of a national park, and the park police patrol it frequently, picking up litter.

It didn't look like the park police had been here in a while.

It didn't look like anyone had. Bushes grew down to the water's edge, and there were moss-covered spaces along the bank where paving stones or bricks had fallen away. Willow leaves floated on the surface, and even that seemed strange, because the water was darker than it usually was, and greener. Not clouded with algae or rotting vegetation but a deep, clear green like the pigments used in watercolors, chrome oxide or viridian. Through the leaves I barely made out a rusty smear of brick, the glint of sun on glass.

I held my breath, and heard the drone and honk of traffic. I was still in Georgetown. Or near it, anyway—the same place I'd been a hundred times, with the same stores and buildings, the same crowded sidewalks and tourists and Metro buses.

Abruptly I wanted to be there again, surrounded by strangers and cement and far away from this strange green place. I pushed my way through the scrim of willow leaves, and saw the stone house.

It was tucked beneath another willow, a tree so huge and gnarled the house appeared trapped in its knobby roots, as though the tree had grown around it. A building not much bigger than a toolshed, its stone walls blotched with moss and lichen, perched precariously on the canal's edge. As I approached, I saw a block of granite wedged between the building and the canal: a stone dock with a rusted iron stanchion for tying up a boat.

Ivy covered the granite, dark-green leaves and tiny yellow flowers. The same vines covered the lockhouse's walls and roof, and the single window that overlooked the water; everything except the wooden door. Paint flaked from the wood, and feathery black mold. In the center was a doorknob with a face on it, eyes and nose rusted away so only the mouth remained. The same face gazed from a metal plate beneath the knob, with a hole in its mouth where a key could fit.

I turned the knob, but it didn't budge. I ran my hand across the doorplate, pressing my fingertip into the tiny metal mouth, then dug in my pocket for the fish-bone key, hesitating before I thrust it into the keyhole.

There are locks everywhere on the C&O, where the water level can be raised or lowered so boats can get through. But I'd never seen a lockhouse in Georgetown before. Maybe it was so decrepit the park police kept it hidden, so people wouldn't break in. It seemed highly unlikely they would give someone like Ted a key. He must have stolen it.

I glanced down at that strangely heavy fish bone with its tarnished silver prongs and, before I could think better of it, jammed it into the lock. The prongs struck something solid. I turned it gently, afraid I'd snap off one of the prongs. It still wouldn't budge.

Then, as though the keyhole really *was* a mouth, it seemed to open wider. Without warning, the key slid forward and twisted to one side. I braced myself against the door and pushed. The wood shuddered and creaked and, slowly, the door began to move, scraping against the floor. I pulled the key out and pushed harder, until the door opened—just a few inches, but it was enough.

I took a deep breath and stepped inside, closed the door behind me, and turned the rusted dead bolt until it clicked into place.

I stood in an empty room, cold and with walls of the same thick gray stone as the exterior. No furniture. No rugs or curtains, no empty bottles or spent cigarette butts or works; no sign that this was a place where Ted might have slept, or homeless people crashed, or teenagers or addicts partied. Nothing except for yellowish dust on the slate floor, and cobwebs and dead flies in the corner, a few brittle willow leaves that crumbled when I touched them.

Yet for some reason it didn't feel abandoned. There wasn't that musty smell you find in empty houses. Instead, I inhaled the same rain-sweet scent as the canal outside, faint as a childhood memory. I crossed to the solitary window, glanced back to see my own footprints in the dust but no others. On the floor was a dark, rectangular spot, marking where a table or bed might once have stood. On the wall above it, someone—Ted?—had scrawled graffiti in white chalk.

Shit on God!

Beneath this was a childishly drawn sun. It looked so much like a crude caricature of my own tag that I flushed: had Ted drawn it to mock me?

But that was impossible. I'd never spoken to Ted before that afternoon, and only Clea and a few of my housemates knew I was the person behind "Radiant Days." I leaned against the wall and stared at the window opposite me, waning sunlight seeping through the filthy glass. Around me dust motes turned in lazy vortices, as though I were trapped inside a darkened snow globe. I eased myself to the floor and closed my eyes.

I must have dozed, waking when the throb of pins and needles shot through my leg. I groaned, then stumbled to my feet in alarm.

On the stone wall glowed a brilliant square, a window I'd somehow missed. But when I looked closer, I saw that what seemed to be luminous glass was actually a square of light reflected from the window on the other side of the room.

The optical illusion was startling. The false window appeared so real it seemed as though it would open onto the woods outside. In the National Gallery I'd seen trompe l'oeil paintings, where the artist fools you into thinking there's a fold of cloth draped across the canvas, or a hidden door embedded in the painting itself.

But I'd never seen anything like that in real life. I pressed my palm against the wall, the stone warm and rough, slightly porous; ran my hand across it to clear away dust and cobwebs. I pulled out my can of spray paint, shook it, and pointed the nozzle at the wall, drawing a yellow arabesque and rayed eye. I signed my tag, set the can on the floor, and stepped back, staring at the image.

Then I reached into my pocket and removed the flannel-wrapped bundle I'd brought from Perry Street. Slowly I unrolled it on the floor. I surveyed the oil pencils, finally picked up the black crayon. I made certain the spray paint had dried, then traced the *A*s in RADIANT DAYS in black, the *I* in Alizarin crimson; picked up the Moorish red crayon and outlined the sun's eye, overlaid this with cobalt so that the colors bled together and a supernaturally brilliant violet eye stared back at me.

I paused, then grabbed the Alizarin crayon and drew first one arc and then another above the blazing words. I thought of Clea and the portraits on the walls of Perry Street: all those paintings that no one would ever see. It seemed right that they'd be obliterated by a wrecking ball.

And suddenly I wished I could destroy those other drawings, all the ones that Clea had taken. Rage fueled me, and fear; loneliness and longing and a perverse exhilaration: because I was here, alone, with no one to see what I drew, no one to judge; no one to critique it or claim it.

I drew as though this might be the last time I'd ever have the chance. I drew for what seemed like hours, the room illuminated by a strange fitful light that seemed to pulse from the words RADIANT DAYS, yellow and onyx and crimson. I heard branches tap against the roof, smelled rust and rain. The ache in my head slowed to the rhythm of my heartbeat and the dreamy sweep of crayon against stone. Only when it finally grew too dim to see did I stop.

In front of me was a whorl of black and red, emerald vines and orange flame, a shifting wheel of shadowy forms like those cave paintings drawn in charcoal and ocher and yellow clay. As I stared, shapes began to emerge from the swirl of color, shapes I'd been only half aware of as my hand moved across the stone: eyes and faces, a hand. Willow leaves and wings, dragonflies and hawk moths.

The longer I looked, the more I saw. Waves, a curve that marked the bend of a river. A crescent moon that was also a boat. The whorl of images seemed to turn, a hurricane brought to life, and the illusion of motion drew my gaze to the center of the painting, where the rayed eye rose from a fiery sea. I reached to touch the center of the eye, and with a cry snatched my hand back.

The stone wall was hot—not sun-warmed, but *hot*. I hesitated, then held my palm a scant inch from the stone.

I wasn't imagining it. The section I'd painted was noticeably warmer than the rest. The center, where the sun was, radiated as much heat as an incandescent lightbulb. Gingerly I touched the eye.

"Shit!"

The wall had *burned* me. My fingertip felt blistered, but the skin was unmarked, not even red. Once more I drew my palm toward the wall. This time it was cool.

I touched the sun-eye: dead cold.

I stepped away and absently thrust my hand into my pocket. A sharp pain shot through my thumb. I yanked my hand out and saw the fish-bone key dangling from it. A silver prong was embedded in the ball of my thumb. Carefully I pulled it out, then replaced the key.

Blood welled from the puncture wound. I turned and pressed my hand against the wall, covering the image of the sun rising from the waves. When I withdrew my hand, a red smear like the imprint of a kiss bloomed across the sun's eye.

I sank to the floor, my head pounding. Maybe I'd imagined that unnatural heat radiating from the wall. The room was now dark. The wind had died, and with it the steady rustling of the willow leaves. Rain pattered on the roof. I cracked the door open and peered outside.

There was no rain. Through the tangle of leaves I saw a sky awash in stars.

I closed the door, yawning. My exhilaration had ebbed with the October light. I felt exhausted. I made sure the dead bolt was drawn, then lay down in front of the door, my head pillowed on my sleeve, the slates beneath me hard and cold as river rock. When I slept, the sound of rain swept through my dreams, and the unblinking gaze of an eye that burned through violet clouds like the sun kept watch.

8

Outside Charleroi

DAWN, OCTOBER 8

LIGHT FLICKERED BEHIND his closed eyelids. Arthur steeled himself against the painful intrusion of morning, but when he opened his eyes, the room was still dim. He held his breath and listened, wondering if someone had entered while he was asleep—the lockkeeper or maybe the tramp he'd seen fishing.

The room was silent. He shifted on the narrow cot, and on the wall above his head saw a swath of silver green, a shining pinwheel spun from the aurora borealis or the watery reflection cast by the canal, sap green, pine silver, minnow bright.

Yet the windows remained dark, and there was no other source of light.

He sat up and rubbed his eyes. The pinwheel shivered and spun, broke apart then joined again like liquid mercury to form a rayed eye rising from a sea, buffeted by waves edged crimson and black.

He didn't stop to wonder if he was dreaming, or still drunk

from whatever it was the tramp had given him: he reached for the wall, covering the image with his splayed palm.

A wave overcame him, a prismatic darkness. His head drooped onto the mattress. His last thought as he plunged back into sleep was that an eye was fixed on him, implacable and radiant as the sun, and that the slate wall had felt strangely warm for October.

PART TWO

STRANGE COUPLE

This time, it's the Woman who I've seen in the City, and I talked to her and she talks to me.

— Arthur Rimbaud, "The Deserts of Love"

9

Washington, D.C.

BEFORE MIDNIGHT, OCTOBER 8, 1978

I WOKE, DISORIENTED, my back aching from the cold stone floor. It was dark, except for a faint gleam from the window. I sat up groggily, then stiffened.

Someone was in the room with me. I held my breath, praying that whatever I'd heard would turn into the soft rustle of a mouse or windblown leaf.

It didn't. I heard a sharp intake of breath and saw a dark shape move on the other side of the room. I swept my hand across the floor, trying to grab something I could use as a weapon, stumbled to my feet and in desperation pulled the key from my pocket, fingers closing around it so that the prongs pointed outward.

"Get out of here!" I screamed, backing toward the door.

The intruder stood, silhouetted against the window, and shouted, "What the hell?"

Only that wasn't what he said. I couldn't actually *understand* what he said—his voice was garbled and heavily accented, and he wasn't speaking English. Yet the meaning was clear, like listening to a car radio trapped between stations, when you catch only fragments of a familiar voice or song or commercial.

Whoever it was, it wasn't Ted. I braced myself against the wall, fumbling for the doorknob as I yelled, "Who are you?"

There was the sharp *pffft* of a match. I sucked my breath in as the figure stepped toward me, face haloed by a flame cupped beneath his chin.

It was a boy. Fifteen or sixteen and about my height, with close-cropped blond hair that looked as though he'd cut it himself in the dark: almost a skinhead, save where unruly tufts stuck out around his face. He shaded his eyes with one hand, the tiny flame guttering in the other, and swore again in that same strangled voice, as though the radio had grown more distorted.

"How'd you get in?" I demanded. "Get out, get out!"

I waved my arms threateningly, but all that did was extinguish the flame. The boy stooped. I kicked out, afraid he'd try to grab my ankles, but there was only the flick of another match being struck. The room filled with a sweetly acrid scent, and I looked down to see him crouched in front of some burning leaves. He lifted his face, the meager flames casting a glow on round cheeks, an obdurate mouth, and very pale, coldly assessing gray-blue eyes.

"Who the hell are *you*?" The words were garbled, the voice a not-quite-broken boy's voice, torn between accusation and wonder. Then it was as though his voice tuned in, like a radio—as though *he* tuned in. I could understand him easily, despite the accent. A dead leaf was stuck to a blondish spike above his left eye. Instinctively I reached for it, and the boy flinched.

"It's just a leaf," I said, and dropped it. I waved away the smoke, coughing. "We should open the door."

I cracked it so that the smoke could disperse, turned to see the boy crouched on his heels, staring up at me with those challenging eyes. I got a better look at his clothes: an ugly overcoat that hung to his knees; dark pants, too short, exposing his ankles; a filthy blue shirt, its cuffs flapping around knobby wrists; heavy boots caked with dirt. His hands were thick-knuckled and raw-looking, big hands for someone so slight. He looked like one of the poorer kids from back in Norville, wearing handmade clothes and daring someone to mention it. He looked like me.

"Who are you?" he said.

"My name's Merle."

"Merle? Merle." He repeated my name as though tasting it, looked at my face, my paint-stained pants, and frowned. "You're a girl?"

"Yes, I'm a goddamn girl. You're a guy, right?"

"Your voice—you sound like a girl. But—" He gestured at my bomber jacket and pants, and gazed at me questioningly.

I stared back, wondering if this was a joke. But he sounded serious. Maybe he was drunk, or tripping. I shrugged. "So where're you from? Are you an exchange student?"

"Exchange?" He shook his head. "I'm from Charleville. The asshole of the universe."

"You mean Charlottesville? I'm from Norville. Greene County. Don't worry, no one's ever heard of it. Maybe the universe has two assholes." I waited for some explanation of his accent, but he continued to stare at me. Finally I asked, "How'd you get in?"

"The door. How did you get in?"

"Ted Kampfert gave me a key. You know him? He hangs out by the river, fishing. He looks like a homeless guy but he's some famous old rock star or something. He knew Bob Dylan."

The boy gave me a blank look, then nodded excitedly. "Yes! I know him—he was by the canal, catching carp. A tramp. He told me to come here. The lockhouse, he said I could sleep here."

"That's what he told me. He gave me this." I held out my hand, the fish bone nestled in my palm. "Did he give you one?"

The boy shook his head, staring at the key enviously, and I stuck it back in my pocket. "So how'd you get in?"

"It was open." He looked past me to where the door revealed a wedge of mist-drenched leaves, brightening from gray to green with dawn. "I'm starving. You want to find something to eat?"

"Yeah, sure. What's your name?"

"Ar-toorr."

"What?" He repeated the name and I frowned. "Spell it."

He jammed a hand into the pocket of his overcoat and withdrew a stumpy pencil and a wad of pages. He wrote something on the corner of a page, angling himself so I could read it. Even in blunt pencil, his signature was surprisingly elegant.

"'Arthur,'" I said.

He nodded again, replaced the wad of paper, and ran a hand across the inch of stubble on his scalp. "In Mazas, they did that," he said. "Shaved my head."

"Mazas?"

"Mazas Prison. In Paris."

"You were in prison? For what?"

"Vagrancy." His tone was deliberately offhand. "And protesting the war, and supporting the revolution."

"Really?" I had no idea what war he was talking about, but I was impressed. "That's cool."

He started toward for the door, then stopped. "What's that?"

The faint morning light fell through the room's single window and rippled across my painting. Arthur stared at it, mesmerized.

"I saw this," he said softly, and touched the rayed eye. "I thought it was a dream."

"No. It was me."

"You did this?" He pointed at my tag. "What does this say?"

"'Radiant Days.' You don't read English?"

"No. Only French."

"Then how can you understand me?"

"Because you are speaking French."

"No, I'm not. You're speaking English."

We stared at each other. After a moment Arthur shrugged. "Maybe we've invented a new language." He turned back to the painting. "It's . . . archaic. Like hieroglyphics. It means something?"

I began to gather my oil crayons from the floor. "I dunno. I mean, yeah, it means something, but . . ." I straightened. "I don't know how to explain it. It's just the way I feel sometimes. Like light. Like I can feel light inside me, and . . ."

I stepped beside him and drew my hand across the stones, the paint and oil pastels slightly moist, like damp clay. "And this is the only way to get it out. You know?"

I expected him to laugh. Instead he stared at the wall for a long time, then nodded.

"Yes," he said. "I feel that way, too. Let's go."

We stepped outside. I locked the door, turned, and looked at the sky in surprise.

It was still night. What I had thought was the pale glimmer of dawn was actually the light from a brilliant half-moon, filtered through dense fog so that everything—tree trunks, willow leaves, even the mossy ground—had an eerie, greenish glow, as though underwater. The muted sound of the canal flowing nearby faded into the rustle of wind in the trees.

Arthur and I started up the long slope, pushing through dripping willow branches. After a few minutes I saw the sulfurous halo of a lone streetlamp. Headlights sliced the darkness as a car sped down M Street, and I stepped from the underbrush onto the sidewalk. I halted when I realized I was alone.

"Arthur?"

I peered back into the overgrown tangle to see him frozen, his face dead white. "Hey, you all right?"

"My God." His voice cracked. "My God, what happened?"

I whirled, expecting to see a shadowy figure with a gun, or a cop.

But the sidewalk was empty. I turned back to Arthur, furious. "What is your problem? Are you completely wasted?"

He struggled through the brambles onto the sidewalk and

walked past me into the street, staring as though hypnotized as a Yellow Cab hurtled toward him. With a shout I grabbed his arm and yanked him safely to the curb. The cab didn't even slow down.

"What the fuck are you *doing?*" I punched his arm. He looked terrified, cringing as another car barreled past. "Are you high?"

"Where are the horses?" he asked in a small voice, and flinched as a third car whizzed by.

"*Horses?* Are you crazy? Listen, you need to calm down, okay?"

I heard the rumble of another vehicle, and shielded my eyes as a car appeared, with lights blazing on top, red and white.

"Shit! That goddamn cop." I dragged Arthur off the sidewalk and into the underbrush. He tried to pull away.

"Let go!"

"*Shut up,*" I hissed, and motioned for him to keep his head down.

The crackle of a walkie-talkie seemed to jolt him: without arguing, he followed me as we pushed our way back through the underbrush, in what I hoped was the direction of the tow-path. When I glanced over my shoulder, I saw the bluish cone of a flashlight slashing through the mist, but as we ran it grew fainter, smaller, until at last it disappeared.

"I think he gave up," I gasped, halting behind a tree. Arthur pressed against me, peering out into the night.

"What was that?"

"Police. Vandal squad, probably—a cop saw me today when I

was tagging a wall down by K Street. They go after people doing graffiti. You know, real threats to society like me. I get ripped off back in Brookland, do the cops give a shit? But no one touches Georgetown with a paint can," I added in disgust. "He saw you playing chicken with that taxi, and then he recognized me. Come on, he can't get a patrol car in here. We'll be okay."

We walked on in silence until we reached the towpath once more. Here beneath the willows everything was dark and still, save for the stirring of leaves. The sound of water in the canal drowned the distant thrum of traffic. I saw no more headlights, just the blurred half-moon shining through the mist. A boulder loomed beside a tree, and I hoisted myself onto it, patting the rock beside me for Arthur to do the same.

"So what happened back there?" I asked. "Why'd you freak out?"

He shook his head, dug into his pocket, and removed a leather pouch. His hand trembled as he opened it and removed a white pipe with a long slender stem, pinched something from the pouch, and tamped it into the pipe's bowl.

Reflexively I glanced around—getting popped for smoking pot would *not* be a good idea. Arthur lit up, striking a wooden match on the side of a small metal matchbox. He folded the pouch, replaced it in his pocket, and took a long pull at the pipe, his face crowned by a bluish, sweet-smelling cloud.

"Is that hash?" I asked.

He twisted the bowl sideways and exhaled. "What?"

"Hash. It smells weird."

He passed the pipe to me. I don't usually get high, but I took a hit, then began to cough uncontrollably. "Ugh, what *is* this?"

Arthur took the pipe back, grinning. "It's tobacco, *imbécile*."

"Tobacco? I thought you had hash! You know, hashish."

"Hachisch?" Arthur choked on a mouthful of smoke and doubled over laughing. "I have *never* met a girl like you."

Me, I'd never seen someone my own age smoke tobacco in a clay pipe. For a few minutes, he puffed away blissfully, eyes half closed. At last he dumped the ashes onto the ground and lovingly put the pipe back into the pouch. "There someplace we can eat?" he said.

"I dunno. Maybe. It's late. Do you have any money? I've only got about thirteen bucks." He shook his head. I thought ruefully of the plastic change purse in my pocket. "Well, maybe it'll be enough for something. But I don't want to run into that cop. If we stay on M Street or Wisconsin we should be okay; there'll be people there. Just don't bolt in front of a cab again or do anything stupid."

"What was that, with the lights?"

"I told you, a police car. What, you don't have cops in France?" He flushed angrily. "Of course. But not trains in the street."

"Yeah, well, they're all over the place here, except when you need them. Like when those kids took off with my bag." We started to walk along the towpath, and I told him what had happened back at Perry Street.

"So now I don't have anything." I picked up a stick and lashed angrily at a bush. "Clea took my best stuff, and those kids stole the rest. It's all probably in a Dumpster somewhere by now."

"They didn't take everything." Arthur tapped the pocket that held my spray can and oil crayons. "Just start over again."

"Sure," I said bitterly, and tossed my stick into the trees.

We reached a narrow dirt trail that led up to M Street, at the entrance to Georgetown. It was nowhere near where I thought we'd come out. Between the moonlit fog and general uncanniness of the last few hours, I'd completely lost my bearings. For a moment I stood in the darkness, just out of reach of a streetlight's sallow glare. Arthur huddled beside me, hands jammed into his pockets, and stared at the stretch of road in front of us, mouth parted and his eyes almost feverishly bright.

The fog had dispersed. The chill autumn wind shook streetlamps and traffic signals, so that the entire block danced with light. Even at this hour there was a steady flow of cars and late-night buses. People spilled from restaurants, from Blues Alley and the Cellar Door, the Biograph and Key movie theaters. Lurid blobs of ultraviolet light glowed in the window of Orpheus Records. A couple leaned against the front of Geppetto's, making out as the manager locked the door behind them. There were plenty of restaurants here, but thirteen bucks would barely get us in the door of any of them.

If they'd let us in the door. I looked down at my bomber jacket, splattered with yellow spray paint, my fingers so crusted with black and crimson oil pastels it looked like I'd jammed them in a blender. Arthur wasn't any better. His overcoat was filthy, splotched with tobacco ash and leaf mold, and his shorn head made him look like one of those skinheads who'd been rioting in England.

"Come on." I sighed and looked up toward Wisconsin Avenue. "I think there's a Miles Long sandwich place here somewhere."

Arthur remained hunched beside a doorway, his expression mingled wonder and horror.

"Where are we?"

"Still Georgetown. Let's go." I started down the sidewalk.

"What is this place?" he shouted after me. "What's happened—what in God's name did you do?"

I groaned. "For chrissake, can we just go?"

He ran toward me, grabbed my collar, and pushed me against a storefront. "Tell me what happened! Tell me what you did!"

I swore and kicked him. "That's it! Get the hell away from me—"

He stumbled backward as I stormed off.

"The moon—Merle, look at the moon!" He ran up beside me, oblivious of a passing couple who glared at us, and pointed at the sky. "It's changed!"

I looked up and saw the same half-moon as before. "No, it hasn't. You can just see it better because the fog is gone."

"No! It's *different*. Before it was full. I know it was, because the tramp said something about how the full moon's best for carp."

"Maybe you just didn't get a good look. I mean, I could barely see it through the fog."

"No! Listen to me—when I left Charleroi last night the sky was clear as water, and the moon was full. I was walking along the canal, *I saw it*." His face twisted into a rictus of fear. "A full moon. I fell asleep beneath the trees, and then I woke up near dawn and saw the *aurore*—"

"The what?"

"*Aurore boréale*. Lights in the sky."

"You mean the aurora borealis?" He nodded, and I sighed, exasperated. "That's impossible. You don't get the northern lights here. It's too far south. And if they had been there, I would have seen them."

I pointed at a bundle of newspapers in front of a shuttered newsstand. "Look, we can check the paper. I can guarantee you, if there'd been an aurora, everyone would know about it."

I walked over and slid a newspaper from the bundle—the *Washington Star*, the evening paper.

"See, the truck dropped these off." I scanned the headlines, flipping to the Metro section. "Nope. Nothing there. I don't know what you saw, but it wasn't the northern lights."

Arthur stared at the newspaper, then jabbed a finger at the dateline. "What does that say?"

"'October 8, 1978,'" I read. "'Sunday.'"

"It's Saturday."

"No, it's Sunday, almost like midnight, but it's still Sunday."

"What does '1978' mean?"

"It's the year." My impatience gave way to unease, the growing realization that this strange boy was genuinely crazy, or maybe something worse. "1978. That's what year it is. 1978."

"No, it's not," he whispered. His gaze darted from me to a

Metrobus trailing clouds of blue exhaust. His pale eyes glazed with fear. "It's 1870." He pulled the sheaf of pages from his pocket, unfolded a piece of newsprint, and handed it to me. "See?"

It was the front page of a newspaper. *Journal de Charleroi, Samedi, 8 October 1870.*

"1870?" I frowned. "It doesn't look that old."

"That's because it's not," said Arthur. "I pinched it this afternoon, from a stationer's."

I moved beneath the streetlamp to get a better look. The paper wasn't yellowed or faded. I pressed my thumb against a column of newsprint, withdrew it, and saw my skin stained black. When I sniffed the paper, I caught a whiff of fresh ink.

"This is so weird." I looked at Arthur. "It's like it was just printed. Where'd you get it?"

"I told you—I lifted it from a place near Charleroi."

"That's crazy." Who would print up a facsimile of a newspaper over a hundred years old? Could he have stolen it from a museum? Though even in a museum, a newspaper this old would show its age. But why lie about something as trivial as stealing a newspaper, unless Arthur was a pathological liar?

In which case, why make the lie so ridiculous that no one in their right mind would believe him?

I handed the paper back. "Why'd you steal it?"

"Why do you think? No money."

"Right." I looked away. His total lack of embarrassment about lying was starting to creep me out, along with that intensely cold gaze. "So, you want to see if we can find something to eat?"

Without waiting for a reply, I started across the street, shoulders hunched against the wind. I didn't check to see if he was behind me. I was hoping maybe he wasn't. I learned in Norville, you never look back if a strange dog starts following you.

But then I heard the squeal of car brakes and a shout.

"What the hell you doing?"

Before I could turn, Arthur grabbed my arm, laughing breathlessly as the car roared off.

"You idiot!" I started laughing, too, as we ran to the curb. "You're going to get killed, you know that?"

Arthur shook his head. "You can't die in a dream. It's impossible—you always wake up right before. I do, anyway."

"You think this is a dream?"

"Who cares? I'm here."

I couldn't argue with that.

10

Washington, D.C.

FOR A FEW blocks we walked without speaking. Arthur stared at everything, especially other people. He'd turn and gape whenever we passed someone who was black, which in D.C. is most of the population. He reacted the same way when we passed a Vietnamese couple, and some teenage girls in skirts up to their ass, and two guys holding hands. Finally I lost it.

"Jesus, stop staring! You're acting like a goddamn hick. I thought you were from Paris."

"Not Paris. Charleville. A shithole in the middle of nowhere."

"But you were *in* Paris, right? You didn't just see it on a postcard or something."

He flashed me an angry look. "Paris is nothing like this. *Nothing* is like this."

I glanced at him, this scruffy kid with his hideous homemade clothes and incongruous baby face. In a way he was beautiful. Not my type, but someone's, when he got older.

He looked at the world like he wanted to swallow it. I was accustomed to paying attention to things that other people didn't notice. A dead sparrow's claws, the way late-afternoon light slanted against the side of a building.

But now I began to see how surreal a stoplight was, strobing from amber to red to green. Plastic bottles, the acid-green wrapper from a bag of potato chips, a broken syringe—all these things are strange and even beautiful, if you look at them long enough.

Once, Arthur stooped to pick up a crushed ballpoint pen. Translucent plastic splintered between his fingers, a bloom of black ink. He turned and pressed his palm against a brick wall, leaving a blotched black handprint.

"There," he said. "Now you."

I looked around. Late as it was, this part of Georgetown still felt exposed and overlit. Not the kind of place you'd bomb, even in the middle of the night. Then I made the mistake of glancing back at Arthur, and got sucked into that blue-gray gaze.

It unnerved me. Young as he was, crazy as he was, he acted like he knew something I didn't, and never would. Clea's taunt came back to me—*Get a decent haircut and some clothes, go home to Norville.*

Arthur would never do that, I thought.

And for the first time I realized, *Neither will I.*

I got out my spray can and shook it, hearing the loose rattle that meant the can was almost empty. With my finger on the nozzle, I felt a rush of adrenaline as neon-yellow paint swirled across the brick wall, a rising sun with a black handprint in its center.

"Yes!" I exclaimed, jubilant.

"Yes!" Arthur swung his arm around my neck and pulled me to him. The empty spray can clattered to the sidewalk and rolled into the gutter. I heard traffic in the street behind us, looked back and saw the familiar crimson blaze of a police car, two blocks away.

I pulled up my collar and steered Arthur along the sidewalk. "Keep going. Keep your head down."

I walked as fast as I could without breaking into a run, but was brought up short when Arthur abruptly stopped in front of the Biograph Theater.

"What?" I said. "We're *not* going to the movies."

I looked up at the marquee: FRENCH NEW WAVE MARATHON. Beneath it was a poster, a black-and-white photo of a girl with very short dark hair kissing an ugly young man in a fedora and suit that were too big for him, a cigarette in his hand. Bright red letters proclaimed *À bout de souffle*.

"We're not going to the movies," I repeated.

Arthur tilted his head. "I like his looks."

"He's hideous." I glanced into the street but saw no sign of the police car. "What's it mean?"

" '*À bout de souffle*.' 'Last breath.' Like a dying breath." Arthur pressed his face against the glass and peered into the lobby, empty except for a man reading behind the ticket counter. "What is this place?"

"A movie theater. They do art films. Foreign stuff." I pointed at the list of titles on the marquee: *Pierrot le fou*, *Les quatre cents coups, Le boucher.* "I went once with Clea; she goes with her husband a lot. Here—"

I pulled him down the sidewalk, to a recessed spot where there was a metal door with a handwritten sign taped to it: KEEP CLOSED FIRE DOOR. "Somebody told me about this. Just keep your mouth shut, okay?"

For several minutes we waited, and were finally rewarded when the door opened and a man stepped out, a smoldering joint between two fingers. He glanced at us and nodded, catching the door before it could close behind him.

"You kids behave," he said as we slipped inside.

I padded down the corridor to another door. Arthur paused to gape at the fluorescent lights buzzing overhead. I yanked him to my side.

"Don't say a fucking word," I breathed. "We could get busted for this, and if you say *anything*, I am out of here and you are on your own. Understand?"

He nodded as I carefully, silently opened the door, gesturing for him to follow me.

We were near the front, a few feet from a row of empty seats. Above us, an exit sign glowed red. Maybe two dozen people were scattered throughout the theater. Some of them looked like they were asleep. On-screen, a black-and-white movie showed the same short-haired girl arguing with the same guy. A white shirt flapped open over his bare chest, and he wore sunglasses even though they were inside a brightly lit apartment. He looked better than he did in the poster, kind of like Mick Jagger. The girl was beautiful. It was a crappy print, the soundtrack rustling with static. The dialogue was in French, and I craned my neck to read the subtitles.

I just talked about myself, and you talked about yourself, the man was saying. *You should've talked about me, and I should have talked about you.*

I glanced at Arthur. He stared at the screen, transfixed, light and shadow washing across his face as the figures moved around the apartment, as though they were performing some strangely detached dance. The man fled the apartment, chasing a sports car in the street. The police arrived seconds later and shot him in the back. Arthur gasped, jumping at the crack of the pistol. The man died as the girl looked on. At the end she turned and stared out from the screen, her beautiful blank face the size of a wall.

"Let's go," I whispered as the credits rolled.

We slipped back into the corridor, joined by a few other people leaving the theater. When we were back out on the sidewalk, Arthur grabbed my hand.

"That's incredible." His face was rapt. "It's a secret?"

I laughed. "Not really. Usually it's more crowded. This is some kind of all-night marathon."

"Merle?"

I turned as someone called my name. "David?"

A figure in a flannel shirt and paisley bandanna stepped over to throw his arms around me: David Fletcher, my friend from the Corcoran.

"*Mon ange,* where have you *been?*" he cried. "I went by the studio one day, and they said you'd dropped out!"

"I got the boot. Flunked out, really."

He shook his head in commiseration. "It's for the best," he said, and we both laughed. David had stayed at the Corcoran for the fall semester but left when he got a walk-on part in a John Waters movie shooting in Baltimore. He was a year older than me, nineteen, with long black hair and a soft-featured face: downy black beard and mustache, slightly crooked teeth yellowed from nicotine. His eyes were lovely—indigo, long-lashed, soulful. He wore a dangling chandelier earring and the bandanna tied, pirate-style, over his head; a blue plaid flannel shirt; and flared jeans that flapped over Converse sneakers that had once been red but were now so encrusted with crud they might have been made of cement.

"I missed you." He kissed my cheek, did a double take when he saw Arthur behind me. "Oh, hello. I'm David—"

David stuck his hand out. Arthur regarded him curiously, then nodded back. "I'm Arthur."

"He's French!" David exclaimed. *"Bonjour, Arthur! Vous êtes français?"*

Arthur took a wary step back.

"He's just visiting," I said quickly to David. "Exchange student."

"Were you homesick?" David pointed at the Biograph's mar-quee. "I just came out to grab a cigarette; I didn't even see you in there!"

"We snuck in," I said. I was trying to decide if it was a good idea or a bad one to stick with David. He always seemed to have wandered in from a different movie from the one that was my own life, which was why it was not really a surprise when he went to that casting call in Baltimore and never came back.

"You snuck in?" David's thick Brooklyn accent gave way to a goofy foghorn laugh at odds with his fey appearance. "Listen, I'm meeting someone—want to walk with me?"

"Yeah, sure. Where you going?"

"Pied du Cochon." David grinned at Arthur. "*C'est un bistro, très bien*. It's open all night, maybe we can get some food."

We headed up Wisconsin. Being with David seemed to confer a sort of invisibility—the few people we passed probably thought we were panhandlers. He talked animatedly about the movies he'd just seen—he'd been in the Biograph since 3:00 that afternoon—but was cagey about who he was going to meet. I understood why when we entered the restaurant, a large, empty room crowded with tables, and a tall older man in an elegant pinstriped suit stood to greet him.

"See you, Merle," murmured David. His hand squeezed mine, and he gave Arthur a good-bye nod. "*Au revoir.*"

The older man embraced David, leaning down to kiss his forehead, then escorted him back out the door. When they were gone, I turned to survey the room. We were the only customers. Waiters leaned against the bar, talking or poring over newspapers. One of them glanced at me and gave a peremptory wave.

"Wherever you want," he called, and turned away again.

We walked toward the back. As we passed a table covered with dirty plates, my hand snaked out to grab some french fries.

Arthur snatched a half-full beer glass and downed it. The fries were stone cold and limp with malt vinegar, but I was so hungry I didn't care.

We settled at a table near the wall. "How was that beer?" I asked.

"Beer is always good. You've got money?"

"Not much."

It was a while before anyone came to take our order. While we waited, we took turns making raids on plates that still had food on them. Arthur polished off the dregs of a few more glasses. When a waiter finally appeared, Arthur glanced at the menu and said something I couldn't understand. The waiter snapped back at him in French, then turned to me.

"Tell your friend he's too young and I will throw him out if I catch him drinking anything else. Do you have an ID?"

"I just want water. And some fries, and I guess some bread." The waiter stalked off, and I raised an eyebrow at Arthur. "What'd you say to piss him off?"

"Nothing. I just asked for a beer."

"Yeah? Nice try. What are you, fourteen?"

"Sixteen," he said hotly. "In two weeks, October twentieth."

"The drinking age here is eighteen."

The food came soon, some fries not much warmer than the leftovers, a stale baguette, and for Arthur a plateful of pigs' feet.

"Ugh? What the hell is *that*?"

Arthur took a bite, pointed at the sign above the bar—AU PIED DE COCHON—and pushed the plate toward me. "Try some—they're not bad. Not as good as my mother's."

"No thanks." I averted my eyes as he began to gnaw at a pig's foot. "The weirdest thing my mother ever made was boiled saltines for breakfast. It was disgusting."

He picked up a second pig's foot. "This place isn't so different."

"Different from what?"

"Everything."

I doused my fries with ketchup. "Well, it's a French restaurant."

"That's not what I mean. All this . . ." He gestured at the window, to where lights shone and flowed with passing traffic. "This *hallucination*. This dream."

"Is that what you think? You're in a dream?" I laughed. "I can guarantee you, this is not a dream. Not *my* dream, anyway."

He cocked his head and recited, "'What if you slept, and what if in your sleep you dreamed, and what if in your dreams you went to heaven and there you plucked a strange and beautiful flower, and what if when you awoke you had the flower in your hand?'"

"That's good." I pushed my plate across to him, and he grabbed some fries. "Did you write that?"

"No. Coleridge. Do you know him? He's fantastic."

"I don't read a lot of poetry. No offense."

"Most of it is shit. Not Coleridge, though. And Paul Verlaine, do you know him? A genius. Everyone else is shit. I wish I had a beer." He polished off the fries. "So, what's your family like?"

"I hate them. My parents, anyway. They divorced a long time ago. I have no idea where my mother is. My father . . ." I stared at my empty plate, drew an arabesque in the ketchup with my finger. "I hate him. I haven't talked to him in months. I'm never going back."

"How did they get divorced?"

"Who knows? It was horrible when they did, especially for my little brothers. But they just fought all the time. My mother was a drunk. Now my father's one, too. I was glad they split up."

"A divorce." Arthur shook his head. "My father disappeared when I was four. I would have run away, too—my mother is a bitch. But divorce?"

"What, people don't get divorced in France?"

"It's a mortal sin!" He gave a caustic laugh. "With my mother, it would have been a good idea. I don't remember my father. He got one thing right: he knew a bitch when he saw one. My mother says he was a drunk, too. Frédéric says he used to let him drink from his cup."

"Frédéric?"

"My older brother. He joined the army this summer. He's an asshole. I have two sisters, Vitalie and Isabelle. They're younger than me."

"My brother's in the army, too. Are your sisters twins?"

"No."

"My brothers are. Roy and Davis. They're twelve now—no, thirteen." I winced. "Shit. I should've called them—I totally forgot, their birthday was last month." I sighed, brushing the hair from my eyes. "Why's your mother such a bitch?"

"All she cares about is money, and me being top student at

school. And working on the farm. It's slave labor, I should call the police on her."

"You live on a farm?"

"In the summers. I hate it, and I hate Charleville." He said it so vehemently that the table shook. "It's a complete shithole, and now you can't even get newspapers or books because of the war. Napoléon's troops, and the Prussians—they screwed up everything."

"Napoléon?" I assumed this was like people continuing to blame Nixon for everything.

"Yes. Frédéric enlisted so he could escape, but I'm stuck." Arthur kicked at a chair. "That's why I took off to Paris last month. Only I got arrested as soon as I got there."

"Is that when they put you in jail?"

He nodded. "I only paid for a ticket that would take me half-way there. When I got off in Paris, I had no money or papers or anything, so they said I was a vagrant." He grinned. "And, you know, they were right. So they threw me in Mazas."

"For how long?"

"Two weeks."

"Jesus." I'd never known anyone who went to jail for more than a night or two, usually for drinking and fighting. "Couldn't you call someone? Didn't your mother bail you out?"

"My *mother*? Christ, I'd rather stay in prison! No—I wrote one of my teachers, and he came and got me. Took him a while."

"You're kidding—a *teacher* got you out of jail?"

Arthur shrugged. "He's useful. I'd never ask my mother for

anything. She's crazy—she used to wait every day outside of school for me and Frédéric, to walk us home. She did that *last year*. At least she's stopped, now that Frédéric's gone. All she cares about is how well I do on my exams." He paused. "I always get first in everything. Except discipline."

"My father's like that too. Totally paranoid if I ever went anywhere by myself; he'd have a heart attack if he thought I was hitching someplace. He'd go through my stuff, my sketchbooks, everything. He didn't even care when I got a scholarship to college—all he cared was it wasn't going to cost him anything. And that I'd be gone."

The waiter made a point of removing our plates and dropped off the bill. I read what was scrawled on it.

"Eleven dollars? Those pigs' feet were *six bucks*!" I counted out the exact amount from what I had. "You have any money? We better leave a tip or they'll come after us."

Arthur fished in his pockets and dumped a few coins on the table. "That's all I've got."

"French money? I don't think they'll take it." I picked up one of the coins, a heavy silver piece with a picture of a goateed man stamped on one side and the words *Empire Français* on the other. The date read 1870, but the coin was smooth and shining as though it had just been minted.

"You should hang on to this," I said slowly, and looked up at him. "This is an antique, right? It's probably worth a lot of money."

"It's worth five francs." Arthur laughed. "Keep if it you want."

We left through the back door and headed across the street. A moment later someone shouted after us.

"Hey! Come back and pay this or I'm calling the police!"

We raced down the sidewalk, darting into the first alley we came to, and cut to another side street before we finally stopped.

"What the hell?" I fought to catch my breath. "I told you he'd be pissed if we didn't tip."

Arthur shook his head and thrust his hand at me. There were the coins I'd left on the table. I stared in disbelief, then laughed.

"And here." With a flourish he pulled something from beneath his heavy overcoat: a bottle, almost full, a cork protruding from its mouth. "Cognac. This'll keep us warm."

"Jesus, you're fast. Thanks."

I pocketed the money, and Arthur made a mocking bow, pointing toward an overflowing Dumpster. "After you."

Behind the Dumpster a narrow alley wound between an overgrown hedge and a brick wall, so encrusted with ivy it was like burrowing into a green tunnel. Moonlight seeped through the tangled branches overhead, and there was a pallid yellow glow from the upper windows of a nearby row house. After twenty feet or so the alley widened into a tiny courtyard surrounded by buildings in varying stages of decay. Cracked flagstones covered the ground, along with dead leaves and several plastic chairs that had blown over. Small tables were pushed against the rear of a warehouse, its windows boarded shut. A tattered CLOSED sign flapped from a door chained with a padlock.

"At least there's no line to get in," I said. I picked up two of the fallen chairs, swiped moldering leaves from their seats, and set them beside the door, out of the wind.

"And no waiter to tip," said Arthur.

We sat, pulling the chairs together. The wind gusted, sending up flurries of leaves as Arthur bit down on the cork, pulled it from the bottle, and took a swig.

"Not bad," he said, and handed it to me.

I drank, my eyes watering. The cognac scorched my throat, not as fiery as whatever Ted had given me, but strong. For a while we passed the bottle back and forth without talking. When Arthur's fingers accidentally grazed mine, he smiled.

"I know what you're thinking," he said softly.

"Yeah, I know," I said, and swallowed another mouthful of cognac.

Around us the moonlit courtyard took on a burnished amber glow. It seemed to burn away something inside me, the toxic fear and rage that had seeped into me during the last few months with Clea. When I thought of her now, I no longer saw the flesh-and-blood Clea but the figure I'd painted on the wall of my room at Perry Street, a woman composed of shadow and shifting light, a woman whose only power came from the pigments and charcoal pencils I'd cloaked her with. Beside me Arthur lit his pipe, his face bright as an ember in the enveloping darkness. A spark fell onto his trousers, burning a hole.

"Look." He brushed aside a wisp of ash. "I invented fire."

He drew on the pipe, then exhaled luxuriously, staring at the gnarled branches that poked above the wall. After a moment he looked at me. "Why do you dress like that?"

"What do you mean?"

"Like a man. You wear trousers, and a work shirt, and this." He flicked at the mangy fur collar of my bomber jacket.

"Everyone dresses like this. I mean, not exactly like me, but girls wear pants all the time. They don't in Paris?"

"Never. That's how you know you're with a woman—you can never find what's hidden under all those clothes."

"I'm not hiding anything."

"I know. That's why I like you." His hand dipped into his pocket, and pulled out the wad of paper he kept there. A page slipped free and I caught it, squinting to read the first line: *Grammaire nationale*.

"Homework?" I asked.

Arthur shook his head. "It was, but I'm writing poems now. I'm a poet."

He smoothed the sheets on his knee, filled with writing in blue ink—real ink, not ballpoint—and a few cartoonish drawings of people. He shuffled pages, then handed some to me. "Here."

His handwriting filled each crumpled sheet. Many words were scratched out, and while I couldn't read French, I could see that the same verses had been painstakingly corrected and copied over and over again. Not just once or twice, but dozens of times.

No one I knew wrote and rewrote like that. I took another sip of cognac and shifted pages from one hand to the other, as though

that might somehow bring meaning to the words. At last I turned
to Arthur.

"I'm—I'm sorry. I told you—I don't understand French."

He gazed at the night sky, finished his pipe, and folded it back
into the pouch. He took the pages from my hand and said, "That's
all right. Listen. This is called 'Romance.'"

"No one's serious when they're seventeen.
—One glorious night, it's good-bye to beer and
    lemonade,
Those crowded cafés all aglow!
You walk beneath the green linden trees on the
    sidewalk.

"The lindens smell sweet on those June nights.
Sometimes the air's so fragrant, you close your eyes;
The wind freighted with noises—the town's not
    far—
The scents of the vine, and beer.

"Then you glimpse a shred
Of deep azure, framed by a small branch,
Pinned by a runaway star, pale and trembling as
It melts away. . . ."

I'd always hated it when people recited poems in school, dron-
ing on or whispering pretentiously in voices that put me to sleep.
But Arthur read as though this was just another part of the

night's long conversation; as though he was speaking to me. I wasn't aware of his voice, or his face; only his words.

> "June nights! Seventeen! It makes you drunk.
> Green sap goes to your head like champagne . . .
> Your mind drifts; you feel a flutter upon your lips,
> A kiss, a butterfly . . ."

I felt as though a veil had been torn away, revealing a landscape at once familiar and unknown. I closed my eyes, and for the first time realized how a poem might be like a painting, each word a brushstroke, a color or flash of motion: words combined the way I mixed pigments, or slashed a sun across a wall in arcs of neon yellow.

> "You're in love. Booked till August.
> You're in love—your sonnets make her laugh.
> Your friends are gone. You're out of your mind.
> Then one night, your beloved writes you!

> "That night you return to the glittering cafés,
> You order beer and lemonade . . .
> —No one's serious when they're seventeen
> And linden trees flower on the sidewalk.

Arthur fell silent. I opened my eyes and stared at the inky sky, a single white star trapped among leafless trees. Somewhere a dog barked.

I drew a finger to my lips. Had Arthur kissed me?

No—he sat with the pages on his knees, and like me stared at the stars overhead. I had imagined it, spurred by the words he'd spoken. The poem's images clung to me like a dream, but someone else's dream, and not my own. It was several minutes before I spoke.

"That was beautiful."

Arthur started as though I'd awakened him; turned and nodded. Carefully, he folded the pages and put them back into his coat. "The poems I'm working on now are better. These are . . ." He paused, frowning. "Old-fashioned. Pretty words and pictures. People want poetry to be a nursemaid. I want to be a murderer and a thief. Art should be like this—" He took my hand, pointing at the fresh scab where I'd cut myself on the fish-bone key. "It should be ugly, and hurt so you can feel it. That's what makes it powerful."

I nodded. "That's what I think! Clea said I need to learn the rules before I break them, but I think that's total bullshit. That's what my tag means—radiant days. Because right now I'm burning and alive, and I don't even fucking know if I'll be here tomorrow. Nobody does. I could die tonight. So I only have this one day to paint, all these radiant days, and when I'm gone my tag will still be there, and my paintings. . . ."

My voice died. I had a flash of Errol running down Michigan Avenue with my bag, of the house at Perry Street reduced to a pile of rubble by a wrecking ball, of the D.C. vandal squad sandblasting graffiti from every brick wall in the city. I shook my head, and said, "It doesn't even matter if my paintings are there. The only thing that matters is that I do the work *today*. That's the only thing I have."

"Exactly." Arthur looked at me, his eyes shining. "Where's that key?"

I pulled it from my pocket and dropped it into his open palm. Before I could stop him, he jabbed one of the silver prongs into the ball of his thumb. He stared as a drop of blood welled, looked at me, and said, "Now you."

I hesitated, then took it and dug the prong into the scab. It felt as though I'd pressed a hot match to my skin. I gasped, dropping the key. Arthur retrieved it, then extended a hand filigreed with blood. He pressed his palm against mine, and I looked down to see dark petals blooming across my hand.

"There," said Arthur. His face was flushed. "Do you know what Plato said? In the beginning there weren't two sexes. There were three: man, woman, androgyne. And each one of them had four legs, not two. Man is child of the sun, woman is child of the earth. But the third sex are people like us, and we are children of the moon.

"The three sexes were so strong that the gods cut them in half. So now each person spends his entire life looking for the missing part. That's why men bed so many women, and why women are never happy once they marry just one man."

"What about the androgynes?"

"They are the ones who can never be satisfied," said Arthur softly. "Because when one of them finds their missing half, they realize that their experience has nothing to do with what goes on between a man and woman. Their yearning is so powerful that no one else can ever understand it. Their souls mingle, and even if their bodies can never again become whole, their souls form one being, and that being can never be destroyed."

He fell silent. Both of us turned to stare at the sky, the moon barely visible now above trees and rooftops.

"Radiant days," said Arthur at last. "And what is this? A radiant night, because our souls set it on fire."

He drew away from me, laughing, and kicked a plastic chair so it flew across the courtyard and crashed into the wall. Seconds later a light flicked on in the next building. An angry voice called down from another window.

"Time to move," I said.

Arthur grinned and pointed into the shadows. "After you."

11

Washington, D.C.

OCTOBER 9, 1978

THE ALLEY WOUND through a labyrinth of back-yards and cobblestoned streets before dumping us back onto M Street, down where the road begins its long curve toward Key Bridge. There was hardly any traffic, just a few cars, and no people except for a handful of figures who stood huddled on the sidewalk a few blocks ahead of us. I was reluctant to pass them, but when I glanced back, the empty black expanse of M Street seemed even more forbidding. I heard the clock from Georgetown University chime once—midnight had passed and I'd missed it. I zipped my bomber jacket and tugged the fur collar around my ears, for good measure looped my arm through Arthur's.

"Stay with me," I said. "Don't say anything. Just try to act normal."

"What? Like you?"

I glared at him, and he shut up.

We hurried on, slowing as we approached the half dozen

people gathered around a streetlamp. Beneath it, a man sat on a dirty white plastic bucket, flanked by a fishing rod and an open guitar case. He was hunched over an acoustic guitar, wearing the same grimy clothes as when I'd seen him that morning.

I halted. "That's Ted."

"That's the man I saw last night." Arthur stopped, frowning. "The tramp. The one who told me to look for the lockhouse."

"That's exactly what he said to me."

We stared at each other, then walked over to the guitar case. A second plastic bucket stood beside it, three-quarters full of water. Two dark shapes moved slowly inside, like a living yin-yang symbol, their scales glittering dull gold.

"Sorry, kids," Ted announced in his gravelly voice. "Technical difficulties, be another minute here."

The body of the guitar had been repaired with duct tape. Ted tuned it, grimacing, reached for an open bottle of beer, and took a swig.

"That's Ted Kampfert," someone whispered. I looked up to see a guy with long hair and wire-rimmed glasses, his arm around a girl wearing a red peacoat. "Know who he is?"

"That guy from the Deadly Rays."

Her boyfriend nodded. "I saw them at the Ontario a few years ago. They were incredible."

"He looks bad," said the girl.

The guy squinted, mimicking Ted's expression. "The years have not been kind to him," he said in a mock-serious tone, and they both laughed.

"Look at him." Arthur nudged me. "He's a troubadour."

I didn't think so. Ted looked like what he was, a homeless man too drunk to stand. Even sitting, he seemed to be having trouble staying upright. His head was bowed so you could see that fringe of gray hair, his badly sunburned scalp. He tapped the body of the guitar with scarred, blackened fingers, and started to play without a word. Everyone fell silent, and he began to sing.

His voice was as hoarse and raspy as his speaking voice, but he didn't sound anything like a middle-aged white man. He sang like an old black man, like someone so ancient it was incredible he still had a voice to sing at all. I couldn't make out the words: something about a man on a river.

But it was beautiful—astonishingly beautiful—and also strange, as though a crow opened its beak to sing like a mock-ingbird. I'd never heard anything like it—that croaking voice and battered face, the scarred fingers dancing across a guitar ban-daged with duct tape. The everyday world fell away like torn sails cut from a shipwreck, and suddenly the ship burst free and I gasped, the cold wind bearing the scent of the sea, of limes, of spilled wine. There was an endless moment when the final notes hung in the air before fading into the night. Then people began to clap and whistle and yell uproariously.

"Thank you, thank you very much," Ted growled without looking up. "You're a lovely audience."

He finished his beer and tuned his guitar again, tipping his head to peer into the little crowd. I stepped off to one side, shy at the thought of being recognized.

Yet he looked past everyone and gazed at me as though the two of us were alone in a small room. He didn't smile or wink, or act surprised. He just stared, his expression impossible to read. Before I could move away again, he rasped, "This is a song for a little friend of mine I just met."

People looked around to see who he was talking about. Arthur pulled me to his side, his heavy overcoat enfolded about us. The song was by Bob Dylan, the one about the girl who's an artist; Ted sang it with his head bowed, his expression invisible from where I stood.

Yet even if he hadn't said a word, I would have known the song was for me—a gift, like the way he'd pointed at the heron the previous morning and said, *Lookit that.* I couldn't make out all the words. I felt on the verge of sleep, and more awake than in my entire life. Then he sang the refrain, and I remembered what he'd told me when we first met.

You can't look back, Little Fly. You lose everything if you look back.

He lifted his face to the night, to where the moon hung above the Potomac, and squeezed his eyes closed, his voice breaking, then turned to stare at me again. A flash of greenish light slid across his eyes, like reflected lightning; but from where?

Because the flare wasn't in his eyes. It was *behind* them, as though Ted's face were a mask. For a fraction of a second someone else had gazed at me, staring through Ted's eyes as if they were knotholes in a fence—someone whose eyes were green, not topaz. I shivered uncontrollably as Ted's voice swelled to fill the air above the sidewalk, above the street, drowning out every other sound—traffic on Key Bridge, distant voices, the ceaseless churning of the Potomac River.

The guitar fell still. There was nothing but a raw wild voice that trembled at the edge of a scream, and at last died away. I heard the people around me gasp. A girl was crying, and a man repeated a woman's name in a choked voice.

Then everyone went crazy, whoops and whistles as Ted nodded, unsmiling.

"I didn't write that song," he said. "But I taught the guy who did."

People laughed. They kept on clapping and calling out, but Ted just sat there. Finally he picked up a bottle in a brown paper bag. He took a long swallow, wiped his face with his sleeve then drank some more.

The crowd broke up. People stepped forward to toss money into the open guitar case. A few stopped to thank Ted. The couple beside me linked arms, and the guy turned toward the street. His girlfriend asked, "Aren't you going to give him something?"

"He'll just buy drugs or beer with it."

"So? That's what *you* do."

She pulled away and dropped a handful of bills into the guitar case.

"Thank you. That was beautiful," she said, and returned to her boyfriend.

A middle-aged woman walked up to Ted. She wore a trench coat with an Hermès scarf and expensive boots, and carried a large handbag.

"I saw you years ago, in New York. It was the best show I ever saw. I met my husband there." She reached into the bag, pulled out a wallet, and handed him a twenty-dollar bill. "Thank you."

Ted mumbled and lit a cigarette. "You still married?"

The woman laughed. "No. But that wasn't your fault."

As she strode off, Arthur grasped my arm. "We need to talk to him. About what's happened—to the time, and the moon . . . to the world."

"Nothing's happened to the world," I said.

But I didn't believe that was true. I wasn't sure what had changed—if Arthur's presence had somehow altered the sidewalks and back alleys around us, the way his poem had shaken something loose inside of me, something I couldn't articulate and maybe couldn't even paint: not so much a different way of seeing the world as a different way of *feeling* it. Maybe because when I was with him, I didn't need to explain who I was; maybe because he seemed even more out of place in the streets of Georgetown than I was. With him, I felt the way I did when I gazed at *The Temptation of Saint Anthony*—as though the world held a secret that I was on the verge of discovering.

I had never felt any real desire for a boy before—in a perverse way, I had never even felt desire for Clea, only the obsessive need to paint her—and now it wasn't so much that I wanted to be with Arthur. I wanted to *be* him, to see things the way he did, as though every traffic light and discarded syringe or empty aerosol can held a mystery inside it.

"You're lying," said Arthur. He pulled me until my face was inches from his. "You know it's changed. Because *I'm* in it, and that means nothing can ever be the same. Even if I go back to Charleville or Charleroi—even after I get back to Paris, it will all be different. *You* will be different—you already are."

He took my hand, the one that had been pierced by the fishbone key, and interlaced his fingers with mine. "Whatever is broken is beauty, for you and me; whatever is scarred. That's how this world was made, by destroying the old one. It scares you, doesn't it, this new world?"

I shivered, unnerved that he read my thoughts. "It's not new to me."

Arthur's pale eyes glimmered. "Oh, yes it is. And *he* knows how it happened."

He pointed across the street. Ted stumbled along the sidewalk, his guitar case in one hand, plastic bucket in the other, fishing rod beneath his arm.

"Come on," said Arthur.

I hesitated, then followed him. We caught up with Ted as he turned down a side road toward the canal.

"Wait!" I yelled. Arthur grabbed at Ted's coat, but Ted angrily pushed him away, shaking his guitar case threateningly. He seemed drunk and also crazed, eyes swollen and his face beet red.

"Hey, sorry," I said, and backed off. As I did, Ted's gaze settled on me, and he seemed to relax.

"Little Fly." He slurred the words; turned aside and spat, then looked at me again. "What'd I tell you? Don't look back."

"I'm not looking back. I just—we just wanted to talk to you. About what happened."

"Yeah?" Ted ducked into a tiny park, with a single wooden bench surrounded by young birch trees still clinging to their yellow leaves. He set down the bucket, water sloshing over its rim, carefully placed the guitar and fishing rod beside it. "And what exactly did happen?"

He took out a grimy cigarette, placed it in his mouth, and flicked his fingers beneath the cigarette's tip. A cobalt spark leaped from his fingertips to ignite the cigarette; he inhaled deeply, then blew smoke into my face.

"That." I coughed, waving the smoke away.

"She's right." Arthur stared at him accusingly. "You did the same thing in Charleroi, along the canal. Lit your pipe without a match or striker."

"There a law against that?" Ted opened his guitar case, fumbled inside, and withdrew a bottle. He uncapped it, took a swallow, and passed it to me. "Not much left. A swallow for each of you, if she don't take it all."

I took a sip and thrust the bottle at Arthur, my eyes watering. He finished it and threw the empty into the shadows.

"Any cognac left?" asked Ted.

"And that," I said. "How'd you know we were drinking cognac?"

"Smelled it on your breath, Little Fly." Ted laughed. "Good work. I didn't think you had it in you."

I decided to take another tack. "How did he get into the lockhouse? I locked it."

"And the moon." Arthur sat on the bench beside Ted. He took

out his pipe and filled it, nodding thanks as Ted lit it with that same eerie blue flame, then gestured at the sky. "When I saw you last night on the canal, the moon was full. You said it was good for carp."

"That's right. Three days before, three days after."

"But the moon isn't full anymore. And yesterday was Saturday, not Sunday."

Ted shook his head. "Kid, if you want to know what day it is, you are talking to the wrong goddamned person."

"And this." Arthur held out the newspaper he'd shown me earlier. "Yesterday's *Journal de Charleroi*. Saturday, October eighth." He paused. "1870."

"Was it only yesterday?" Ted rubbed his chin, then nodded. "Yeah, that sounds about right."

"That's insane," I said, as Arthur moved aside to make room for me on the bench. "Today's Monday—the clock struck one. And it's 1978."

"I told you, I'm not so good with dates." Ted scowled and tossed his cigarette. "Look, I don't know if I can explain this to you. But I'll try. Have you ever noticed how minutes or hours seem to speed up sometimes, but other times they go really slow? And how you remember things that happened a long time ago and it was like only yesterday? Ever think that maybe it doesn't just *seem* that way? That time really *does* speed up and slow down?"

I didn't say anything, and glanced at Arthur to see how he was taking this. He'd leaned back against the bench, his legs

outstretched—long legs for someone not much taller than me—
and was smoking his pipe, head cocked thoughtfully.

"I've felt that," he said after a moment. "In Charleroi, everything takes forever. But Paris—that passed in an eyeblink." He
stared wistfully at his pipe. "And when I was in Douai with my
friend's aunts, that seemed like a year. But tonight . . ." He turned
to me, puzzled. "Tonight is like a dozen nights, all run together."

I nodded slowly. "It all seems . . . stretched out. From this
morning until now, it seems like more than one day. Especially
tonight."

Ted picked up his fishing rod and began to untangle a knot in
the line. "That's because time is a river, and you can travel back
and forth in it. But only sometimes, and only if you're in the right
place."

"Like the lockhouse?" I said.

Ted was silent, the line taut between his hands and gleaming
in the moonlight. "Sometimes" was all he said.

For several minutes no one spoke. Arthur smoked; Ted
worked through the knotted line with a patience at odds with
the slurred voice and unsteady gait he'd shown earlier. I slipped a
hand into my pocket and ran my fingers over the oil pastels. The
leaves on the birch trees stirred, gilded by waning moonlight;
fallen leaves at our feet rose and fell as the wind gathered them. I
shivered, cast adrift upon that midnight sea, the bench bearing us
someplace farther than I had ever traveled, someplace I couldn't
begin to imagine.

In the plastic bucket, one of the carp thrashed. Murky water spattered my face. I shook my head, the dream broken, and leaned over to peer inside the bucket. The two fish floated side by side, their strangely prescient black eyes staring back at me. One of them turned lazily, exposing an underbelly that flickered red-gold and amber before it righted itself and rose until its head broke the surface of the water. Its beaklike mouth opened and closed, its liquid eye fixed on mine, before it slowly sank to the bottom once more.

I looked away, unnerved, and saw Arthur gazing at the carp. "You caught something," he said.

"Sometimes you get lucky." Ted brought the fishing line to his mouth and bit it in two. "Plus you got to know where to look for 'em. What's important is to keep your eyes open and keep moving. Don't ever stop. And don't look back. Looking back is deadly."

He tossed the knot aside and threaded the line along the pole. When he was finished, he held it out at arm's length and eyed it as though setting his sights upon a target. After a moment he nodded and, grunting, got to his feet.

"Okay. Time to see a man about a dog." He tucked the pole under his arm and picked up his guitar case, weaving slightly. "See you two later."

He hoisted the bucket in his free hand. Arthur hopped to his feet, knocking the ashes from his pipe. "Wait, I'm coming."

"No can do." Ted's voice was gruff. "Time waits for no man. Sorry, kid. Beat it."

Again he shook the guitar case threateningly, lurched from

the tiny park, and began to walk downhill, toward the canal. Without a backward glance at me, Arthur headed after him.

I hurried to catch up. But as my foot touched the sidewalk, light blazed around us, a blinding red flare. I fell against Arthur, shading my eyes.

"Stop right there." A staticky voice crackled from a bullhorn. *"District Police."*

Arthur grabbed me and we raced down the sidewalk after Ted. He continued to walk unsteadily, water slopping from the bucket, seemingly unaware of anything behind him.

"It's that cop," I gasped when we caught up with him. "That same guy from before, I think it's him."

Ted glanced back at me, and then at the black figure silhouetted in the glare behind us.

"Ted." The voice echoed through the empty street. *"Hold it right there, please."*

Ted narrowed his eyes. "Jesus wept. Here, Little Fly." He handed me the bucket of carp. "Hang on to this—be careful, and for chrissake don't drop it."

I grabbed the metal handle and winced—the bucket must have weighed thirty pounds.

"Here." Arthur's hand closed over mine. "Let me."

"Now get the hell out of here!" Ted commanded. "Both of you, go!"

I stared at him blankly. "But—"

"Stick together." He clasped my shoulder, and for a moment I glimpsed that same leaf-green flare within his eyes, incandescent in the cruiser's headlights. "Find the lockhouse. And whatever you do, don't drop my goddamn fish."

He pushed me away, turned, and strode into the street, holding his guitar case as though it were a machine gun and shouting, "You'll never take me alive, coppers!"

Beneath the bullhorn's crackle I heard a laugh. *"Stay right there, Ted. And you two—"*

I hesitated. A flashlight's beam moved across my face as Ted yelled, "Don't look back, Little Fly!"

I turned and fled.

12

Washington, D.C.

OCTOBER 9, 1978

I CAUGHT UP with Arthur at the corner, glancing nervously back at the cruiser. When there were no cars in sight, we crossed, Arthur doing his best not to spill the bucket. We walked as quickly as we could, leaving a trail of black water on the asphalt.

"God, this is heavy," Arthur gasped when we finally reached the curb.

"We can do it like this." I grasped the handle. "Both of us together."

It was difficult to carry it between us, but we did, breaking into an awkward trot when we spotted a stand of trees near the river's edge. The ground beneath us shifted from concrete to pounded earth to brittle grass, ankle high and studded with trash—bottles, crumpled glassine envelopes that had once held dope, a wisp of cloth, all strewn like sea wrack on a beach.

But beneath the trees, the grass was soft and unlittered by anything save dried bracken and scattered leaves. The moon was invisible here. The air smelled of the river, of granite and moss and mud. There was a strangely charged tension to the encroaching darkness, as though we'd stumbled onto a stage immediately before or after a performance. Instead of traffic, I heard only the purl of running water and the wind in the trees.

"Thank God." Arthur set the bucket down and flopped onto the grass, his slender form enveloped in shadow. "How could two fish be so heavy?"

"I don't know." I settled beside him, glancing into the bucket. "Shit. The water's almost all spilled out."

We knelt and stared into the bucket as though it were a magic mirror. Only instead of our own faces staring back, we saw the two carp struggling in a scant few inches of water, fins and tails thrashing, their mouths making desperate Os as they fought to breathe.

"They'll die." I looked at Arthur, fighting panic as I recalled the carps' prescient onyx gaze and Ted's command, *Whatever you do, don't drop my goddamn fish.* "We need to get more water."

We turned and stared past the trees, down to the Potomac. Without speaking, we each grasped the bucket's handle and headed to the river. A tumbledown stone wall ran alongside the water's edge, overgrown with moss. We set the bucket down and I clambered to the top of the wall, sneakers sliding on the slick rock. Arthur followed with the bucket.

"I don't remember this." I tugged at the collar of my bomber jacket and shivered. "It's all wrong."

Above the trees on the far shore hung a full moon, so brilliant it cast a shining path across the river, a phantom road that rippled with the water's passage and ended on the shore, a few feet from where we stood. There was no sign of Key Bridge; no sign of the glittering high-rises in Rosslyn, or of traffic moving behind the scrim of trees.

"The moon." Arthur gazed at it, enraptured. "It's as it was last night." He looked at me, his eyes candled with moonlight. "The world has changed again."

Before I could stop him, he jumped from the wall onto the sandy ground at the water's edge. Ted's bucket swung wildly from his hand.

"Wait!" I scrambled after him, but my foot skidded across damp moss and I fell, crying out as I slammed onto the ground. Arthur ignored me; he had already stepped onto a flat stone in the shallows, and stretched one long leg until he could hop onto a smaller rock in the center of the silvery passway, maybe ten feet from shore. I watched as he balanced precariously, teetering back and forth. He caught his balance and turned to look at me, his face radiant in the moonlight.

"Look, I'm on fire!"

He grinned and batted at an imaginary blaze. As he did, the bucket slipped from his hand. Twin arabesques spilled from it, twisting and gleaming gold as though he'd summoned flames from the night. I had a glimpse of a thrashing tail, a glint of onyx as first one carp and then the other struck the surface of the water and disappeared.

"No! You can't do that!"

I stumbled to the river's edge. I saw Arthur poised on the rock, staring at the river with disbelief and unabashed delight. Without a farewell word or glance at me, he jumped.

The air blurred into a haze of silver-white, like the watery mirage that appears on the road on a blinding-hot summer day. Arthur hung suspended in that quicksilver light, eyes wide in astonishment.

Then, as though a sudden gust swept the night, the blaze was extinguished. He was gone.

"Arthur!"

I waded into the river, screaming his name and floundering until I reached the rock. Water flowed around me, barely knee-deep. I stepped onto the rock, dazzled by moonlight, and looked around in vain for any trace of him; waded out until the water reached my waist and the current began to tug at my legs.

I saw no sign of Arthur. He had disappeared, as though he'd been a stone cast into the river. Fighting tears and now shuddering with cold, I somehow made my way back to shore, and collapsed on the stony ground.

PART THREE

EXILES

I realized she must have returned to her
everyday life, that the stars would fall before
this gift would be repeated. She has not
returned, she will never return. . . .

— Arthur Rimbaud, "The Deserts of Love"

13

Outside Charleroi, Belgium

DAWN, OCTOBER 9, 1870

HE STOOD ON tiptoe, teetering slightly as he gazed into the moonlit river. Behind him he could hear the girl's warning—*No! You can't do that!*—her voice shrill as his mother's when she caught him working on poems and not his homework. Anger flickered through him, gave way to amazement as he saw a carp staring up at him from the rippling water, its round black eyes intent and curious as a child's. Its mouth parted: a bubble escaped, iridescent as a green pearl, burst in a crystalline shimmer that released a scent of apple blossom and a breathless command.

Jump.

The sound shocked him. He lost his balance, at the last moment lifted his arms so that he seemed to lift into the air, as he did in dreams, suspended between sky and silvery current, sleep and waking.

Then water filled his nostrils; not water but something gelid, icy-cold, racing through his mouth and veins until his mouth opened wide and wider still, until he felt as though his jaw would snap as a fish's jaw is broken in the fisherman's grasp. He tried to scream, struggling to free himself; but whatever clasped him would not let go until, abruptly, his arms thrashed and he sat up, gasping, on a narrow bunk.

There was no river, no girl; no wondrous city, no beckoning carp. He was inside the lockhouse he had entered after meeting the tramp fishing along the canal.

"Merle?" he called. There was no reply.

He rubbed his eyes and gazed at the wall beside him, a faded frieze of rust-colored stains and black splotches that, as he squinted, resolved into faint depictions of waves, a blurred eye. He pressed his hand against the stone, recalling the strange heat that had radiated from it right before he fell asleep.

But now the wall was cold, the room around him empty. His mouth tasted sour and his stomach roiled, like the sick aftermath of too much wine. He stood, light-headed, and all in a rush the long, strange night came back to him: the terrifying rapture of the northern lights, and then the girl with her bizarre clothes and manner, a city like an opium dream, poised between the *Arabian Nights* and Jules Verne; golden carp and a road made of moonlight; a tramp whose music sounded as though it were plucked from an instrument strung from his own sinew and bone.

"Merle." He whispered her name again and stumbled to the door, flung it open to stare out at the canal, green-gold in the morning sun. Ravens clacked in the trees, a cricket sawed beneath

a drift of oak leaves. The air smelled of autumn and the year's
death. He held his hands before his face and stared through the
latticework of fingers—blue sky and russet leaves, a flash of black
wings.

Was it possible to dream into being a world beyond one's own
imaginings? Was he truly awake now?

He slipped a hand into his pocket and felt the sharp prongs of
the fish-bone key. He rested his head against the doorframe, gazing at the crosshatch of grime on his knuckles and ink on his fingertips, squeezed his eyes shut, and saw a night sky that erupted
into a rainbow of flame, horseless omnibuses roaring through
a broad avenue, a girl who dressed and cursed like he did, and
painted radiant suns on crumbling walls.

He held his breath and waited to see if the dream would
recur, straining to hear the girl's voice, a drunk old man playing guitar.

But he heard nothing but the wind in the trees, and the plaintive cry of geese high above him heading west toward the sea.
Finally he went back inside. He sat on the bunk and for a long
time stared at the wall, the shadowy afterimage of a rayed eye that
was all that remained of Merle's painting, and of Merle herself.

He would bring her back. She had summoned him once; now,
he would summon her.

He lit the pipe Leo had given him, pulled the wad of pages
from his overcoat, and smoothed them out on the bunk, sorting
through them until he found one that was not yet covered with
words. He found the nub of pencil at the bottom of his pocket,

sharpened the tip with a filthy thumbnail, and began to write, reworking a poem he'd begun months before.

> *On the calm black wave where the stars sleep*
> *White Ophelia floats like a great lily,*
> *Floats so slowly, laid to rest in her long veils. . . .*
> *In the woods, you hear a distant fanfare.*

He paused, felt a twinge as he recalled Merle's desperate voice calling after him.

No! You can't do that!

Not anger, as he had thought; not a command but genuine fear, as she saw him poised to leave her. He had broken their unspoken contract, abandoning Merle to whatever private grief had led her to summon him from his own world and time.

> *O pale Ophelia, beautiful as snow!*
> *Yes, you died, borne away by that river. . . .*
>
> *Because the wild sea's voice, a vast death rattle*
> *Broke your child's heart, too human and too gentle.*
> *Because one April morning, a pale handsome prince,*
> *Poor fool, sat silently at your knees.*

Hours passed. The sun crept high enough to ignite dust motes in the room around him. Arthur rubbed his eyes, his stomach rumbling. For the first time he realized how hungry he was. He'd last eaten at the bistro with the girl; why, if he was going to eat a visionary meal, couldn't it have been a better one?

Sighing, he read over what he'd written, then rolled up the pages and stuck them back in his pocket. He gathered his overcoat about him and stepped outside, chilled and famished and with a distinct hangover. Poets wrote of the wine of dreams, but he'd never heard that it gave you an aching head the next morning. He wandered back and forth along the towpath, hoping to meet the tramp again; unwilling to give rein to a more foolish hope, that the girl might miraculously reappear.

But he saw only a grebe paddling in the canal, its russet feathers mirrored in the tea-colored water, and a single carp, swimming lazily just beneath the surface.

HE WALKED ON, STOPPING IN CHARLEROI FOR A FEW DAYS, THEN continued to Brussels, where he stayed for a week or so with a friend of Izambard's. He borrowed enough money to buy some new clothes, including a top hat that added eight inches to his height, and a one-way ticket to Douai. Georges was still living with the three aunts. Paris was under siege; schools remained closed because of the war, so there was no reason to return to Charleville.

"Does your mother know you're here?" Georges eyed Arthur dubiously. "That hat looks ridiculous."

"Of course she does." Arthur walked past him into the drawing room, where the aunts erupted into warbles of delight. "Who do you think bought it for me?"

"You're lying," Georges said after the aunts bustled off to the kitchen for coffee and pastries. He grabbed Arthur's top hat and threw it onto a divan. "I was in Charleville last week; I dropped by to see you and your mother said you'd taken off again. She accused me of kidnapping you! She'll kill you when she finds out you're here."

Arthur shrugged, regarding Georges with icy blue-gray eyes. "She'll kill me no matter what."

"Yes," said Izambard grimly. "And she'll kill me, too. I don't care how many times you run away—you're still a minor. She could have me arrested if she wanted to."

Arthur walked to the door and peered into the kitchen. "If you don't write her, she won't find out. Look, my birthday's almost here—let me stay till then, at least." He smoothed the cuffs of his new shirt, then gazed up at Georges pleadingly. "Please? I swear I'll be good."

"God save me from another promise from Arthur Rimbaud!" Georges smacked himself on the forehead. "Next time it will be *me* in Mazas Prison, for harboring a fugitive."

"And I'll visit you every week. Please, let me help with that!" Arthur hurried to take a plate filled with tarts from a beaming aunt. "God, I missed you all!" he said, and kissed her cheek.

"Not as much as we missed *you*," she replied, as Georges groaned and sank back into his chair.

The rest of the month passed quickly. The aunts baked a cake for his sixteenth birthday, and gave him a sheaf of expensive writing paper and a new pen.

"Thank you, thank you, thank you," he cried, hugging each in turn and hiding his face so they wouldn't see how his eyes welled.

"For your poems," one said, smiling.

"And to write to your mother," added another.

"Here." Georges handed him a neat bundle wrapped in butcher paper and tied with twine. "These cost a fortune, so be careful with them. Demeny got them for me; they were smuggled out of Paris."

Arthur sank onto the divan. He undid the twine, unwrapping the brown paper to reveal a stack of newspapers, the front page of each a brightly colored, engraved caricature.

"*L'Éclipse!*" Arthur stared rapturously at the broadsheets. "Really, Demeny smuggled these out for me?"

Georges nodded. "Yes, God knows why. He also said maybe he'd look at your poems again someday."

"To publish them?"

"He didn't say *that*. Don't push your luck—he could've done prison time if he'd been caught with those." Georges gestured at a caricature of a bedbug clad in royal raiment.

One of the aunts peered at the drawing and frowned. "Is that by André Gill?" she said. "I thought he was arrested."

"He was censored," said Arthur, grabbing back the newspapers. "I think he's brilliant. That's what I'm going to do—become a political cartoonist."

"I thought you were going to be a poet," said the aunt.

Arthur nodded absently. "That too."

"Don't you think you should develop some artistic talent first?" asked Georges.

"There's seventy newspapers in Paris," retorted Arthur. "One of them will buy my drawings. And Demeny said he knows André Gill, right? After I sell the first cartoon, the rest will be cake. All I need is a foot in the door."

Georges sighed. "Try keeping it out of your mouth. That might help."

Arthur spent the next few weeks writing and rewriting seven new poems. He also wrote a number of letters to the local newspaper, calling for the overthrow of the government and signing Georges's name. One evening Demeny arrived for a visit, and he and Georges and Arthur walked to the café for drinks. After several bottles of wine and myriad glasses of beer, Demeny turned to Arthur.

"I gather you have spent these long autumn evenings consorting with the muse Euterpe?"

Arthur raised an eyebrow and glanced at Georges. "Do you understand what he just said?"

Georges poured himself another glass of wine. "He wants to know if you're still writing poems."

"Oh. Of course." Arthur turned to Demeny. "Why? Are you ready to publish them?"

Demeny laughed. "What, with all the great poets begging to be published? Why should I waste paper on the laureate from Charleville?"

"Maybe because I'm better than they are," said Arthur. "Better than all of you."

Demeny leaned across the table. "What about Baudelaire? 'Alas, my poor muse, what's wrong with you this morning? Your cavernous eyes are filled with nightmare visions. . . .'" Sounds like what you write."

Arthur scowled. "I would never write that shit."

Demeny tapped his chin. "Edgar Allan Poe?"

"More shit."

"Banville?"

"*Incredible* shit."

Georges pulled his chair closer to Arthur's. "What about Paul Verlaine? You wrote me that you liked his book. Is he shit, too?"

"Verlaine's a genius. You know why?" Arthur pounded the table, knocking over an empty bottle. "Because he's not afraid of sounding like an idiot. He's not ashamed of anything. Like me."

He picked up Izambard's glass of wine and emptied it in one long swallow, sank back into his chair, and gazed defiantly around the table.

Demeny snorted. "Verlaine. Can you quote one line of his?"

"No, but here's one of yours." Arthur belched, and Georges threw a napkin at him.

The next afternoon a letter arrived, addressed to Georges Izambard and with a postal stamp from Charleville. He read it, wincing, then handed it to Arthur.

"Well, that's it. Your notice of execution has arrived."

"Very funny." Arthur stared at his mother's handwriting, his jaw clenched. "I'd rather go back to prison. I swear to God, I'd rather die in Mazas than spend another day in Charleville."

"It won't be that bad." Georges put his hand on Arthur's shoulder, turned him gently to face him. "Listen to me, Arthur. You can't stay here. She's contacted the Douai police chief and made arrangements for him to escort you to Charleville. I should have sent you home the day you arrived—she could press charges against me if she wanted to, and I really might spend time in prison."

"I know." Arthur balled up the letter and tossed it viciously across the room. "But I'm not staying in that shithole—I'm just telling you that right now. I'm going to Paris. I'll get a job at Gill's newspaper."

"That would be wonderful." Georges smiled sadly. "Maybe next time, I'll see you there. After the war. When your book's published. I'll even let you pay for the drinks, how's that?"

In the morning, he took Arthur to the police station. "Don't even think about getting on a different train," he warned him as they stood outside the station door. "Write me as soon as you get home, and we'll make plans for when I come back to Charleville. The war can't last forever; they'll reopen the school soon."

Arthur nodded silently. He and the aunts had cried when he said good-bye. Now he felt sick to his stomach at the thought of what awaited him in Charleville.

"Come on," said Georges softly, and steered him through the door. "'If it were done when 'tis done, then 'twere well it were done quickly.'"

Inside, Georges greeted the police prefect and gave him the money for Arthur's fare.

"We'll take good care of him." The prefect regarded Arthur through narrowed eyes. "Your poor mother. What kind of a son is so cruel to the person who loves him most in all the world?"

Georges turned and shook Arthur's hand. "Until next time, my friend."

Arthur watched him leave, fighting tears, then sat and waited for the officer who would accompany him back to Charleville.

14

Washington, D.C.

OCTOBER 9, 1978

I DON'T KNOW how long I huddled there beside the river. It seemed like hours, but when I finally lifted my head, the sky was still dark and filled with stars. I stood shakily, turned, and saw the familiar garland of lights that marked Key Bridge, and on the far shore of the Potomac the spires of Rosslyn's skyscrapers. The world was as it had been: only Arthur was gone.

I trudged back toward Georgetown, legs aching with cold. My pants were wet, my sneakers soaked through. I needed to find someplace to crash, if only for the night. I dug in my pocket for the fistful of coins Arthur had returned to me. There was barely enough for a meal, let alone a motel room, but maybe I could find a pay phone and call Clea, beg her to take me in long enough to shower and dry my clothes.

But I had no idea what time it was, other than late, and the thought of waking Clea in the middle of the night—or worse, waking her husband—and pleading for help after she'd dumped me was more than I could stomach. I decided I'd rather freeze, and stuffed the money back into my pocket. The oil pastels had dissolved to a smear of green and yellow that stained my fingers. I had no idea how to find any of my friends—I'd written all their numbers in one of the sketchbooks that had been stolen.

The sudden memory of my lost bag made my eyes tear up. I thrust the thought aside, kicked furiously at a rock and sent it bouncing across the street. Clea, my bag, my drawings, my home—was there another fucking thing that I could lose?

That was when I remembered Ted's key. Frantically I searched my pockets, and started to retrace my steps when I halted beneath a streetlamp. I turned my hand to the light, gazing at the fresh scab on my palm, where I'd jabbed it with one of the tarnished silver prongs. Then the key had fallen and Arthur picked it up. He'd never returned it.

The lockhouse was lost to me now too, and Ted as well—he'd never speak to me again. I turned and began to run blindly back to the Potomac, not stopping till I reached the river's edge and climbed atop a concrete pier that thrust out into the black water.

It looked deeper than before, much deeper and faster moving. I knew the water would be cold, but maybe that would make it easier to die. I thought of Clea and how she'd immediately fall apart when she found out I was dead, and as quickly get over it. I thought of my younger brothers crying inconsolably.

But they'd forget, too; they were so young, and my father would do nothing to preserve my memory. My paintings and drawings were gone. Even my tags would fade, or be painted over by the vandal squad. The river would take me and I would leave no trace. Nothing would show that I'd ever been alive, that I'd created beautiful things and experienced a miracle—a boy from out of time who had seen my work and recognized it; a boy who'd seen and recognized me.

I took a deep breath and stared at the water below. My own face stared back, pale as the moon. Something splashed and sent ripples across my reflection. For an instant it seemed as though another face gazed back at me, and I heard Arthur's voice, half chanting.

We are children of the moon . . . the ones who can never be satisfied. Because when one of them finds their missing half . . . their souls mingle, and even if their bodies can never again become whole, their souls form one being, and that being can never be destroyed.

I let my breath out and sank into a crouch. Something splashed again, a pattering of icy drops across my hand. In the water a carp gazed up at me, its head as big as mine, its eyes inky black. I cried out and the fish disappeared, its golden tail flicking across dark water.

"'Mother, may I go in and swim?'" pronounced a gravelly voice behind me. "'Yes, my darling daughter. Hang your clothes on a hickory limb, and don't go near the water.'"

I scrambled to my feet and turned to see Ted.

"That water's radioactive," he said, taking a drag off a cigarette. "I wouldn't swim in it."

"I wasn't," I said, embarrassed. "I thought you got busted."

"Nah. They just like to keep an eye on me. 'Specially in cold weather, they check up on folks sleeping rough, make sure you don't freeze to death on their watch. Of course they'll push you right out of Georgetown into another precinct, but I don't bear them no ill will. They're just doing their job, like I'm doing mine."

He pulled out the leather canteen, opened it and took a swig. "What happened to the boy?"

"I don't know." I stared miserably at the river. "We were both here, and then he jumped. The carp—he let them go by mistake."

"And he went after them?"

I nodded, unsure if Ted sounded admiring or angry. "I waded in but I couldn't find him. I mean, it was impossible—the water wasn't deep enough for him to drown. It doesn't make any sense."

"My band made four brilliant albums and never had a single goddamn hit. We were supposed to be the American Rolling Stones, and we couldn't get more than five minutes of airplay. Does that make sense?" Ted stubbed out his cigarette.

I sighed. "I just want everything to go back to how it was before."

"You can never do that, Little Fly." Ted shook his head. "You can't step into the same river twice. Water's always moving. And so are you." He held out the canteen. "Here. That'll warm you. Come on, I'll take you someplace you can dry out."

I followed him, my relief undercut by anxiety. What would he do when he found out I'd lost the key to the lockhouse? He was empty-handed; maybe he had an extra key, or maybe he'd stashed his guitar case and fishing gear and planned to retrieve them now.

But as it turned out, we weren't headed for the lockhouse. Instead Ted plodded along beneath the Whitehurst Freeway, turned up onto 30th Street, then led me down alleyways and narrow sidewalks, until we once again reached the C&O Canal. There was a lock, one I'd never seen before, concrete pilings stained with rust and mold, and an ancient-looking streetlight that gave off a sulfurous glow. Willows overhung water smooth as black marble. An overturned metal trash can had been converted into a makeshift barbecue grill, the ground beneath it littered with fish bones. A trio of feral cats scrabbled and fought over these, darting into the underbrush as we approached.

"Home sweet home," announced Ted, and walked toward the canal. A boat was tied off to an iron post. Not a canoe or dinghy but a proper canalboat, twenty feet long and nearly as wide as the canal itself: a replica of one of the mule-drawn boats that used to bear goods and passengers to Great Falls and beyond. In the summer, they were still used to tow tourists through Georgetown, but it didn't look like this one had gone anywhere in a while.

I was amazed it wasn't at the bottom of the canal. Boards were missing from the sides, and paint peeled like lichen from the prow. Newspapers were stuffed into a fist-sized hole above the waterline. I looked around for a building or shed, or another lockhouse, but saw nothing.

"Welcome aboard," Ted said, and hopped over the side of the boat. He held out a hand and helped me clamber after him, then stumped toward a small hatch and disappeared down a wooden ladder missing most of its rungs. I hurried after him, climbing hesitantly down into a cramped cabin. A battered kerosene lantern hung from a lethal-looking iron hook; as Ted lit the lantern, his head nearly grazed the ceiling.

"Is this your boat?" I asked.

"Friend of mine lets me crash here. Retired park police; he'd lose his pension if anyone knew, so just keep a lid on it, okay? Give me that guitar."

Empty bottles littered the floor, clinking softly as the boat rocked, along with several large white buckets. A filthy sleeping bag covered the bunk, the porthole above it scabbed with dirt and cobwebs. The air reeked of stale beer, cigarettes, and dead fish. Yellowing gig posters covered the walls, advertising ancient shows by the Deadly Rays, a few solo gigs by Ted. The most recent had taken place eight years ago.

I found the guitar and handed it to him. Ted sighed, and settled with it on the bunk. "Make yourself at home."

I looked around in vain for a spot on the floor that was free of spilled beer or moldy clothing, resigned myself, and sat. I was relieved that the guttering lantern kept much of the room in shadow.

"So." Ted opened his guitar case, pulled out a bottle, and took a long drink. I huddled on the floor and tried to avoid looking at him, fearful of that uncanny flare of green behind his eyes. Finally he stood and shuffled across the cabin, moving aside buckets filled with scrap wood and old newspapers until he revealed a tiny potbellied stove, so small I could have cradled it in my lap. He crouched and opened the door, poked around inside, humming to himself; stuffed the firebox with crumpled newspapers and kindling, then leaned back on his heels before extending his hand. A tendril of cobalt lightning leaped from his fingertips to a shred of newsprint, flickered into leaves of golden flame that, within minutes, grew to a steady blaze.

"There." He closed the stove's door and beckoned me over, swiping his hand across the floor to clear it of bottles. "Have a seat."

I knelt in front of the stove and luxuriated in the sheer joy of heat and light after the seemingly endless October night. For a long time neither of us spoke. Now and then a blue flash would spill from Ted's fingertips as he lit a cigarette; he'd pass me the canteen of fiery liquor and I'd take a mouthful, until at last my clothes were dry and I felt as though I'd swallowed one of the embers burning behind the stove's isinglass window. I took off my bomber jacket and turned.

Ted sat on the bunk with the guitar in his lap, eyes closed and mouth slightly parted. His hands stroked the guitar's body, lovingly, as though it were a person and not a thing of wood and steel wire. After a moment his eyes opened and he stared at me, irises shot with emerald sparks, each pupil a glowing pinpoint.

"Sorry," he muttered, and set the guitar aside. "Forgot I had company."

I looked away, embarrassed. "Do you—is this where you live?"

"Sometimes. I move around a lot. Occupational hazard. What about you?"

"I don't know." Without warning, without wanting to, I began to cry. "I told you, I got kicked out of the place I was living."

"Right. I remember now. Booted out of college, booted out of your house, your girlfriend dumped you, and some punk kid took off with your art supplies. Bad day at Black Rock." He picked up the canteen and took a drink. "You have my sympathy."

"It's not a fucking joke!" I grabbed an empty beer can and threw it at him. "I've lost *every* goddamn thing in *one goddamn day*."

Ted caught the beer can, crushed it in one hand, and threw it back at me. I ducked. It bounced off the woodstove, and Ted scowled. "Screw that, Little Fly. You lost everything? Big fucking deal. Boo hoo. You said you were an artist, right? Well, this is where it starts to get interesting."

"But I don't have any paint. And my sketchbooks—all my drawings, my brushes, my charcoal pencils—"

"You don't need that stuff. I've seen your tags. You need another aerosol can? Steal it. Wouldn't be the first time, I bet. Steal everything you need. If you're good enough—if you're great—they'll forgive you. And if you're not good enough?" His eyes narrowed. "In that case, Little Fly, nobody cares."

I said nothing. Overhead, the kerosene lantern burned with a steady dull ocher flame. The boat rocked softly, and I heard the patter of rain against the porthole window. Ted continued to stare at me. Finally he spoke.

"'The poet must be a thief of fire.' Someone I know said that. What do you need to draw, anyway? A charcoal pencil? Here—"

He stood and crossed the cabin in two steps, opened the door to the woodstove and thrust his arm inside, grabbed something, then withdrew his arm and closed the door again.

I gasped as he held his hand out to me. In the palm was a glowing ember, runnels of flame still licking across it.

"Here," he said. "Take that—go ahead."

"But—"

"You're complaining about nothing to draw with. You said charcoal, right? Take it," he commanded. "And don't drop it."

I gritted my teeth, then gingerly picked up the glowing coal. Heat seared my fingers, but almost immediately the ember cooled. The tiny flames died to wisps of smoke. I blew on my fingertips, afraid they'd blistered; but there were no marks and, after that first fiery surge, no pain. I held a lump of charcoal that left soft black smudges across my palm.

"See?" said Ted. "Not so hard. Now . . ." He strode to the opposite side of the cabin, halting in front of one of the tattered gig posters. He pried out rusted thumbtacks, carefully peeled the poster from the wall, and handed it to me. "There," he said, pointing at the back of the sheet. "Draw on that. Plenty more where it came from."

The paper was mottled with stains, and in some places images and words from the printed side had bled through. But I smoothed it onto the floor, weighting the corners with beer bottles, and for a few minutes sat gazing at it.

"I don't know if I can do it," I said at last. "Everything I was working on—all my best stuff—it was all paintings or drawings of her. Clea."

"Gotta get back on that horse, Little Fly," Ted said softly. He stood behind me, and for an instant I felt his hand touch my hair. "Remember what I said? Don't look back."

I shook my head. "I can't forget her—I don't *want* to forget her."

"I'm not saying you should forget her." He crouched beside me. He looked impatient, but also immeasurably sad. "I'm saying you shouldn't waste your energy on looking back. Because what happens then is you lose her all over again. The only way you keep it alive—whatever it was that made you want to paint her—is if you keep working. That's all that matters."

"What about you?" I asked, not meeting his eyes. "You and your band—you were supposed to be so great. But you stopped."

"Yeah, well, them's the breaks. I stuck it out for a long time. Too long, probably. And I let other stuff get in the way. You want to know something, Little Fly?" Ted touched my wrist, and then the piece of charcoal in my hand. "None of this lasts. None of *us* lasts. But that"—he pointed at the empty sheet of paper—"*that's* what matters. That's what'll be around after you're gone. Not you or Arthur; only the stuff you leave behind." He fumbled a cigarette from a battered pack and held it to his fingertips. A blue flare; he took a drag and exhaled. "Your paintings. His poems. That's what's left."

I stared at the cigarette. "Jesus, how the hell do you *do* that? Is it—is it some kind of magic?"

I thought he'd laugh. Instead, he shook his head and said, "Magic isn't something you do, Little Fly. Magic is something you *make*. Now get to it." He stood and walked unsteadily to the ladder. "I gotta piss."

When he was gone, I sat and gazed at the paper. I made a tentative sweep with the lump of charcoal, leaving only a grayish smear. I swore under my breath and tried again, pressing harder. The tip broke into soft pieces. I flung it down, grabbed one of the beer bottles, and threw it across the room. It struck the bunk, knocking something to the floor. I swore again and scrambled to my feet, afraid I'd hit Ted's guitar.

But it wasn't the guitar. It was the jawbone of a large animal, a bone as long as my forearm, from a horse or cow, or maybe one of the mules that used to tow boats like this one. Weathered gray as a piece of driftwood, with four deeply furrowed teeth still implanted in its long curve, and blackened strings that stretched between the two ends of the bone crescent.

I counted the strings—seven—and ran a finger along one. It made a very faint sound, not the twang of a plucked guitar but a sort of hushed sigh, like the release of a long-held breath.

Behind me the ladder rattled as Ted climbed back down. Quickly I set the bone instrument onto the bunk and dropped to the floor.

"Don't look like you got much done," Ted observed, glancing at the empty sheet.

"I'm thinking."

Ted stomped over to the bunk, picked up his guitar, and sat. I picked up the lump of charcoal, studied it for a moment, then began to scrape at one end with my fingernail. When I'd shaped a blunt point, I gently touched it to the paper and drew a line fine as the vein of a leaf; took the other, thicker end of the charcoal and drew jagged rays pulsing from a black sun.

I sat back, studying my work, and glanced up to see Ted with his guitar, his scabbed fingers turning pegs and tapping strings. He coughed and spit onto the floor; then began to play, so softly that I had to strain to hear. A wordless song that reminded me of something from long ago, a wash of yearning that must have come from a dream, because I could find no name or face to attach to it.

Above us, the lantern swayed as the boat rocked, and I sat, charcoal still clasped in my hand. I no longer saw Ted's face in the near-dark; only the curve of his skull and lamplight shuttling across his fingers like thread upon a loom. If it hadn't been for the sound of the guitar, I might not have known a man was there at all, just a play of light and shadow. I felt as I had when Ted played for that small crowd, at once dreamy and more awake than I had ever been. I half expected him to stop, to make some wry remark or light another cigarette. But it was as though he were alone, completely oblivious to me and everything around us.

Minutes passed, maybe hours, and still Ted showed no sign of stopping. I shifted, careful not to make a sound, lowered my head to stare at the sheet of paper in front of me and the solid black shape in my hand. I rubbed my fingers across the charcoal's tip and began to draw. I drew Ted where he sat sideways on the bunk, cradling his guitar and playing a song I can still hear some-times, late at night or early in the morning when the sky has a faint greenish tinge. His face looked ancient, seamed with lines like cracks in a marble statue, his eyes bloodshot and the stubble on his chin more white than gray.

But as he played, the lines gradually smoothed away. There were still deep grooves alongside his mouth, and two furrows between his eyebrows. Yet he seemed younger—almost another person. After some minutes he turned and stared back at me.

For an instant those other eyes gazed out, the deep unclouded green of a lake in spring, at once ancient and childlike, just as he was at once Ted and someone else, his face ravaged by sorrow and some indescribable joy.

But then he turned back to his guitar, calm and detached as though he sat alone in the tiny cabin.

I stared at the sheet in front of me, and began to move the charcoal across it. The page dissolved into light and shadow, black hollows and empty space; a crosshatch of fine lines around his eyes and beneath his chin, a darker wedge where the guitar touched his chest; more empty space where the lantern light rippled across broken fingernails and guitar strings. I smudged edges with my fingertips, and leaned down to blow away charcoal dust like ash.

I don't know how long it took. All I know is that when I was finished, I knew that it was the best thing I'd ever done.

For a few seconds I felt dizzy, almost sick. Then Ted's words came back to me in a rush. I let my breath out, not knowing how long I'd held it, touched my hand to the page, and realized, for the first time, that what Ted had told me was true.

Magic isn't something you have, or find. It isn't something that happens to you, or something you do. Magic is something you *make*. And if you don't make something and leave it behind, it's not just that it's gone. *You're* gone.

Yet if you create something truly great, there's no need to look back—because it will remain, and live on its own, without you.

I looked up. The cabin had fallen silent. Ted sat on the bunk, watching me.

"Look at this," I said. I moved the bottles, picked up the sheet, and brought it to him. He set aside his guitar, took the page in both hands, and stared at it for a long time.

"That is beautiful," he said at last.

"I know."

He smiled and handed the picture back to me. I looked at it again, then placed it carefully on the floor beside the wall. "I wish Arthur could have seen it," I said.

Ted began to play again, another song without words, sweetly plaintive. I yawned.

"Tired?"

I nodded. Ted rose, his fingers still moving across the strings, and inclined his head toward the bunk. I climbed into it, pushing aside flannel shirts and rumpled sheets to pull up a worn wool blanket laced with holes. Ted crossed to the far end of the cabin and pulled a stool from the shadows, sat and continued to play.

As I pillowed my head on my arms, my hand grazed something: the bone harp. My fingers closed around it as the memory of Ted's song echoed inside my head, along with the soft slap of water against the boat's hull.

It seemed then that Ted began to sing, though somehow it was not a song but a net of words, a silvery fretwork of names and shapes, trees and birds and spangled fish; a boy who looked like Arthur, trudging across a golden desert; a girl who looked like me, standing in a crowded room with a wineglass in her hand. I saw all these things and a thousand more, saw them and heard them, too, tumbled together in a shining, tinkling heap within the folds of a net strung with stars and fish's scales, glowing liquid streaming from it as unseen hands pulled the net from an endless, indigo sea, and I felt myself tumble into that shining web.

PART FOUR

≪੭≪

STATE OF SIEGE

By the thousand, above France's fields

Where yesterday's dead lie sleeping,

Whirling in winter

So that passersby don't forget—

You'll sound the alarm,

Black birds of death.

— Arthur Rimbaud, "The Crows"

15

Charleville, France

NOVEMBER 2, 1870

To Georges Izambard, Douai

—FOR YOUR EYES ONLY—

I'm back in Charleville, at my mother's doing nothing. She says she's going to send me to boarding school in January.

You made me promise to come back, so here I am.

I'm dying here, rotting away from boredom. What did you think would happen? All I want is to be on my own. I should have left this morning—I could have, I've got new clothes and I could sell my watch. I'd be free! Grab my hat and coat, hands in my pockets and I'm out the door! But I'll stay, I'll stay—I didn't promise that, but I'll do it to prove to you I've been worth all this trouble. You'll see.

I can't thank you enough for everything you did for me, I feel it more today than ever. I'll make it up to you someday. I'll do something even if I die trying—I swear. I have so much to say.

That "heartless" A. Rimbaud

School was still closed. He didn't hear back from Georges, or Paul Demeny—mail delivery was all but halted by the war. Even newspapers were hard to come by, and when they arrived, the news was always bad. He spent his time hanging out with friends in town, drinking and smoking, shoplifting books until the bookstore closed for lack of trade; also stealing a bottle of cognac that he hid beneath his bed. At home he fought with his mother constantly, arguing over chores, his failure to find a job, the weather.

"I think you should go back to Paris and live on the streets," his mother announced one morning in early December. He was still in bed. Snow blew against his window and the house was cold, because he'd forgotten to bring in any firewood the night before. "I can't afford to keep you anymore."

"Fine, I'll go," he retorted, voice muffled as he burrowed deeper into the covers.

But for the moment, he stayed. He was restless and miserable. Yet perversely he found that unhappiness was a spur to write. His life in Charleville was a void, an absence: writing created another life, gave substance to another being, someone who was at once Arthur and someone else, his daemon self.

It didn't even take entire words: mere letters could invoke that other world and daemon other. Late that night, after his mother had gone to bed, he stole downstairs and retrieved the oil lantern with its gleaming glass chimney, brought it up to his room, and set it on the plain wooden table he used as a desk. He lit the lantern, keeping the flame low so that it wouldn't burn out, and angled it so that the window threw back the light's meager reflection and that of his own face, mouth grim beneath baleful eyes.

Outside, snow covered the courtyard and distant fields. It was a clear night, the sky like polished jet and so bitterly cold that the stars winked in and out of view, as though momentarily obscured by clouds. Arthur pulled on his greatcoat, then reached beneath his bed for the stolen bottle of cognac. He took a swig, set it beside him, and huddled over the table.

He took out a fresh sheet of the expensive paper the aunts had given him in Douai, warmed the little bottle of India ink between his hands—it was so cold it had grown viscous, too thick to write with. He stared out at the glittering stars and recalled the October night when he had seen the northern lights, that spectral wash of scarlet and emerald and lapis lazuli: as though gems had been melted, like lead in a blazing athanor, then splashed across the sky.

After several minutes, he dipped his pen into the ink and drew a crude eye of Horus at the top of the page, followed by a few random letters and words. He paused, overcome by the odd vertigo that struck him sometimes when he most wanted to write—a feeling that he was poised to jump into a terrifying yet inescapable abyss. Once he plunged, there would be no turning back.

He squeezed his eyes shut, rubbed them until bright jots of

orange and red appeared on his eyelids, the eerie tracery of blood vessels. When he opened his eyes, the afterimages hung ghostly in the air before him, as his pen nib scraped the creamy paper and he wrote.

> *A black, E white, I red, U green, O blue: vowels,*
> *One day I'll tell of your hidden birth:*
> *A, black shaggy corset of glittering flies*
> *Buzzing around horrendous stinks,*
>
> *Shadowy pits; E, guileless mists and canopies,*
> *Proud glacial spears, white kings, shivering blossoms;*
> *I, purples, spat blood, laughter of beautiful lips*
> *In anger or raptures of regret;*
>
> *U, wheels, divine vibrations of viridian seas . . .*

Letters burned upon the page and silvery petals blossomed across the windowpane as he released each breath, until the glass held as many stars as the sky outside.

> *O, final trumpet with its unearthly clamor,*
> *Silent wastes of worlds and angels,*
> *O: Omega, the violet radiance of Her Eyes!*

Shivering, he set down his pen. The bottle of cognac was nearly empty. He drank what was left in a fiery mouthful, gazed out at the sky in rapture. A torrent of memory and words and desire surged through him, and his head pounded: a dike had been breached. The membrane that separated him from the written world dissolved, a white flame that burned away flesh and hair and bone so that only words remained and he was there and not there, sole creator of a world that contained only him and the wheeling stars: Alpha and Omega, *I* and *somebody else*.

His breath caught in his throat. It was not a revelation but a life sentence, not rapture but rupture.

"I" is an other.

The blood pounded in his ears. He no longer felt the chair beneath him or his hands on the scarred wooden table; didn't hear the soft thump as the empty cognac bottle rolled to the floor. He felt nothing but the shock of realization that he possessed this secondary self, cupped within his consciousness like an egg in its shell: the Arthur that the world tore through like a gale and the Arthur who gazed steadily and unblinking at the glittering night sky, opening himself to that tumult like a sail: voyager, visionary.

Poet.

When his sister Vitalie came to wake him next morning, she found him slumped across the table, the lantern cold, splinters of frozen ink covering his fingers like black feathers; and his eyes wide and bloodshot, as though he had stared too long at the sun.

16

Charleville

IT WAS A brutal winter. Snow sheathed Charleville's streets, too deep even for horse-drawn sledges to pass. The rivers and canal were locked in ice. The air rang with the sound of axes as bargemen smashed the frozen canal, cursing when chips keen as flints struck their cheeks, sharp enough to draw blood. Arthur and his sisters wandered the fields outside town, scavenging fallen trees for firewood, but no matter how much they gathered, the house was always cold.

As the year wound down, the fighting drew ever closer. Men released from military service began to limp back to Charleville, and sometimes came to the door begging for food. Many were missing legs or arms, and if the Mouth of Darkness was gone, Arthur would let them in and give them sips of brandy beside the woodstove. The school became a makeshift hospital, reeking of carbolic soap and ether. Often he would hear screams, and once while scrounging for firewood he discovered a corpse huddled against a tree, eyes frozen shut and its uniform in tatters.

Very early one morning near the end of February, he went downstairs. Paris had signed the armistice with Prussia a month before: he no longer needed to worry that he might be conscripted into the army.

His mother eyed him coldly as he walked into the kitchen. He was wearing almost everything he owned—heavy boots, trousers, woolen vest. His greatcoat was stuffed with paper and pen and Leo's pipe lovingly wrapped in flannel; the fish-bone key was in his trouser pocket, along with the watch he'd won as a translation prize at school. He took some bread from the cupboard and began to eat it, spilling crumbs on the floor.

His mother stared at him suspiciously. "You're up early. Did you find a job?"

"I'm going to Paris to work for André Gill's newspaper. Tell the girls I'll write to them."

When she started to argue, he stormed out the door. But for once she didn't follow, and he didn't stop until he reached the train station.

He sold the watch to a pawn shop on a drab Charleville side street. The money barely covered his train ticket. He had no way of contacting Gill, no money, nothing but the address of Demeny's bookshop. It was a start, anyway.

17

Paris

THE TRAIN DREW into the station in midafternoon. The air held the violet tinge of winter twilight and stank of piss and charred wood. People mobbed the platform—women and children, injured soldiers. A one-legged man using his rifle as a cane spit at a group of Prussian soldiers as they clambered from the first-class carriage.

"Watch we don't take the other one!" a Prussian shouted, and kicked away the rifle. The wounded soldier collapsed. The Prussian turned to see Arthur staring at him.

"You too?" he yelled, and grabbed for Arthur's arm.

Arthur fled, elbowing through the crowd until he reached the street outside the station and stopped, gazing in disbelief.

The beautiful old trees along the boulevards were gone, cut for firewood during the siege. Gas lamps lined the streets, but only a few were lit. Windows held the smeared yellow gleam of tallow candles or petrol lamps. People stumbled past heaps of dirty snow, their pinched faces the same lilac-gray as the twilight. The city's marble statues had been swaddled in black cloth, like winding sheets. Everyone Arthur saw looked bruised, and most of them looked famished.

"Spare something for a soldier, friend?" A man with a caved-in face lurched toward him, extending a hand.

Arthur pulled up the collar of his overcoat and ran across the street. After a few blocks, he stopped and ducked within the skel-etal doorway of a building that had been bombed. He pulled out the bundle of paper in his pocket, shuffling through pages until he found where he'd scribbled the address of Demeny's bookstore.

Night had fallen by the time he located the shop, in a shabby neighborhood on the Left Bank. There were bomb craters every-where, and rubble-filled blocks where buildings had once stood. On a street corner, two boys sat with a filthy oilcloth spread before them. Three dead rats were lined up on the cloth, along with some twisted metal fragments and what looked like a shriv-eled mushroom.

"Three francs a rat," one of the boys said as Arthur approached. "That's a bargain."

"Thanks. I'm not that hungry." Arthur nudged a shard of metal with his boot. "What's that?"

"Piece of a bomb. Five francs. That's a good souvenir. Can't eat it, though."

Arthur bent to examine the shriveled mushroom. "What about this?"

"That's a Prussian's finger."

Arthur started to pick it up, but the boy stopped him. "That's ten francs. One sou if you just want to touch it."

"No thanks."

He found the bookshop on the next block. Demeny wasn't there, of course, but a young clerk was, huddled under a blanket behind a tall desk covered with battered volumes and old issues of *La Lune* and *L'Éclipse*.

"I'm a friend of Paul's from Douai." Arthur shoved his hands into his pockets, shivering. The shop wasn't much warmer than the street. "I'm a wartime journalist from Brussels—said you'd be able to give me some work until I find a permanent position."

"Oh yes? Lots of luck."

The clerk pointed out the grimy window to where a half dozen young men lumbered down the middle of the street, gesturing excitedly as they passed a bottle back and forth. "See them? That's the staff of *The Red Pages*. Which suspended publication today. Everyone's too busy planning the next war to bother about the last one. Why don't you get back to school, huh?"

Arthur scowled. "What about Gill? He around? I told him I'd be here this morning, but I got held up."

The clerk stared at him dubiously. After a moment he nodded. "André dropped by around noon, but I haven't seen him since then. You know where he lives?"

Arthur memorized the address and left. On the curb, the boys had rolled up their oilcloth. One of them dangled a rat by its tail.

"Two francs," he yelled after Arthur. "I'll even skin it for you!"

The windows of Gill's studio were dark when he arrived. It

had begun to snow. A single streetlamp glowed feebly, stinking of petrol and casting barely enough light for Arthur to read the name on the door. He knocked, his knuckles aching from the cold.

Nothing. He called out Gill's name and pounded harder.

Still nothing. He glanced down the empty street, then tried the knob. The door opened, and he went inside.

"Hello?"

His voice rang loudly through a darkened space that smelled of ink and damp. Bundled stacks of newspapers wobbled beside the door. In a corner a ghostly form materialized into a coat rack holding stained smocks and an overcoat nearly as filthy as Arthur's. There was a drafting desk, a tall stool and, beside the coatrack, a horsehair chaise longue covered with a frayed piano shawl.

Arthur picked up a cracked plate with a blob of dried mustard on it. He licked it clean, sank onto the chaise, and pulled the piano shawl over his lap. He closed his eyes and saw the two jeering boys, a mummified finger that swelled into his mother's face, ratlike as she shook him, shouting.

"Who are you?"

He cried out and woke with a start. Above him stood a man in a snow-covered overcoat, fist raised to strike. Arthur scrambled from the chaise, but the man grabbed his shoulder and pushed him roughly against the wall.

"Who are you? How'd you get in?"

"The door—it was open, I just—I'm a friend of Paul Demeny.

He sent me. And the bookstore, the clerk told me I could stop by." Arthur swallowed. "You're André Gill, right?"

"Yes, I'm André Gill." The man glowered. He had long, waving black hair dusted with snow, and a luxuriant mustache. "Charles sent you? From the shop? That idiot. You could be a spy. I may have to kill you."

"I'm not a spy!"

"No?" Gill stroked his mustache. "Prove it."

"I don't even know anyone in Paris! That's why I came here!"

"Ah, but how would you have known to come here, unless another spy sent you?" Gill tapped the side of his nose and smiled. He appeared to be rather drunk. "Demeny is an idiot. Terrible poet."

Arthur nodded. "He is."

"And you are?"

"Arthur Rimbaud."

"Rimbaud, Rimbaud." Gill peeled off his coat, revealing a worker's blue smock riddled with burn holes. "You're the child poet."

Arthur frowned. "I'm not—"

Gill clamped a huge hand on his shoulder and squeezed. "No? Well, which is it? Spy or child poet?"

"Poet," gasped Arthur.

"Excellent!" Gill released him and rubbed his hands gleefully. "Of course we kill poets too. But it takes a bit longer. Why in God's name did you come see me?"

"I want a job."

Gill laughed. "So would we all! What, did you arrive by balloon? Because otherwise you might have noticed that everyone in Paris is starving or recently emerged from a basement. Have you heard about our little siege? Our bombardments? Conflagrations, small children blown to bits in their beds, that sort of thing?"

Arthur flushed. "I live near Mézières—we were bombed, too."

"Oh, poor thing." Gill rolled his eyes, stifling a yawn. "I forget how sensitive child poets are. You took the train, then?"

"Yes. I arrived this afternoon. I—"

A wave of dizziness struck him, and he flopped back onto the chaise. A moment later he blinked to see Gill's mustache twitching a few inches from his face.

"You do look sickly, even for a poet." Gill shook his head. "Have you eaten?"

"Some kids outside tried to sell me a rat for three francs."

"Three francs! Highway robbery. One shouldn't pay more than eight centimes for a rat these days. Come on—"

Gill helped him to his feet. "I couldn't offer you a job if I wanted to. Times are hard for all of us, my friend. Revolution is in the air, and I wasn't making a joke about spies. Well, I *was*, but—you know. Can't trust anyone these days. The Prussian soldiers have moved out but everyone's still in an uproar, and"—his voice dropped as he drew Arthur to the front door—"I will whisper this in your ear, friend, a word to the wise. There are plans afoot to overthrow the city government. A winter under siege, starving to death and getting bombed by the Prussians . . . it wears on you.

"And rats aren't the worst of it. Last month the menu at the Jockey Club featured poodle for a week. But rat isn't half bad, especially braised, though don't ever order black rats. Gray rats have a much finer taste. Now . . ."

Gill opened the front door and with a flourish indicated the street. "The City of Light awaits you. I suggest you go to the Chapeau Noir—that's just two streets over."

He lowered his voice to a conspiratorial whisper. "It's a Red Club. You've heard of them? Where we meet to plan a new government to replace this corrupt one. The proprietor is a friend of mine. I recommend the rabbit *sauté au chasseur*. Here's ten francs; forget we ever spoke. Be careful of the company you keep, trust no one, take notes. If you are truly a poet, we will meet again, I'm sure. If not . . ." Gill shrugged. "That is your loss, not mine. Good luck, and remember: when it comes to rats, eight centimes. Not a sou more."

With a thump, the door closed in Arthur's face. He blinked, then counted the coins Gill had shoved into his hand. Shivering, he pulled his coat tight and began to walk.

He found the Chapeau Noir, a glass-fronted building that might have been cheerful once upon a time, before the siege. Inside reeked of petrol, though the only illumination came from tallow candles in empty bottles. But the tables were crowded with blue-smocked workmen, drinking and talking animatedly, and bearded student types who wore red caps or crimson sashes.

And there were women, too. Arthur had never seen so many women in a café, tossing back glasses of beer and making more noise than the men. Some had faces brightly rouged, skirts hiked to show a white flash of ankle or the muddy hem of a petticoat. Others wore black *pantalons* and bumblebee-yellow dresses with black hoods, as though they were in costume for a pantomime.

"M'sieur?" A waiter in a long white apron appeared, and showed Arthur to a table.

He took Gill's advice and ordered rabbit and a glass of beer. The food arrived quickly, a fragrant platter of meat and herbs. It was so good he ordered a second helping and a loaf of bread, also more beer; then sat for a long time sucking the rabbit's tender bones.

The beer was strong. Only after his fourth glass did he realize that a mere three francs remained of what Gill had given him. He sipped what was left, and devoted himself to eavesdropping. He learned that the bumblebee women called themselves Amazons and were plotting against the National Guard. Armed with hatpins dipped in prussic acid, they would entice soldiers to their death. He also listened, rapt, as a cloaked man spoke in urgent whispers of a revolutionary communal government. Another man, his mustache as impressive as Gill's, outlined a plan to blow up the city's monuments.

Arthur considered joining them. But the combination of fatigue, beer, and rabbit *sauté au chasseur* was too much. He pushed himself from the table, walked unsteadily across the smoky room to the door, and staggered outside.

It was close to midnight. A single lamp shed sulfurous light onto the street, and threw into nightmarish relief the outlines of shattered buildings. Arthur stepped behind a pile of rubble and pissed, then headed toward the river, following a canal that emerged from beneath an armory where a handful of sleepy-looking soldiers stood guard. The wind picked up. He could smell the Seine, a stink like a fish market and a latrine.

He staggered along a street that ran roughly parallel to the Canal Saint-Martin. Twice, exhausted, he tripped and almost plummeted into the frigid water. He looked for a place to sleep, somewhere out of the icy wind. But every alley and tunnel he peered into had a tramp or ragged soldier already resting there; or a whore servicing a client; or a half-starved mongrel that growled and stared at him with vulpine eyes.

At last he sighted a barge tied up not far from a narrow bridge. He hurried toward it, shoulders hunched and teeth clenched so they wouldn't chatter. Back in Charleville, bargemen were usually good for a potato roasted in hot coals and a few swigs of brandy. Occasionally one demanded payment with a kiss or something more, and he'd usually obliged willingly enough.

Here, he saw no sign of a lockhouse, and no evidence of a bargeman; only the long black silhouette of the boat. It rested low in the water, weighted down by a tarpaulin-covered mound sifted with snow. An acrid smell caught in his throat, overpowering the stagnant reek of the canal: coal.

He glanced over his shoulder, quickly hopped on board, and walked the length of the deck, searching for a cabin or alcove where he could take shelter from the relentless February wind.

But he found nothing save a series of cleats around the barge's perimeter, where ropes leading from the canvas tarpaulins had been tied off. He yanked aside the edge of one tarpaulin and crawled beneath, coughing as he inhaled coal dust. He curled up beside the heap, and did his best to tug the stiff canvas around him like a blanket. It did nothing to warm him.

Still, he was out of the wind, at least; and after a few minutes of shivering, he fell into a restive sleep.

18

Paris

FEBRUARY 26, 1871

I WOKE FROM a dream of a parade: martial music, drums; a trumpet that wavered between a blare and a bleat. My ears ached as though someone had thrust frozen rods into them. I blinked, opened my eyes to darkness fading to gray, and a cold so penetrating I couldn't feel my fingers or toes. Shuddering, I tried to burrow deeper into the bunk.

But the layers of worn sheets and clothing that had pillowed me were gone. I felt only cold wood beneath my hands, and the ceaseless rocking of the boat. Some kind of stiff coverlet had been flung over me: I huddled beneath it, warming my hands beneath my bomber jacket and trying to summon the courage to stand. Finally I pushed aside the coverlet, crawled out, and clambered to my feet.

Thin sunlight blinded me. I shaded my eyes, looking around for Ted; shook my head, thinking, *I'm still asleep.*

Because Ted was gone. So was the bunk where I'd slept, and the little cabin with its swaying kerosene lantern and trash-covered floor. I was outside, standing on the deck of a much larger boat, surrounded by some kind of cargo covered with dirty gray canvas. A freezing gust buffeted me and I fell back onto the canvas tarp, cried out as the canvas heaved and rippled and someone staggered out from under it. I grabbed a lump of coal, and flung it at the figure in front of me.

"Ow!" he yelped as it struck his arm, and he began shouting and cursing. His words were gibberish. My head pounded: I had a flash of déjà vu that wasn't déjà vu but the memory of a slight figure looming in the darkness of the lockhouse, his voice garbled and discordant as a broadcast from the surface of the moon. Abruptly his words shifted, and I could understand him.

"Get away from me!"

My entire body went cold. "Arthur?"

He fell silent, staring at me. After a long moment he croaked, "Merle?"

His voice had changed; everything had changed. I no longer gazed into his eyes but had to look up, into a face thinner than it had been, crowned by an unruly nest of thick dark-blond hair. His coat was the same, but he wore bigger boots, encased in gray mud. His shirt was white, not blue; his overcoat flapped open so I could see the jacket he wore underneath, and dark wool trousers that ended above his ankles. Only the eyes were the same, that unnerving, unwavering gray-blue gaze, icy as the water around us.

"Arthur," I said in a hoarse whisper. "Arthur, *what did you do?*"

I thought I might be sick.

"Merle." He reached out to touch my hair, and I saw his hand was trembling. "Are you—are you real?"

"I think so." I laughed shakily, for the first time turned to glance around. "Are you?"

We were on a barge tied up alongside a narrow walkway, beyond it clouds of thin vaporous haze. As I stared, the haze burned off, revealing shadowy impressions of buildings. Church spires began to appear, faint at first but growing darker and more solid, the boulevards and sidewalks and alleys of a city taking on color and depth, like a painting transferred from gauze to heavy canvas.

But the city wasn't D.C., or even New York. It wasn't any city I knew.

Or, rather, it was a city I half recognized, from photographs and movies and paintings in the National Gallery of Art, sepia images or ones that had darkened with age. Yet this place was flooded with color—a blue sky pale as Arthur's eyes; fluttering scarlet banners trailing from a moss-green lamppost; blackened trees and ivory monuments defaced with mustard-yellow paint. A city crowded with uniformed men, women in long dun-colored skirts and white caps, and darting children in blue smocks or jackets, all of them laughing and whooping as they marched down a broad street. Distant sounds echoed toward us: the clatter of carriage wheels and *clonk* of hooves upon cobblestones; awnings flapping in the wind; the brooding tone of a church bell tolling nine o'clock. No cars; no buses or taxis.

No structure that looked as though it had been built within the last hundred years, or more.

My mouth went dry. "What is this place?"

Arthur looked at me as though I were mad. "Paris." He wiped a hand black with coal dust on his trousers. "Come on, I want to see what's happening."

He climbed over the boat rail and hopped onto the sidewalk, as an afterthought turned and waited for me to do the same.

"What is it?" I asked breathlessly as he took my arm and headed for the marching throng.

"I don't know. An execution, maybe. Hey—"

He dropped my arm and grabbed a young woman wearing loose pants tucked into high-buttoned boots and a billowing, orange-striped black dress. "What's going on?"

The girl looked us both up and down, then said, "A unit of the National Guard is marching. Jules Andrieu is supposed to make a speech—stirring up shit, as usual." She grinned at Arthur. "Hey, weren't you at the Chapeau Noir last night? I thought so. You better move—don't want to miss Jules. Just be careful—the police are out in force, they'll smash your skull open if they have the chance."

She spun on her heels and hurried toward the crowd, glancing back to see if Arthur followed. He started after her. I had to run to catch up—his long legs seemed to have grown by at least four inches since I'd last seen him. "Who's Jules?" I gasped.

"Another poet. A radical."

"Is that who they're going to execute?"

"God, I hope not." He glanced back at me, slowing to a trot. "You haven't changed."

I shook my head. "It's only been a few hours—a night, I guess. For me, anyway."

"That's stupid—it's been four months."

"Have you seen Ted?"

"Who?" he said, distracted. "Look, let's head over there, that looks like where everyone's going."

He began to elbow his way through the crowd. I followed, fighting to get past a knot of women in wooden clogs and mud-stained aprons.

"Wait," I said desperately. "The key—the fish-bone key. Do you still have it?"

He pursed his lips, then dug into his pocket and held it out. "This?"

"Yes." I grabbed it and stuffed it into my pocket. Arthur looked annoyed, but when he saw my panicked face, he grinned.

"Better move quick, or you'll miss everything. Whatever it is," he added, and ducked past a lumbering man in the ragged remains of a military cap and jacket.

I stuck with him, but seeing anything was hopeless. There were just too many people, a stinking, fast-moving river that bore us along like insects. I saw nothing but bedraggled women's hats and the bright red caps of men who looked like laborers, with chapped, sunburned faces and raw red hands.

But after a short while, the crowd began to fan out and Arthur slowed to a trot. We'd reached an open area, a broad plaza with a tall monument in its center. A freezing wind tossed up flurries of dead leaves and tattered broadsheets. Beneath the monument, a ragtag crew of uniformed soldiers marched back and forth, many of them limping and some covered with soiled bandages.

"Who are they?" I asked, fighting to catch my breath.

"National Guard," said Arthur. He shaded his eyes and squinted. "Citizens' militia, guys who were soldiers and ordinary people. The government's not protecting us, so we've taken it into our own hands."

Four men led this beggars' parade. Two played battered horns, the others a drum and tin whistle. Filthy children ran alongside them, shouting and cheering and sometimes throwing rocks. Occasionally a soldier broke rank to chase them off. The men carried rifles and wore crimson sashes around their waists. The drummer was missing an arm. As they marched, boys and old men and even some women joined their ranks, arms linked as they chanted.

"Bread or blood!"

"Property is theft!"

"Long live the Commune!"

More and more people thronged the plaza, streaming in from alleys and the main boulevard. The impromptu parade threatened to become a riot. It was difficult now to see the soldiers through their mass of supporters. The chanting chorus grew louder and more angry.

"Bread or blood!"

"Blood!"

Arthur turned to me, face flushed and eyes shining. "Let's try to get closer to the river—I think we can see better there."

We fought our way through the crowd, the hot stench of sweat and sour wine at last giving way to a blast of cold air that smelled sweet in comparison, despite the muddy stink of the river. We dodged a man hobbling on homemade crutches, and were free.

We stood at the far end of the plaza. To one side, the canal ran toward the river. Before us, the ground rose toward an embankment that overlooked river and canal alike, and afforded an open view of the crowd. The wind carried snatches of chatter.

". . . all damned . . ."

"Couldn't see her for the blood."

". . . lost him, I couldn't stop . . ."

I thought we'd at least stand still long enough to catch our breath, but Arthur immediately headed toward the embankment and began to stride up the grassy slope. A solitary old man with a fishing pole stood at the top, his line dangling into the murky Seine. My heart leaped.

"Ted!" I shouted. The man didn't move. I started to call out again, but Arthur silenced me roughly.

"Leave him alone. He's just some tramp."

As though the man had heard, he glanced over his shoulder. He was younger than Ted, and shorter, and one eye was covered with a white patch of cloth.

I turned and trudged after Arthur, hunching against the wind. He stood at the other end of the embankment, silhouetted against

the wintry blue sky. Fifteen feet below us, an ancient stone culvert spewed foul-smelling water into the canal, which a few yards
farther on joined the river. A crumbling pier jutted above the
culvert. Arthur pulled himself atop it, leaned down to help me up
beside him. We turned and looked back at the plaza.

The soldiers continued to march—I could pick them out
from the encroaching mob by the glint of sunlight on their rifles.
All around them, the mass of onlookers fought and shoved. I
watched as a pickpocket stole a man's watch. Another man lifted
a woman's skirts; she whirled to punch him, and he crumpled to
the muddy ground.

No one looked up at us. Arthur turned to me, his face exultant.

"We've climbed the highest tower!" he shouted above the
wind.

I laughed, my exhaustion and terror and bewilderment burned
away. I felt invisible, invincible; godlike. I stooped to strike my
palm against the concrete pier and said, "I wish I could tag this."

Arthur grinned. "I know. It's amazing, isn't it?"

I straightened and stared out across the plaza, at shops and
rows of houses along the wide boulevards, bomb craters and
warehouses and stables, smoking chimneys and rubble-strewn
streets. But no skyscrapers, no electric plants, no power lines. The
tallest building was a cathedral. In the distance, where the river
curved, I saw a series of arched bridges, the spires of churches,
and a shining white dome. I picked out the charred stumps of
trees, a formal garden filled with broken statuary.

It all appeared small and eerily unreal—like a diorama, only moving and alive. Thumbprint clouds moved across the sky. Horses pulled carriages, tiny as if glimpsed through a backward telescope. Minute people in old-fashioned clothes walked side by side, as children played with a hoop. Rats no larger than ants scurried along the riverbank. My skin prickled with fear, and an eerie sense of recognition. It took me a moment to realize what, exactly, this view reminded me of.

But then it was like peeling back a sheet of tracing paper to see the original image beneath: the painting I'd fallen in love with at the National Gallery, *The Temptation of Saint Anthony.*

Only of course it wasn't the same. There had been no cathedral in the painting, no horse-drawn carriage or couples on a promenade, no ragtag soldiers and jeering crowds; just as now there were no men peering from trees, no goblin-like figures or boats rowing across the gray-white clouds.

Yet in some way that I could neither explain nor understand, I knew they were both visions of the same thing.

"Merle, look—"

I started, glanced up to see Arthur pointing at the canal. Its bank was strewn with flotsam—weathered boards, wooden spokes that had once formed a carriage wheel, a slimy mound of rope. A group of boys played with the detritus, making boats from old newspaper and launching them into the water, where they invariably capsized and floated past in sodden gray lumps, until the canal joined the river and they were lost to sight.

"Do you see him?" Arthur said, drawing up beside me and inclining his head. "There—a policeman."

A few feet from the boys a man stood, back to them as he

surveyed the crowd. He wore a crisp blue uniform with a bright yellow belt and observed the militia's drill with grave interest, frowning as he smoothed his mustache. Now and then he would remove a small red notebook from his breast pocket and write something, then put it away. Behind his back, the boys looked over their shoulders at him, making faces and sniggering. One made oinking sounds. Another furtively tossed a pebble at his hat.

The policeman started. He patted his hat and peered up into the sky, then turned, scowling, toward the canal bank.

But the boys appeared all innocence, intent upon their make-shift regatta. The policeman turned away again, continuing to observe the demonstration and take notes. Every few minutes, one of the boys threw another pebble at his hat, and the puppet show repeated itself.

"Like teasing a cat." Arthur shook his head. "You'd think they'd get bored. Or he would. Ah, there he goes—"

The policeman cast a final, affronted glance at the boys. He crossed his arms and stepped toward the crowd, brow furrowed. A few people turned to heckle him.

"Why aren't *you* marching?" shouted a heavyset woman in a black cap. "Scared?"

The policeman said nothing.

"Too good for us, huh?" Another woman jostled up along-side the first. As though she were a conjuror, she reached into the crowd and yanked an ancient man to her side, stooped and wizened as a stork. "*He* volunteered to join up, but they wouldn't take him because he's ninety-three years old."

The old man gave the police officer a mock salute and grinned, displaying a single tooth. The policeman raised an eyebrow but remained impassive.

"Maybe they wouldn't take him," said the first woman. Beside her loomed a giant of a man, wearing a blue smock, a red cap, and heavy hobnailed boots. "Marcel here, he's in charge of volunteers—maybe you should talk to him, eh?"

A small crowd had broken away from the demonstration to watch, laughing as the old man capered and saluted the policeman again and again. Several men pushed their way forward to stand beside Marcel.

"You know, I don't recall seeing him at any of the Red Club meetings," one drawled.

The boys had abandoned their boats to watch. Beside me, Arthur shifted to get a better view.

"We need a few good men." Marcel stepped toward the policeman, towering above him. "You can join up now if you like, how's that?"

More raucous laughter as people hurried to see what was happening. The horns and drums grew silent as soldiers broke formation and ran over. The policeman stood, unperturbed, and fingered the end of his mustache, lost in thought. Finally, he reached into his breast pocket and once again withdrew his red notepad and pencil. He opened the notebook, with a few neat strokes wrote something, and raised his head.

"Marcel . . ." He stared up at the big man. "Your last name, please?"

Marcel gaped. "My name?"

"Yes. These demonstrations by the militia . . ." The policeman gazed blandly at the soldiers, who stared back with open hostility. "They encourage revolutionary thought. It's a threat to the stability of the government. It is my duty to report all of you."

"Report us?" someone cried out in disbelief. "To whom?"

"To the proper authorities. One at a time, please." The policeman pointed his pencil at Marcel. "I must ask you again—your name, sir."

"I'll give you my name." Marcel's massive arm swung out to strike the policeman and sent him sprawling. "It's Langois. That's L—A—"

As he pronounced each letter, he kicked viciously at the fallen man. The policeman grunted, then cried out in pain.

"N—G—"

"*Stop, please!*"

"—O—"

"*I beg you, pl—*" The policeman raised a hand feebly, his face awash with blood. His hat tumbled into the canal and bobbed toward the embankment.

"Shut *up!*" Marcel kicked him again. The policeman shouted in anguish, his cry swallowed by deafening cheers as Marcel pumped his fist. "Solidarity!" he bellowed. "Long live the Commune!"

I lost sight of the writhing figure on the ground as the mob surged around him.

"Here!" A boy dragged a long board from the rubbish, calling to Marcel. "Get that rope!"

I watched in horror as the boys and Marcel tied the doomed

policeman to the plank. He struggled uselessly, his back against the board, his body swathed in gray coils.

My stomach roiled; I tasted blood where I'd bitten the inside of my cheek.

Yet I couldn't look away. It was as though two Merles stood there, side by side: the one that numbly observed the man's torment and the one that recorded every detail of it, noting the play of light and shadow across the man's face, the crosshatch of hemp fibers and blotched flesh. There was me, and somebody else.

That somebody else watched motionless as the crowd lifted the plank with the policeman bound to it, carried it a few steps, and flung it into the canal. There was a report like a cannonshot as the board struck the water's surface. For an instant it was submerged. Then the plank bobbed back to the surface, and began its descent to the Seine.

"My God," whispered Arthur.

I glanced at his rapt face and swiftly turned away, repelled and sickened: did I look like that?

Below us the boys darted along the canal path. Whenever the plank floated toward the shore, someone ran to the bank and pushed it off again. A small group began to drunkenly sing, linking arms, when a trumpet fanfare rang out.

The boys halted and looked back. An angry voice shouted a command, followed by another fanfare and more shouting. The soldiers groaned, shouldered their rifles, and trudged back toward the center of the plaza. Drumbeats sounded, and a sergeant's call to order. Murmuring, the rest of the crowd turned to follow the militia. The boys ran after them.

Only Arthur and I remained on the embankment, watching as the current bore its human vessel toward the river. The man's face had collapsed into a ruin of violet flesh. For a fraction of a second his gaze met mine. I stepped away from the edge of the embankment and turned toward Arthur.

He was gone.

"Arthur?" I scanned the embankment and saw no one, glanced down at the plaza and spotted a lanky form, black-clad, running across the cobblestones to where the crowd had gathered to watch the militia's drill.

"Arthur!" I shouted, but my words were swallowed by the wind. I started to run down the grassy hillside but almost immediately drew up short. Already he had disappeared within a throng that had now swelled to thousands, many of them bearing rifles or lethal-looking farm tools. I scrambled back to the top of the embankment, numb with despair.

I was trapped. Even if I could find Arthur again, he'd shown little interest in me, and had raced off without even a cursory good-bye. The thought of facing people who had tortured and murdered a policeman as calmly as they would have cut down a dead tree made me think that standing on such an exposed spot might be suicidal.

Yet where could I go? If I left the embankment, sooner or later I'd run into someone whose language I didn't understand, in a world that had existed almost a hundred years before I was born.

I shivered, slowly walked to the other end of the promontory, and stared at the river below. It moved swiftly, tawny water green-flecked in the thin sunlight. I could just make out a small black shape, moving with the current downstream.

I slid a hand into my pocket and fingered the fish-bone key. I thought of Arthur, leaping into a river that had, somehow, brought him here; remembered how I'd stood upon a concrete pier above the Potomac and thought of how easy it would be to jump and drown in that icy water.

I no longer wanted to die. I wanted to be back in the city I knew, among the noise and fumes of rush-hour traffic with a satchel full of oil pastels and virgin sketchbooks; wolfing down a Reuben sandwich and a beer at the Blue Mirror; drawing Ted as he played his guitar on M Street; squatting in a warehouse in downtown Manhattan; clutching a can of neon-yellow spray paint as my tag glowed across a crumbling storefront:

RADIANT DAYS

I drew a deep breath and took two more steps, until my toes hung over the turf, twenty or so feet above the river.

Below me, the water brightened from muddy brown to amber to gold. In the distance, I could still see that tiny jot of black, rising and falling with the current. I watched until it was nothing but a black speck, until it might have been a grain of dust in my eye; watched until it all became one thing, water and sky and shadow turned to fire as the world blazed around me. A sound rose above the soft rush of water, a plangent note that faded into the memory of a plucked string, a word that might have been my own name.

A blue flare slashed at the corner of my eyes, blinding me. The plaintive note rang out once more: no longer faint but deafening; not a name but a command. I stuck my hand into my pocket and ran my fingers across the cold prongs of the fish-bone key; took a deep breath and stared straight into the dying sun, consumed by a corona of indigo flame; and jumped.

19

Paris

ARTHUR REMAINED IN Paris another twelve days. Sometimes, he'd recall Merle and feel a twinge of longing, regret that he hadn't tried to make her stay with him, or attempted to return with her to the night city.

But he knew that world was gone forever, along with the boy who'd lived in it. He was someone else now: he had watched a man die and felt not only revulsion but also detached curiosity. It turned out that fear, like misery, could spur him to write. So could desire, and the growing awareness that he was aroused by the very things that disturbed his sleep.

He joined the Communards who met at the Chapeau Noir, plotting a new regime that would overthrow the one that had abandoned the citizens of Paris during the siege; but grew impatient with the amount of time and energy it took to organize a revolution. In March, as winter began its slow death, he left Paris and began the weeklong walk back to Charleville. By the time he reached home, he had influenza.

He remained there for a month, long enough to recover from his fevers and to replace his disintegrating boots with new ones. The Mouth of Darkness burned his vile clothes, though he saved his frayed overcoat, a treasured souvenir that gave off a faint odor of café smoke when it rained. At the end of April he left again for Paris, where he became a runner for the Communards, bearing messages across the Left Bank in the guise of delivering paper to one of the tabloids that sprang up then disappeared, sometimes overnight.

After a few weeks he returned home again. He hated Charleville, loathed it with a passion that bordered on obsession. But, perversely, he could write there, boredom and rage distilling his memories of Paris into poems. Every evening he'd get drunk, close his eyes, and will himself to be someplace else. He'd write throughout the night, adding to the sheaf of poems he'd already penned, the notes he'd scrawled after witnessing the policeman's murder in the Place Vendôme. He wrote until his eyes watered, until the pen fell from his fingers and his hand ached; until he felt sick and nauseated from exhaustion.

> *sour apples . . .*
> *green water pierced my hull, stains of blue wine, vomit,*
> *   a drunken boat . . .*
> *that vile sun a mystic horror . . .*

He was the boat, borne into an unknowable distance; and he was the poet, writing on a crumpled piece of paper. When he finally plunged into sleep, he rode waves upon a sea of stars that overtook a paper boat, where a man bobbed like a cork among isles of blue and gold.

> *Sometimes, I bathed in the Poem*
> *Of the Sea, steeped in milky stars, devouring azures and*
>   *greens;*
> *Where sometimes a drowned man floated past,*
> *Ghastly, enraptured, and sank into the depths. . . .*

By day he wrote to Georges and to Paul Demeny, long letters that continued a conversation that had never really begun: more a conversation with himself about poetry, madness, the destruction of all the established writers whose work he disdained. He sent them poems as well, fragments of things he'd begun, lists of what he'd been reading. He was building a bridge between Charleville and the world outside, an escape route composed of words and loss and longing.

By autumn he knew he could no longer stay. His arguments with his mother had become screaming matches; once he had attacked her, and if his sisters hadn't pulled him away he might have killed her. He gathered the poems he'd been working on—"Vowels," a long poem called "The Drunken Boat"— and composed a letter to the one poet whose work he admired, Paul Verlaine. Verlaine was ten years older, married, comfortably settled in a flat in Paris. Arthur had never met him, or even corresponded.

But they had a mutual friend who lived in Charleville, and so Arthur decided to throw himself on the older poet's mercy. He sent Verlaine several poems. When he received no response, he wrote another letter and sent him a few more. Finally, he composed a brief note on the last of the paper he'd received from the aunts in Douai.

To Paul Verlaine, Paris

Charleville, September 1871

> *I've been trying to write a long poem, and I can't write in Charleville. And I can't come to Paris—I'm broke. My mother's a widow, extremely religious: my only money is the ten centimes she gives me every Sunday for church.*
>
> *I promise not to be any trouble....*

> *A. Rimbaud*

He hoped the older man might be a soft touch; also that Verlaine might have a soft bed with, perhaps, room in it for an enfant terrible masquerading as a child poet. A few days later, he finally received a reply.

> *Come, dear great soul, we summon you, we await you....*

❊   ❊   ❊

ONCE AGAIN ARTHUR GRABBED THE FEW THINGS THAT WERE PRECIOUS to him—his clay pipe and tobacco pouch, the wad of poems, his pen. The next day he left for Paris, where he would be proved right about Verlaine's soft bed.

As for causing no trouble, he couldn't have been more wrong.

PART FIVE

⟡

FAREWELL

Autumn already! But why long for an eternal
sun when we're searching for divine light, far
from those who die with the seasons.

— Arthur Rimbaud, "Adieu"

20

Washington, D.C.

OCTOBER 9, 1978

LIGHT STABBED MY eyelids, counterpoint to a throbbing pain in my arm. I groaned and turned onto my back, rubbing my eyes as I fought to untangle myself from a dream of ragged soldiers and a drowned man, a boy in the moonlight pressing his hand against mine as a drop of blood spilled into a silvery river where carp with human faces gazed up at us then disappeared. I stared at the ceiling of my room, searching for the familiar constellation I'd painted, Clea's feline face amid a progression of radiant suns.

But my paintings weren't there. I wasn't at Perry Street. I sat up in a panic, disoriented; jammed a hand into my pocket and withdrew a glittering silver coin and a tarnished key shaped like a fish bone. One of the key's prongs brushed against a small cut on my thumb, and I winced.

With that flare of pain I realized where I was: on the bunk in Ted's ramshackle boat. Pale sunlight fell through the porthole;

the kerosene lantern swung gently from the ceiling, its flame extinguished. The window of the potbellied stove was black with creosote, the cabin so cold my breath stained the air. I pulled a frayed blanket around my shoulders and stood. I saw no sign of Ted, no guitar, no fishing rod. I called out a few times but heard no reply.

At last I wrapped the blanket around me against the cold and headed for the ladder to the deck. A note had been thumbtacked to one rung.

Had to go find something that got lost. Take care—Don't look back!—

Ted

I swore under my breath: he'd gone in search of the lockhouse key. I stuck the note in my pocket and quickly climbed the ladder. If I hurried, I might be able to catch up with him, or at least find him at the lockhouse. That was presuming I could actually *find* the lockhouse.

I stepped out on deck, Ted's blanket around my shoulders. A saffron glow suffused the sky as an early-morning sun shower swept across the water. Rain fell like fistfuls of glitter. Clouds raced across the sky, so low they seemed to catch in the leafless trees along the riverbank. I could hear the faint drone of dawn traffic, and the bell in the church tower at Georgetown University tolling eight.

I hopped back on shore, pushing through brambly under-growth until I found the towpath. The rain stopped. Sunlight streamed through the trees, igniting puddles at my feet. Now and then I paused, scanning both sides of the canal for the field-stone wall and white birches I'd seen when I first came upon the lockhouse. Mourning doves cooed as they fed alongside the path, erupting into a flurry of gray wings when a siren wailed nearby. There were hardly any trees here, just heavily trodden grass and gravel, the barred windows and doors of row houses. I passed another lock, footbridges, and a few spindly saplings, and came to a spot where the canal ran beneath the street, emerging into sunlight again on the other side.

But no lockhouse. I stopped and raked my fingers through my hair in frustration. The siren wailed again, louder this time. I clutched the blanket tighter and started walking. An amplified voice crackled nearby, and I looked up.

On the street above the towpath, a policeman leaned over the rail and gazed at the canal, speaking into a walkie-talkie. An ambulance and two patrol cars were parked behind him, red lights flashing. A few yards ahead of me, several people in EMT uniforms crouched on the bank of the canal. A cop spoke to a man in jogging clothes, taking notes. Two more EMTs walked down the path, carrying a stretcher.

I walked toward the emergency crew, feeling as though my blood had been replaced with helium, and saw a figure on the ground, motionless. My entire body went cold as I ran the last few steps. The cop glanced at me as the crew arrived with the stretcher. They began tossing things onto the ground—an oxygen tank, tubes, and blankets.

I halted, staring at the man beside the canal. He lay on his back, one arm flung out, his flannel shirt pulled up to expose his chest, white and slack as a deflated balloon.

"Ted." For a moment I thought it was someone else talking. *"Ted!"*

One of the ambulance crew turned to me and shouted, "Get her out of here!"

Someone grabbed my arm. "Come on, get out of the way!"

"No." I tried to pull away, found myself staring at a cop. "You can't! You—that's *Ted*."

The cop looked over his shoulder at the jogger. "Just hang on a minute, okay?" He turned back to me. "Were you with him last night?"

"What?" I shook my head, dazed.

A second cop came up behind the first. "Get back to the guy who found him. I'll talk to her." He stared at me, a man about my father's age, with close-cropped hair and a black mustache. The badge on his uniform jacket read PIERI. He inclined his head toward the crowd of EMTs and police surrounding Ted. "How do you know this guy?"

I stared at him blankly. Finally I stammered, "Ted Kampfert—that's Ted Kampfert."

Officer Pieri nodded. "That's right. Homeless guy, lives on the street." He gave me a quick once-over, and I realized that, with my filthy clothes and frayed blanket, I looked like I'd been living on the street as well. "Were you with him last night?"

"Last night?" I repeated stupidly. The first cop joined us, trailed by the jogger. I turned to see the EMTs kneeling around Ted. They lifted him, with as little effort as though he were a child, and placed him on the stretcher. I looked back at Officer Pieri. "Is he—is he okay?"

Annoyance faded into a sort of resigned pity, and he shook his head. "No. They pronounced him dead a few minutes ago."

"No! They can't—he was *fine*!"

The jogger gave me a sympathetic look. "A lot of the kids around here knew him," he said to Officer Pieri. "He'd buy them beer and cigarettes. He was some kind of street musician. I saw him all the time, that's why I thought he was sleeping first time I ran by. Second time, though, he just didn't look right."

I stared through my tears at the man on the stretcher. He looked smaller and frailer, as though he'd aged decades in one night. As the crew bore the stretcher up toward the ambulance, I saw a few things littering the ground where he'd lain—cigarette butts, brown paper bags, a white plastic bucket. His fishing rod and guitar case.

And something else, a shapeless brown object that still bore the imprint of where his head had rested.

My satchel.

Before Pieri could stop me, I darted off, dropped to the ground, and grabbed it, my heart pounding as I flung it open.

There were my bundled drawings; my sketchbooks and oil pastels and watercolors; the cracked plastic box of brushes and pencils; my palette and notebooks and gum erasers. I remembered the note tacked to the ladder on his boat.

Had to go find something that got lost.

"Hey!" A hand closed around my shoulder and pulled me to my feet. "What the hell do you think you're doing? Hand that over—"

"It's mine." I hugged it to my chest. "Two kids stole it from my house!"

"What house? You live here?" Officer Pieri eyed me skeptically.

"No—Northeast. Brookland."

"What's your name?"

"Merle Tappitt."

"Merle Tappitt." He regarded me for a long moment. "You were with him yesterday, down by the river. The kid who's been painting that stuff all over town. Radium something."

"Radiant Days," I said automatically, then winced.

"Right, Radiant Days. I never heard of a girl doing that kind of stuff. Graffiti. I thought you must be a guy." He held out his hand. "Okay, Merle. Hand me that bag, please."

"But it's mine!"

"We'll determine if it's yours or not. Right now, you need to come with me to the station house." I started to argue but he cut me off, waving over another cop. "I want to ask you some questions and try to figure out what happened here. Mind emptying your pockets?"

I handed him my bag, defeated, and turned my pockets inside out as he watched. They were empty, save for the change purse and fish-bone key. Officer Pieri examined the key, then handed it back.

"You said Ted was fine? Well, as you saw, he's not fine now. I want you to come and answer some questions about Ted. We'll determine who this purse belongs to. And it'll be warmer at the station, I can promise you that," he added, gesturing at the blanket draped around my shoulders. "How old are you, Merle?"

"Eighteen."

"Eighteen." His walkie-talkie crackled again. He turned away and spoke into it, signed off, and took my elbow. "Okay, Merle. Let's go."

He guided me up the sidewalk toward the street. A few people had gathered near the ambulance, craning their necks as the crew bundled the stretcher into the back. The crowd stared as Pieri escorted me to the patrol car, as though I might be a criminal, the kind of teenager who would kill a homeless man. I avoided their eyes and slid into the back of the cruiser. Officer Pieri slammed the door after me and got into the front seat. I pressed my face against the window while he called in to the station, watching as the ambulance pulled away in silence.

21

Washington, D.C.

OCTOBER 9, 1978

AT THE POLICE station, exhaustion and grief overcame me, and I got the dry heaves. Officer Pieri had me put my head between my legs until I felt better, then made me recite the alphabet backward and take a Breathalyzer test.

"What day is it?" he asked.

I hesitated. "Monday?"

"What month and date?"

I thought of Arthur, a moon turning from crescent to full in a single night. "October ninth? Um, 1978," I added for good measure.

"You don't sound too sure of that." Officer Pieri leaned back in his swivel chair. "Did you take anything, Merle? Any drugs?"

"No. I don't do any of that stuff."

"Well, good for you," he said drily. He reached into the bottom drawer of his desk and retrieved a brown paper bag, opened it, and handed me an orange and a sandwich wrapped in plastic.

"You like tuna fish? You look like you could use a bite."

I tried not to wolf it down while Pieri stepped into the hall, returning with a paper cup of water.

"Here," he said. "Don't make yourself sick. So what were you doing with Ted there yesterday by the river?"

"Nothing. Just hanging out. Talking."

"Talking about what?"

"I dunno. Art. Painting, music, stuff like that." I ate as he recorded my answers onto various forms. After a few minutes I tentatively asked, "Do they know what happened?"

Officer Pieri finished filling out a sheet and set his pen down. "They'll run toxicology tests and do an autopsy. Probably he died of exposure. Or liver failure. Acute alcohol poisoning. It could have been anything." He sighed. "Ted had his issues."

"You knew him?"

Pieri nodded. "Sure. I used to keep an eye on him, make sure he got something to eat when I could. Tried to get him to go to a shelter, but he always seemed to have someplace he'd disappear to. Maybe he went to his brother's; I don't know." He twisted his chair to gaze at the wall, his expression sorrowful. "I saw him and his band once. Back when I was in college, they did a show in Trenton. Best live concert I ever saw, even better than the Stones. They played for four hours and when they were done a bunch of us followed them into the parking lot, stayed out all night with a case of Rheingold. Ted and his brother got a couple of acoustic guitars out of their van and sang—we all sang." He shook his head. "Everyone stole from Ted. You're too young to know about that, but it's true. Bob Dylan, Neil Young, that guy Tom Waits. Bruce Springsteen. All of 'em. He was the best damn guitarist in the world. It broke my heart to see him out on the street, but some people, they just decide what they're gonna do and there's nothing you can say to change that. You ever see him play?"

"Just last night. On M Street."

Officer Pieri continued to stare at the wall for another minute. Finally he swiveled around again and picked up another form. "Did you have any other contact with him? Did you see anyone else who was with him?"

When he finished questioning me about Ted, he pulled another sheaf of papers from a drawer and began asking about how my bag had been stolen. I told him what I knew, but didn't mention Errol's name. There was no point in getting a twelve-year-old in trouble. All I wanted was to get my bag back.

"How did Ted Kampfert come to have your purse?" Pieri tapped his pen against the desk. "You said some kids took off with it in Northeast yesterday. How'd it show up with Ted this morning?"

"I have no idea," I said.

"You have any ID on you?" I shook my head. "What about inside the bag? No? Can you describe its contents for me?"

I rattled off everything I could think of. Pieri opened the bag and rummaged inside. At last he closed it, set it on the desk, and pushed it across to me.

"Okay, Merle. Looks like this belongs to you."

"Thank you." I took the satchel and held it on my lap. "Is it okay if I go?"

"Not yet. Your graffiti—you know that's a crime, right? Vandalism, defacing government property. I should give you a summons right now." I started to say something but he cut me off. "Now I shouldn't do this, but you seem like a nice girl—like I said, I thought some guy was putting those up everywhere. Radiant Days." He sat musing, then leaned across the desk to stare at me pointedly. "You've got some real talent. Why are you wasting it on graffiti?"

"Maybe it's not wasted." I stared back. "Maybe it's just different."

"Different?" He sighed. "Well, Merle, I better not catch you again being different in my district, okay? Hold on—"

A light on his phone blinked. He punched it, picked up the receiver, and listened before setting it back in the cradle. "There's someone here who wants to talk to you. Robert Kampfert—he's Ted Kampfert's brother."

"What?"

"He's next of kin; he just arrived from the hospital. Someone at the front desk told him you were with Ted last night. Would you be willing to talk to him?"

My expression must have indicated clearly that I was not. Officer Pieri hesitated, then said, "You don't have to, Merle. But it would be the kind thing to do."

I stared at my bag, and nodded. "Yeah, sure."

Officer Pieri escorted me to a small room with flickering

fluorescent lights, pointed to one of two battered metal chairs, and said, "Wait here, I'll be right back."

I waited. The door had a glass window with wire mesh in it. There was a poster that demonstrated the Heimlich maneuver, and a dead cockroach on the floor beneath. After a few minutes Officer Pieri returned with a middle-aged man dressed in jeans and a beat-up leather jacket. His eyes were red, his dark hair uncombed.

"Merle, this is Rob Kampfert, Ted's brother." Officer Pieri showed him into the room. "I'll be across the hall in my office. Just tell me when you're done."

He stepped out, leaving the door open. The man looked down at me, then settled in the other chair. "You're Merle?"

I nodded. He looked like Ted, but younger, his hair brown and graying around his temples. His eyes behind wire-rimmed glasses were dark brown, not amber.

But they were deep-set, like Ted's, and while his face wasn't weathered by exposure, he had the same deep grooves beside his mouth, and the same pattern of creases when he at last gave me a tight, unhappy smile. Under his worn leather jacket he wore a flannel shirt, newer and cleaner than Ted's. He smelled strongly of cigarette smoke. He looked drained and heartbroken, and when he talked, he sounded almost exactly like Ted, his voice deep and gravelly.

"Well, Merle, I'm Rob."

He stuck out his hand. I took it and he held it for a few seconds before dropping it. He looked like he had no idea what to do or say next. He glanced at my face, then at the bag in my lap. He cleared his throat and asked in that rasping voice, "Someone out there told me you were with Ted last night?"

"Yeah."

Rob sighed and ran a hand through his graying hair. "Look, I'm not here to interrogate you or anything. I know Ted bought kids booze, but I don't give a rat's ass if he bought you the whole goddamn bar, okay? I just want to know if he was all right. What he did, was he having fun. Was he happy, what was he doing, you know? We—we hadn't talked in a while." His voice cracked, but his gaze remained fixed on me. "That's all I care about, Merle. So . . ."

I shrugged, miserably. I couldn't tell him what really happened. But I had to tell him something.

"No, he was fine," I said. "I mean, we just kind of hung out, me and—"

I checked to make sure Officer Pieri wasn't listening. "Me and a friend," I went on softly. "Someone I just met last night. We were walking along M Street late and Ted was there playing his guitar for people and we hung out and listened to him." I paused. "His guitar—he was amazing."

Rob Kampfert smiled. "Yeah. He was the best."

I recalled what David had said, that Ted and his brother had started the Deadly Rays in high school; that they hadn't spoken for years. "Was he—do they know what happened?"

"Yeah, probably. They still have to do an autopsy, but the ER doc said it was alcohol and exposure." For a moment he shut his eyes. "Business as usual. Asshole."

"I'm sorry." I started crying. "I'm sorry, I'm so sorry. . . ."

Officer Pieri poked his head into the room. "Everything okay in here?"

Rob nodded. "Yeah, thanks, I'm about done."

Officer Pieri withdrew. Rob Kampfert touched my shoulder and got to his feet. "Thanks, Mary—"

"Merle."

"Right, Merle." He stopped, slid a hand into his jacket, and pulled out a scroll of paper. He unrolled it and held it up: my portrait of Ted. "You do this?"

I flushed. "Yeah. Last night."

"No shit. Huh. That's really good."

"Thanks."

"It was in his pocket when they found him. That and a couple of fish hooks. My brother loved to fish. Fishing and the guitar, that was pretty much his whole life. And booze," he added. "But this is a great picture. I've got photos of Ted but they're mostly old ones. When we were both kids. And a bunch with the band. But your picture, you really nailed him." He laughed. "And my brother is a hard guy to nail down."

I thought he was going to return the drawing to me. Instead he rolled it back up and slid it inside his jacket.

"Thanks for talking to me," he said. "There's going to be some kind of memorial service, probably Saturday. Maybe you can make it."

He nodded at me and left. I waited a few minutes, gathered my bag, and did the same.

Officer Pieri gave me a perfunctory wave as I passed his

office. My steps slowed as I approached the waiting room: I had
no idea what to do now—where to go, how to get enough money
for food and a place to live. The notion of going back to Norville
was the only thing worse than that of spending a night out on the
street, alone. I could continue to search for the lockhouse, but I
couldn't bear the thought of being there without Arthur or Ted.

And suddenly it hit me that I'd be spending the rest of my life
without them. Ted Kampfert was dead, and Arthur as well—
unless time really did flow backward and forward, something
that was impossible to believe in with both of them gone. I wiped
my eyes, determined not to walk through the waiting area in
tears, and stared resolutely at my feet as I strode across the room.

I was halfway out the door when someone ran up breathlessly
alongside me.

"Merle! Hey, Merle, wait up—"

I stared in disbelief. "David?"

"Jesus, I waited in there for like an hour, and then you almost
got away!" He hugged me, so tightly I could smell his musky
aftershave.

"But how'd you find me?"

"I heard what happened when I went to get coffee. A guy said
Ted had OD'd or something, and that the police had brought in
a girl for questioning. I remembered seeing you last night and, I
dunno." He hugged me again. "I just had a feeling. I'm so sorry,
Merle."

"Thanks." I drew back and winced. "I must smell awful. I
haven't had a shower in—well, you don't want to know."

David laughed. "Yeah, I figured that when I saw you last night. You and that guy, you seemed like you had other things on your minds. And Ted, too—God, that's so sad. Were you with him? Do you know what happened?"

I did my best to fill him in as we walked. I left out the more arcane details, though I did mention seeing that odd green flare in Ted's eyes as he played. When I was done, David took out a joint and lit it, tossed the match to the curb, then took a long hit. "Man, you had quite a night. All I can say is, it sounds like Ted went out with a bang. I mean, at least he died happy, right?"

"I dunno. Did he? Does anyone actually die happy?" I kicked through a patch of brown leaves. "I just can't believe he's dead."

"What about Arthur? Does he know?"

"Probably not. I mean, no. He just . . . took off." I gestured vaguely in the direction of the Key Bridge. "I doubt I'll ever see him again."

"Hey, you never know." David passed me the joint, but I waved it away. "But what you said about Ted's eyes, that weird green thing—I've seen that."

"You have?"

He nodded. "Yeah. Ted was the one who set me up with John Waters, did you know that? Well, no, you wouldn't, but he did. I always felt that he was always sort of out there, pulling strings in this weird way. Other people have told me shit like that about him, too. Couple guys in a band, this girl who went to New York to study acting with Stella Adler. Ted always seemed to know someone who could help you out."

"Well, he didn't know someone who could help me," I said with a trace of bitterness.

"That's why I'm here, darling." David put his arm around me. "Listen—there's this little room at my place, it was like a maid's room or something. I've just got boxes in there now, books and stuff, but there's a daybed, and you're small enough you could sleep on it."

. "Oh, David, really?" I grabbed his neck and kissed him, over and over. "Oh my God, you're an angel—"

David pulled away, grinning. "Be warned, it's a tiny room. Peter said I should use it as a closet, but I wanted to see about making it into some kind of office or something."

"Is Peter the guy you were with last night? Does he know about this—is he going to mind if I crash at your place?"

"Yeah, he's the guy. And no, he won't mind. I don't think so, anyway," he said vaguely. "He's paying for my place, but he doesn't live there—he's got a house up in Tenleytown. I'm a kept man, Merle." He burst out with that goofy foghorn laugh. "At least until I get work in another movie and become famous."

David wasn't lying—the room was tiny. But I would have been happy with a broom closet, if it had access to hot water and a pillow. As soon as we arrived I dumped my bag on the floor and took a shower, getting out only when David barged in and announced I'd used up all the hot water.

"Here." He held out an armful of clothes—jeans and corduroys, flannel shirts and T-shirts, and a sequined vest. "Something in there'll fit you. We can go down to the Junior League Shop or

Goodwill later and find some girl clothes if you want."

"I don't need girl clothes." I grabbed a Roxy Music T-shirt, a pair of black drainpipe jeans, and a silky black polyester shirt covered with purple medallions. "I'll take these."

"Here." David tossed me a long cotton-candy-pink scarf. "A token girl thing. So your neck doesn't get cold. Come on, I made breakfast."

We went through an entire skillet of scrambled eggs and chives, a platter of bacon, toast, and coffee, and orange juice. Afterward I was so tired I could barely walk to my room without stumbling. David had removed most of the boxes and stuck an old Windsor chair beside the daybed. He'd saved one carton as a makeshift nightstand with a lamp balanced precariously atop it.

"Good night, sweet princess," he said as I crawled under the covers and groaned in pure joy. "I'll be out for a couple of hours—see you when you get up."

When I woke, the room was filled with a lavender glow, the trees outside the window etched black against the twilight. For a moment I was disoriented, my mind clicking through all the places I might be—the squat on Perry Street, Ted's boat, the lockhouse, Paris. . . .

I bolted up in a panic: where was my bag?

Then I saw it on the carton beside the bed. I snatched it to my breast, thought of Ted and whispered, *"Oh, thank you thank you."*

David was still gone. I foraged in the fridge for something to eat, and returned to my room. I sat on the daybed with my satchel and meticulously began to remove its contents.

There was the sketchbook with all my drawings of Clea; there was my notebook. There were my charcoal pencils and the prismatic array of oil pastels—violet, indigo, crimson, saffron, black. There was the very first sketch of what became my tag, fractal stars exploding into the eye of the sun.

Nearly everything was arrayed before me on the bed. I stuck my hand into the bag one last time, in case I'd missed a pencil or gum eraser, and my fingers closed around something unfamiliar—a paperback book.

I pulled it out, trying to remember if I'd stuck a book in there in the last few months. On the cover was a black-and-white reproduction of an old photograph. Something about the image was familiar. I stared at it, frowning, then snatched my hand back, as though the book might burst into flame.

It was a photograph of Arthur. Not the round-faced fifteen-year-old I'd first met in the lockhouse, but the young man of a few months—for me, a few hours—later. His mouth was tight-lipped, almost grim; his tousled hair swept back from a high forehead. He wore a dark suit jacket and high-collared shirt with a knotted tie askew at this throat. It was inconceivable.

But it was him. Those pale eyes were unmistakable, staring at some impossible thing, unseen by anyone else: an unblinking gaze, and utterly cold.

ARTHUR RIMBAUD: SEASONS IN HELL
COLLECTED POEMS

My neck prickled, and I skimmed the back copy.

> The young rebel Arthur Rimbaud changed poetry
> forever . . . his precocious involvement with the Paris
> Commune . . . violent aftermath of his notorious
> affair with poet Paul Verlaine . . . Rimbaud's abrupt
> abandonment of poetry at the age of nineteen, followed
> by years of exile . . .

I opened the book. There were French words on the left-hand
pages, English translations on the right.

> Sometimes, I bathed in the Poem
> Of the Sea, steeped in milky stars, devouring azures and
>   greens;
> Where sometimes a drowned man floated past,
> Ghastly, enraptured, and sank into the depths. . . .
>
> I know skies slashed with lightning and waterspouts,
> Riptides, tidal waves. I know twilight,
> Exalted dawns exploding with doves.
> I've seen what men have only imagined they'd seen!

I continued to leaf through the book.

> Then the woman disappeared. I shed more tears than
> God has ever asked for . . . She hasn't returned, and she

will never return, the Beloved One who came to my
room—something I'd never dared to hope for.

My companion, beggar girl, child monster!

My hand shook as I turned the page.

This is the friend, neither passionate nor weak. Friend.
This is the loved one, neither tormentor nor tormented.
   Beloved.
Air and the world, unbidden. Life.
So it was this?
And the dream returns.

"Hey, you're up!"

I turned.

David stood in the doorway, his brow furrowed. "You okay, Merle? Did something happen?"

I said nothing, just stared at the book in my hands. David walked over and took it from me, glanced at the cover, then nodded in approval. "Rimbaud! He's incredible, isn't he?"

"You—you've heard of him?"

"Yeah, sure. He was amazing. A total rock star. All the Beats were into him—Kerouac, all those guys. Jim Morrison, Bob Dylan. He was gay—Rimbaud, not Dylan—he was living with this guy named Verlaine, another poet. Verlaine tried to kill him, shot Rimbaud in the hand. Crazy as shit. Rimbaud wrote some stuff after that, but then he gave up on poetry and disappeared. He worked for the emperor of Abyssinia as a gunrunner."

He paused and gave me an odd look. "That French guy I saw you with last night—his name was Arthur, too, right?" He gazed at me expectantly. I remained silent, and finally David shrugged. "Just seems kind of weird, that's all."

I nodded. "Yeah, weird." I pointed at the book. "What happened to him? Rimbaud. How—how did he die?"

David frowned. "I'm not sure. Cancer, I think. He died kind of young. But the insane thing is that he was so young when he wrote all this stuff. By the time he was nineteen, he was finished."

"Nineteen." I stared at the charcoal pencils and oil pastels on the bed. After a moment, David moved these aside and sat beside me, thumbing through the book.

"Here." He handed it to me. "Read that."

To Paul Demeny, Douai

Charleville, May 15, 1871

Here's some prose on the future of poetry. . . .
"I" is somebody else. . . . This is clear to me: I witness the birth of my own thought: I see it, I listen to it. . . .
I say one must become a visionary, make yourself a seer. The Poet becomes a visionary through a long, immense and deliberate derangement of all the senses. All forms of love, of suffering, of madness, he seeks these

out, he exhausts himself with every poison, he sucks their essences. Unspeakable torture that demands all his faith and superhuman strength, where he becomes the sickest of all men, the greatest criminal, the most damned— and the supreme Knower—because he arrives at the unknown! *Since, more than anyone, he has cultivated his already rich soul! He arrives at the Unknown; and when, maddened, he loses the meaning of his visions, he has still seen them! So what if he destroys himself in this leap into the unheard of, the unnameable—other dreadful workers will come, they will start from the horizon where the other has collapsed. . . .*

The poet is really the thief of fire. . . .

You're a shit if you don't write back—fast, for in eight days I'll be in Paris, maybe.

Au revoir.
A. Rimbaud

"He was only sixteen when he wrote that," David said. "Can you believe it? Sixteen fucking years old."

I remembered Ted's words. *"The poet must be a thief of fire." Someone I know said that.* I handed the book back to David.

It was too much to even begin to think about: like learning the guy sitting next to you in class was Shakespeare, or Picasso. I remembered the drunken boy who'd read his poems to me beside the C&O Canal, the boy who'd said, "We are children of the moon," and pressed his bloody palm against my own; the same person who watched, rapt, as a man drowned in an icy river, and later wrote a poem about it.

"Hey, are you sure you're okay?"

I looked up and saw David staring at me in concern. "Yeah," I said, and forced a smile. "Just kind of wrung out, that's all."

He nodded. "I got a check today. C'mon, let's get something to eat. I'll pay."

"You sure?"

"Yeah, absolutely. Anywhere you want, you name it."

I stood, pulled on my bomber jacket, stuffed the book into a pocket, and followed him to the front door. "Pied du Cochon?"

"Perfect." He grinned, linking his arm through mine, and we walked out into the night.

22

Washington, D.C.

OCTOBER 14, 1978

THE FUNERAL WAS in Northeast, at the Cathedral of the Archangels and Saint John the Divine. David went with me. We got there early, but even so the place was packed.

"How does Ted rate a funeral here?" I asked, staring at the vast and dementedly ornate building that loomed above us.

David shrugged. "I guess he had friends in high places. Or high friends in other places."

As we stepped inside, a man handed us each a memorial booklet.

THEODORE LAWRENCE "TED" KAMPFERT
A CELEBRATION OF HIS LIFE AND MUSIC

On the cover was my drawing.

"Holy shit." I winced in apology as the man frowned, then whispered, "David! Look—that's my portrait!"

"Wow." He stared at the cover. "That's *fantastic*, Merle."

Despite my sorrow I felt a kind of happiness I'd never experienced before. Seeing my drawing like that, professionally printed—it made my work look *real*. Not student work, not graffiti painted in a rush before the cops arrived, but a portrait by a real artist. Something beautiful; something that would last.

We found a pew near the middle of the cathedral and squeezed in. There were a lot of folks my father's age, but some were older—Ted's relatives, I assumed, or neighbors from when he and Rob were growing up. But I was surprised by how many people were my age.

"Jeez. How did all these people know him?" I asked David.

"Fans," said David. "The Raisins had a huge cult following. Hey, look—" He gestured excitedly at someone who'd been on the cover of *Rolling Stone* a few months earlier. I glanced back, then turned my attention to the altar. There was no coffin, no sign of his fishing pole or guitar. David whispered that Ted had been cremated, his ashes scattered along the Potomac River. "But don't tell the priest that. Catholics say you have to be buried in sacred ground."

"I think the river was sacred to Ted," I said.

"No kidding. His fishing pole, too."

Propped around the altar were blown-up photos. Ted as a kid with Rob and their parents, wearing a cowboy outfit; pictures of him with the band in their heyday. The PA played rock music as people continued to file in, and I vaguely recognized some of the songs that David had played for me in the studio. None of the music sounded anything like what Ted had sung for me.

Finally the service started. A priest came out and gave a brief invocation. After that it was all people who knew Ted—friends and family, the surviving members of the Deadly Rays. David whispered the names of those he recognized, and pointed out Ted's ex-wife and three of his old girlfriends, which surprised me.

But of course he hadn't always been homeless or old. The photos showed a man who wasn't handsome, exactly, but someone you might fall in love with, especially if he had ever sung to you alone.

The service went on for a while. So many of the stories were funny that it was hard to tell if people were crying from laughter or sorrow. Finally, Rob Kampfert stood up, and the room fell silent.

He talked about how he and Ted grew up in the Maryland suburbs; how they had been altar boys and constantly in trouble. When I shut my eyes, I could almost imagine it was Ted speaking. Rob Kampfert told some great stories, stories I couldn't imagine telling in a church, let alone a cathedral.

"I have to be honest," he finally said. "I was always afraid of something like this happening. Every time the phone rang in the middle of the night—and you know, he had a couple of really close calls. But he always came back, so he thought he was fucking immortal. After a while, I started to think he was immortal, too. But he wasn't."

He wiped his eyes. "My big brother's gone. He's fishing up there somewhere. . . ."

He looked up into the cathedral's vaulted ceiling. For the first time I noticed a narrow balcony above the altar, to one side, with a small pipe organ but no people. "He's up there fishing, and I sure as hell hope they're biting."

He stepped back from the lectern. People rustled in their pews, uncertain whether this was the end of the service.

Then a recorded song began to play, a sweet cascade of notes from an acoustic guitar. I sat bolt upright, and so did everyone else. People let out small cries, of sorrow or recognition or delight.

It was the song Ted had played the night before on the canalboat, the song I thought he'd made up just for me. Now, seeing the reactions around me, I realized that everyone felt that way. David was weeping openly. The woman on my other side grabbed my arm.

"Oh, this song," she whispered, tears streaming down her cheeks. "My God, this song."

On the tape, Ted's voice chimed in with the guitar, that same gravelly tone but softer, younger. And while I hadn't been able to remember the words before, I remembered them now, the way that, sometimes, something in your waking life summons back a dream you'd forgotten.

He sang about how he'd once stood on a bridge, and fallen in love with a woman he saw walking beside the river below. Day after day he returned, hoping he'd see her again.

But he never did. He roamed the city, searching every place he thought he might find her. She was never there.

And so he returned home; and one day as he walked along the river, he looked up and saw her, high above him on the bridge.

He stood and watched as she walked away, and then she was gone forever.

It's the saddest song I have ever heard. Though now, I know there is something far sadder than never meeting someone you've only glimpsed from far away.

And that is to meet someone just once, and not know until afterward that it was the most important night of your entire life, and that it will never happen again.

Crying uncontrollably, I looked above the altar, at the small balcony with the pipe organ.

A man stood there. Even at that distance I recognized his face, his worn flannel shirt and black T-shirt, the grooves along his mouth and his deep-set eyes. He stared down at the crowd in the cathedral, his expression sorrowful, almost pitying; then lifted his head slightly and stared right at me. His eyes flared from amber to emerald as he raised his hand, holding up something in a gesture of farewell. His guitar, I thought, until it blurred into something else: a bone-white crescent strung with silver. I gasped and stood on tiptoe, struggling to see.

The balcony was empty. The last echoes of Ted's voice and guitar trembled in the air and faded. For a minute, the cathedral was silent.

Then people began to move again, quietly at first. Soon they began to talk, turning to greet old friends and hug one another. Slowly, in ones and twos, we walked into the aisles and began to file out of the cathedral, back to where the October sun shone in a cloudless sky and the chilly air smelled of burning leaves and chrysanthemums and woodsmoke.

David held my hand and drew me through the crowd, greeting people he knew and stopping to introduce me to John Waters. We passed Rob Kampfert in the middle of a tight knot of people, smoking a cigarette.

"Hey," he called. "Merle, come here."

We walked over, David for once saying nothing. "This is the girl who did that portrait of Ted," Rob said, and pulled me toward him. "Merle—what's your last name?"

"Tappitt," I said.

"Merle Tappitt." He dropped his cigarette and ground it out. "Sorry I didn't ask if I could use that drawing, but I didn't know how to get in touch with you. You got a phone number?"

I gave him David's number. Somebody made a crack about him robbing the cradle, and Rob shook his head. "Nah. Like I said, this is one kick-ass artist. Maybe someday I can use you." He copied the number onto the back of one of the memorial booklets. "Okay, thanks. See you. . . ."

He turned, and David and I headed toward the Metro station.

"Fucking A, Merle," he said when we were out of earshot. "I can't believe you just gave Rob Kampfert your phone number!"

"He's not going to ask me for a date, you idiot. Plus, he's not my type."

"Yeah, well, he could be mine."

From the station came the hum of an approaching train. We ran to catch it, neither of us casting a backward glance at the mourners who remained outside the cathedral.

PART SIX

❧

RADIANT DAYS

Arriving forever, setting out for everywhere.

— Arthur Rimbaud, "To Reason," *Illuminations*

23

Washington, D.C., New York City, and London

1978—1984

"HEARING FOOTSTEPS." THAT'S a saying my father used when I was a kid and he'd be knocking back a case of Miller while watching the Redskins on TV. It's what happens when the player running with the football gets so spooked at the thought of someone coming up behind to tackle him that he drops the ball.

I quickly realized that I couldn't listen for Arthur Rimbaud's footsteps. If I did, the sound would drown out everything around me, until I was deafened. Still, I spent weeks, then months and finally years, learning to live with the memory of that night. Not just the long shadow cast by the knowledge of Arthur's genius, but what it all meant—Arthur and Ted and myself, meeting then losing one another within the space of twenty-four hours. That's one of the things you never read about in books—what happens after the magic ends, and life goes back to normal?

Ultimately I simply accepted it. I had the fish-bone key and a

century-old French coin to prove it had not been a dream. The
key I had made into a pendant that I wear around my neck; the
coin is in my pocket, always. No matter how broke I was, I never
sold it. I knew that I had been given a great gift: the ability to see,
for a moment, that place where art and love and desire and loss all
come together like the bands of color in a rainbow.

And what makes a rainbow so beautiful is that it can't last. In
the end, that night was only one night out of my entire life.

Still, there was one thing that made my memories of Arthur
almost unbearably sad; also mysterious, even unbelievable.

How could he have stopped writing poetry when he was only
nineteen? *Why* did he stop writing?

Nobody knew. Nobody knows.

DAVID HAD A FRIEND WHO WORKED AT THE ATLANTIS, A PUNK CLUB
in D.C.'s old downtown. She said they were looking for a part-
time waitress, so I went to a vintage clothing store and bought a
pair of red alligator cowboy boots, some button-front jeans, and a
bunch of 1950s bowling shirts. I combed my hair into a modified
ducktail, went to the club, and got the job. I worked only three
days a week at first, but since I had no distractions besides drawing, I was able to focus on being a really good waitress, which is
harder than it seems. After a few months I was given the highly
desirable weekend shift, which meant more money in tips. By
the following spring, I was spelling the bartender and had saved
enough money to get my own apartment in Adams Morgan.

I'd made some new friends by then, people I met through the

Atlantis and d.c. space, a nearby bar and artist's space where a lot of local live acts performed. On my nights off I'd hang out and sketch the regulars—members of Bad Brains and other D.C. acts like Vernon Reid, the Velvet Monkeys, and the Slinkees, a band started by a kid named Ian MacKaye who worked at the Georgetown Häagen-Dazs with another kid named Henry Rollins. I transformed the sketches into oversized canvases that ended up in the Punk Art exhibition by the Washington Project for the Arts, a show that went on to Manhattan's School of Visual Arts and, the following spring, a gallery in Amsterdam. Two of the paintings sold, one of guitar hero Dale Williams, the other based on my Radiant Days tag. The Williams portrait went to Anna Greenhouse of the Nemo Gallery, and as a result got mentioned in the *SoHo Weekly News* and *Art Scene*. That was when my career really began.

I got even more mileage out of the portrait of Ted Kampfert. About a year after I moved to Adams Morgan, I got a phone call from Rob. That famous integrity must have finally cracked: he and the surviving members of the Deadly Rays had signed with a record company to release a double album. One disc would be devoted to outtakes and rare demos of the Rays' work, the other to Ted Kampfert's solo career.

"We'd like to use that picture of yours for the back cover art," Rob said. "And I'd like to commission you to do the cover."

He also mentioned the possibility of a Raisins reunion, and said he'd call me if and when that came off. I didn't make a lot of money for that cover, but I got major street cred.

"You knew Ted Kampfert?" a girl asked one night when I was tending bar. By then the Atlantis had become the 9:30 Club, ground zero for the city's burgeoning punk and hardcore scene.

I nodded and pushed a beer across the bar. "Yeah."

"That's your painting on the new album, right? It's amazing. Why the hell are you working here?" She shook her head: a slight, dark-haired punk named Felice. She worked at a tattoo parlor—this was back when tattoos were still rare, especially on women—and knew a lot of the younger bands.

"Because working here pays the bills." I'd stopped doing graffiti by then. I was painting as much as I could, but had yet to sell another canvas.

Felice sipped her beer. "Well, it doesn't pay anything, but I think you should do gig posters. What you do is a shitload better than most of what I see."

So I started doing posters. It combined the stuff I loved—portraits, graffiti, music. I learned how to silk-screen and bought time at a studio to produce my work. The bands couldn't afford to pay me, but after a while some of the clubs did. My posters became ubiquitous, first in the D.C. area, then in NYC, always signed with my tag, RADIANT DAYS, and a sun-eye. People stole them from wherever they were posted—telephone poles, bars, clubs—so I decided I'd start selling them. There's a market for that kind of thing, especially if you're doing posters for well-known bands.

Which, by that time, I was. I'd run off signed, numbered editions of my prints and sell them at shows. It wasn't much money, but the posters acted as ads for the few dozen canvases that now leaned against the walls of my apartment. When that Raisins reunion finally came together as a one-time-only event at the 9:30, I designed the limited-edition posters for it, and the cover art for the live album that followed.

Felice and I started to go out. I was fascinated by the tattoo studio, probably more fascinated than I was by Felice. She had a steady job, and she was calm. You need steady hands and focus to be a good tattoo artist, and Felice had both.

After a year we split up, but amicably. As a parting gift, she tattooed my back with a gorgeous rendition of my tag—azure and violet and turquoise waves, the rayed eye reflected in a sea where, if you looked closely enough, you could just make out a tiny boat. I designed it, but Felice made it part of me.

"There." She blotted blood from between my shoulder blades. "Now you won't forget me."

"Like I would," I said, and hugged her.

By then the first tremors of the 1980s art boom were being felt. Anna Greenhouse bought another of my paintings. Because I'd started out doing graffiti, my name was mentioned alongside those of New York City painters like Keith Haring and especially Jean-Michel Basquiat, the artist formerly known as SAMO. I moved briefly to New York, squatting in a loft in the meatpacking district, but I felt constrained and slightly repulsed by the amount of money being thrown at the people around me.

So I saved my money, got a passport, and moved to London. My plan was to study at the Slade School of Fine Art. I was twenty-two by then, old to be a first-time student, but I wanted to learn some aspects of my craft that I had been too young and arrogant to understand that I needed to learn, if I was going to become as good as I wanted to be.

And I wanted to be not just good but great.

I had enough money to live on. I found a room in a squat in Crouch End, in North London, with a bunch of anarchists who spent their days screaming about Margaret Thatcher and their nights shooting up. One of them had silk-screening equipment; I started designing T-shirts for bands, and got more work doing gig posters for Dingwalls in Camden Town. I set up a makeshift studio in the basement of the squat, and made money for a while as a messenger, delivering packages to posh addresses in Kensington and Belgravia. Drugs held no romance for me, especially after I found one of my housemates dead in the bathtub, a needle in the crook of her arm like a macabre fishing lure.

I quit the messenger job. I had enough money to buy a roll of canvas, some brushes and acrylics. I spent three weeks painting for fourteen or fifteen hours a day, stopping only to bolt down some boiled eggs and lager. I put together a portfolio and sent my application for the Slade. After a month I received a letter: I had been rejected.

"Screw that," I said. I got drunk and tore the rejection letter into pieces, glued them onto a canvas and painted around them, slashes of orange and gamboge and fuchsia forming the outline of an ornate building in flames, with my own face peering from one of the windows.

I called the painting *Art School Burnout*. When I had a dozen

completed canvases, I schlepped them around the city. I told gallery owners I'd shown with Anna Greenhouse. I gave them silk-
screened T-shirts of Margaret Thatcher dancing with a skeleton,
and Jah Wobble as the Mona Lisa with a spliff hanging from his
mouth. It took a year, but I finally got into a group show in Far-
ringdon. I was the only artist who sold a painting.

I began to make contacts in the small, closed world of gallery
owners and collectors in the city. The 1980s art-grab had made its
way to London: I told everyone I was from New York, and that,
along with my T-shirts and the fact I lived in a building slated
for demolition to make way for council housing, gave me more
street cred.

Even though I still couldn't get a solo show, I continued to sell
my paintings, and was invited to gallery openings, where I'd stash
hors d'oeuvres in my satchel and drink as much cheap white wine
as I could before the crowds thinned.

It was at one of these that I met a tall, sweet-faced blonde who
worked for a catering company. After I'd snagged my fourth
plastic cup of wine, she sidled up to me with her tray and whispered, "If you come out back afterward, I'll just give you a fucking bottle, okay?"

I flushed, but she laughed and added, "I mean it. They just
chuck this stuff unless someone takes it."

I hung around till the gallery closed, then slipped out to a catering van idling beside the back door. The waitress stood beside it,
still in her work livery of cheap black pants, white blouse, black
vest.

"Here." She held out a half-full bottle, but when I reached for it, she stuck it behind her back. "I have a better offer. How 'bout I buy you dinner?"

"You can afford that?"

She raised an eyebrow, grinning. "Who says it will be an expensive dinner?"

We went to a small bistro in Islington. Her name was Olivia. She had taken ancient Greek at the University of Reading; the catering job was a part-time gig while she worked on her doctorate. When I stood to go to the ladies room, I picked up my satchel and the dog-eared paperback of *Seasons in Hell* fell out.

"Rimbaud, huh?" Olivia picked up the book and handed it to me. "You know he lived near here? Camden Town, on Royal College Street. I'll show you, it's just a few blocks from the flat."

I shook my head. "You're kidding, right?"

"No, it's true. He and Verlaine, they had rooms in a house there. There's a blue plaque on the building, I see it every time I walk past."

"That's incredible," I said, and slid the book back into my bag. I'd long ago stopped listening for Arthur's footsteps—but without knowing it, I'd been following them.

Dinner turned into drinks after dinner, and then into a hot make-out session outside the Highbury Fields tube station.

"Your tattoo is beautiful," she murmured. "You want to see mine?"

She drew away from me, tugging at her sleeve to display a symbol inked upon her bicep. I went cold. "What—what is that?"

"Christ, you look like you've seen a ghost!" She traced the tattoo's outline with her finger: an archaic-looking bone crescent with seven lines drawn between its points. "It's the lyre of Orpheus—that's what my dissertation is on, Orphic studies. You know Orpheus, right?"

I stared, stunned, at her arm. "Yeah, I mean—vaguely."

"Ah, the advantages of an American education! Well, in ancient Greek myths, Orpheus is the greatest singer and musician on Earth. He could charm anyone and anything through his music—rocks, birds, gods, and men. His wife was Eurydice, who some sources say was the daughter of Apollo. When she was bitten by a poisonous snake and died, Orpheus was so grief-stricken he went to the Underworld and pleaded with Hades and Persephone, the rulers of the dead, to return Eurydice to him. He played his lyre and sang so beautifully that even Hades wept, and finally agreed that he would allow Eurydice to accompany her husband back to the daylight world—the only time Hades ever permitted one of the dead to leave his kingdom.

"But he set one restriction: Eurydice could follow Orpheus to the overworld—but if Orpheus looked back at her even once, no matter how briefly, she would be doomed to return to the dead."

I fought to keep my voice calm. "And?"

"They made it as far as the entrance to the Underworld. Orpheus could hear Eurydice a few steps behind him, but as the first light shone into the tunnel he couldn't bear it anymore: he had to make certain she was still there.

"So he looked back—and lost her forever. She struggled to

reach for him, but her arms clasped empty air; she whispered farewell and died once more, this time for eternity. That's what Ovid says, anyway."

"What—what happened to Orpheus?"

"Some say he killed himself out of grief. Afterward he became the patron of artists, and the lyre of Orpheus was the symbol most associated with him. Then the Orphic mystery religions sprang up. Most of them have some sort of ritual in which initiates are forbidden to look behind them. That's what my dissertation's about—Orphic survivals in early Coptic texts."

Something in my face stopped her. Then she laughed. "Merle, you look like your dog just died! It's only a myth—Orpheus wasn't a real person."

"Yeah, sure. Just, you know . . . it's so sad." I gave her a broken smile. "Did he—is there anything in the myth about—well, about him fishing?"

Olivia gave me an odd look. "That's very strange."

"What?"

"That you'd ask that. About fishing. It's what I'm arguing in my dissertation: that early Christians stole that symbol—the fish—from the Orphic mysteries, and attached it to their own religion. It's fairly obscure, but there's quite a bit of evidence on vase paintings. The ones I'm studying all have a symbol representing a fish, and many show Orpheus in a boat with a fishing pole. You can see them on some vases in the British Museum. The lyre of Orpheus, too—not the real lyre," she added. "That doesn't actually exist. But the symbol does."

I leaned against the wall of the station. "Holy shit."

Olivia grinned. "You mean 'Holy fish.' Don't they teach you this stuff in American schools?"

"Not really."

"But you've been to the British Museum, right?"

"Not yet. I haven't had time."

"Hmm." Olivia put her arms around me and leaned forward, until her forehead touched mine. "I can see there are huge gaps in your education, Merle Tappitt. The sort of things that only a worldly Englishwoman with a degree in classics can explain. So I think we'd better start right now, don't you?"

"Oh yes," I murmured, and kissed her.

24

Camden Town, London

DECEMBER 1874 / DECEMBER 1994

HE RETURNED TO London—he and Verlaine had lived there after they fled Paris. Now Verlaine was in prison in Belgium, sentenced for two years after shooting Arthur in the hand: a lovers' quarrel that had ended in disaster. The memory twisted Arthur's insides, guilt and desire and loathing tangled into an inextricable knot that had unraveled into his poetry. While he had taken other lovers since Verlaine's imprisonment, he knew that there was one knot inside him that would never be undone.

The last of his money was gone. His tobacco pouch was empty; even his pipe was barren of ash. Walking was the only intoxicant that remained to him.

So he walked, for miles upon miles, and slept in ice-covered fields; visited taverns where he cadged beers from workmen or sold himself inside horse-drawn cabs for the price of tobacco and a ploughman's lunch. He was thin, almost gaunt, and taller, his blond hair so sun-bleached it looked gray. Only his big hands and icy pale eyes betrayed something of the tousled boy who had been startled awake in a lockhouse a few years before.

After several days he reached the village of Hampstead, just north of London. He strode across the heath until he came to the Kentish Town Road, then headed south, through Kentish Town and on to Camden Town, where he and Verlaine had lived on Great College Street. He continued on to the Regent's Canal, with its stone bridges and placid water, which reminded him of the canals in Charleville and Paris and his dream city. Some nights he dreamed that the canals were all linked, deep below the surface of the earth; other times he dreamed that they flowed through him, deep within his arteries and veins.

He walked beside the canal path, pausing to watch a carp break the smooth green water. In the distance, a tramp fished from a stone span. Arthur waved at him: the tramp lifted his head and nodded, sunlight glinting from his topaz eyes as Arthur hurried along.

He was so lost in thought that, when he first saw her mark, he thought he imagined it. He drew up short, reached to push aside the tangle of mulberry bushes that covered a wall. There was a brilliant yellow sun-eye.

"Merle," he whispered, tasting the old name as though it were a mouthful of absinthe. He traced the words with his finger, then pressed his palm against the brick.

It was warm—not warm, *hot*. He stepped back onto the path and walked more quickly, until he spied her second mark—the same glowing rayed sun. Gingerly he touched it and snatched his hand back. The brick had burned his fingers.

He turned and broke into a run. Beneath his feet the canal path began to shimmer as with heat; he heard a faint ringing sound, the clamor of distant bells. He looked up, and saw a radiant eye gazing down at him from the arch of another bridge spanning the canal. Beneath it, a set of stairs led up to the High Street.

A painted sun-eye blazed from each step, rising from a painted sea. He laughed, his own words thrown back at him like a handful of dead leaves.

> *Found!*
> *What? Eternity.*
> *The sun vanished*
> *With the sea.*

He raced up the stairs. A boy sprawled across the top step, drunk. Arthur stepped nimbly over him and strode down the sidewalk. Strange vehicles filled Camden High Street, magically propelled: sleek omnibuses, metal cars like those he'd seen with Merle in the dream city, glittering velocipedes. Lights flashed from red to amber to green; sirens wailed; his ears hummed with the din of trains. Far overhead something gleamed across the gray sky—a flying machine like a silver dart, trailing white smoke.

He gazed up at it, his heart pounding with joy: the great dream had engulfed him again. He turned in a circle, dizzy, heedless of those who pushed him aside as they hurried in and out of glass-fronted stores, or clambered onto red omnibuses the size of small buildings.

Yet strange as it all was, he recognized it: he had lived here. He knew the pub on the corner. He knew these buildings, though none of them resembled the shops where he had bought beer and fresh-baked bread, writing paper and brandy.

Everything was different, except for her mark, that radiant eye beckoning him from walls and buildings, sidewalks and the sides of buses. Like the trail of crumbs left by the boy in the fairy tale: a trail of golden eyes led him from the High Street onto a narrower way, past shops that sold exotic perfumes and jewelry, dresses and trousers that hardly resembled clothing at all.

The trail ended in front of a building with tall windows and words painted across the glass.

GALLERY SYBILLA

Illuminations:

Merle Tappitt

Inside he found a crowded room lit by brilliant electrical lanterns. Huge canvases covered the walls. Knots of people stood before them, holding champagne flutes and talking excitedly. No one noticed him as he strode to a painting twice his height, a green swath stippled with jots of scarlet and emerald, orange and violet and indigo. A pair of gray-blue eyes rose above a cloud-like promontory, with tiny capering figures inside the irises. At the lower right-hand corner of the canvas, a golden sun-eye was stamped beside a signature.

Merle Tappitt

He stood and stared at it, then wandered to another painting, a blaze of vermilion through which he could discern the outlines of a city, with the same signature and sun-eye in the corner.

They were all like that, cities and shadowy rivers with half-seen figures on the shore, on bridges, in boats. The scale of the canvases made it seem as though he stood inside them, as though he inhaled the haze of yellow and umber and pale green like smoke. He moved from one painting to the next, so absorbed he never saw their titles, printed on white cards beside each of them.

Une saison en enfer. Alchimie du verbe. Voyelles. Le bateau ivre.

It was as though she had captured his dreams.

Near the back of the room, he came upon three canvases that were different from the others. No rivers, no spires or towers or flying machines. Instead each depicted a desert, vast reaches of sky and sand, a dazzle of lacquered blue and vermilion interrupted by a bundle of bleached bones, the black strut of a rifle bore; the recurring image of a bone harp, hanging in the sky like a crescent moon.

He gazed at them entranced, until his head began to ache. Around him the gallery had grown more crowded, the buzz of conversation and laughter loud enough to break his reverie. He felt a pulse behind his eyes, that strange vertigo he experienced sometimes when writing. He turned to look for a way out.

She was on the other side of the room, surrounded by people in spare black clothing. They held glasses of champagne and listened raptly as she spoke, her voice throatier than it had been; more confident, accustomed to an audience.

"It's not just that I love his work." A sudden hush allowed the words to rise above the *tink* of glasses. "He changed my life when I was young and didn't think I would ever become a real artist. His poetry saved me. *He* saved me. I painted these to honor him."

Her hair was dark, cut close to her skull, and she wore a sleeveless shift over loose black trousers. She was older than she had been, older than he was—thirty, maybe—her face pale, her eyes dark with kohl. Her bare arms were covered with tattoos, images that might have sprung from his poems: towers and waves, eyed suns and an arched rainbow, leaping fish and a man who carried a harp of bone. She had her arm around a tall woman whose fair hair was bound upon her neck in a loose chignon. Each of them wore a plain gold band upon her left hand. As he watched, the tall woman bent her head, and Merle raised hers. Their faces touched, and Merle kissed the tall blond woman on the mouth. The people around them laughed and raised their glasses.

As though he had spoken her name aloud, Merle turned.

For an instant their eyes met. Her mouth parted in a stunned, joyous O of recognition. Arthur nodded, smiling, and she raised her hand, a gesture at once greeting and farewell.

Arthur lifted his hand, mirroring her gesture. A man walked

in front of him, and when he stepped away Merle was gone, swallowed by the crowd.

It was time to leave.

Arthur looked around for a door. Crowds made him jumpy; he wanted a drink. He turned and walked to the back of the gallery. A long corridor stretched there, dim save for a faint yellow glow that grew brighter and larger as he approached, until it blossomed into a great rayed eye.

The eye erupted into a blinding vista like molten gold: a desert where instead of sun or moon a bone lyre hung in the blazing sky, a signpost to show him that, indeed, this was the way. He walked through the passage, the flash of heat upon his skin erupting into a shimmer of quicksilver light, the dying plaint of bells and horns drowned by the rush of time past and time present mingling into an endless, enveloping stream that bore him away.

The heat burned his skin like fiery rain and dissipated. The quicksilver light faded into chill December mist, the rumble of carriage wheels and the impenetrable yellow haze of London's winter twilight. He sidestepped a beggar whose teeth had rotted to stumps, paused to let a horse-drawn carriage pass, its well-dressed customers staring out at him with contempt.

Arthur didn't notice them, or the coal-dust darkness pressing down upon the street. He walked quickly, as he always did, and he did not stop or look back again.

He didn't need to: he knew the way. His life was still before him. Night would fall soon enough. Right now, he was on his way to Paris.

AUTHOR'S NOTE

"Rimbaud cannot be duplicated. He does not
suffer any disciples: Do not go to see if he is there,
but to feel your own self."

—Alain Borer, *Rimbaud in Abyssinia*,
translated by Rosemarie Waldrop

There was only one Rimbaud, just as there was only one Shakespeare, and there is no substitute for reading his work in the original French. Rimbaud's poetry was famously allusive, using puns and neologisms, many of which don't translate easily (if at all) into English. And of course, much of it was written in elaborate rhyming sequences, sonnets and the like.

The translations of Rimbaud's poems are my own, and I have loosely transcribed and edited his letters for brevity. I tried to give a sense of the flavor of Rimbaud's work for an American reader: there are many far better and more elegant translations, and I've listed some in the bibliography.

In 1870–1871, Prussia was the most powerful state of an empire we know today as Germany. Under Napoléon III (not *the* Napoléon, but his nephew) France declared war on Prussia—a big mistake. The Prussian army retaliated and marched through the French countryside, and ultimately laid siege to Paris. Cut off from the rest of the country during the winter of 1870–1871, the residents of Paris survived bombing and starvation, the latter by eating dogs, cats, horses, and yes, rats.

ON ARTHUR RIMBAUD

Rimbaud may be the patron saint of young writers: he wrote nearly all of his poems before he was twenty years old, and many of them between the ages of sixteen and eighteen. I first stumbled upon his work when I was seventeen and a junior in high school. That was when I read (in English) his extraordinary *Lettres du voyant*, known in English as the *Letters of the Visionary* or *Letters of the Seer*. Rimbaud wrote them when he was sixteen, on May 13 and May 15, 1871, to his teacher Georges Izambard and the poet Paul Demeny. Graham Robb, Rimbaud's biographer, calls the first of these "one of the sacred texts of modern literature." The letters' most famous pronouncements are "'I' *is somebody else*" and this:

> *I say one must become a visionary, make yourself*
> *a* seer. *The Poet becomes a* visionary *through a long,*
> *immense and deliberate* derangement *of* all the senses.

A year after reading the "Letter of the Seer," I heard Patti Smith chanting, "Go Rimbaud, go Rimbaud!" on her landmark album *Horses*. I was hooked.

Rimbaud's creative impact didn't begin in the 1970s, of course. He influenced generations of writers and poets and artists, as well as musicians and songwriters, including Smith, Bob Dylan, Jim Morrison of the Doors, Richard Hell, Tom Verlaine (who took his name from Rimbaud's lover, the poet Paul

Verlaine), Nick Cave, KT Tunstall, Tom Waits, the Clash, Beth Orton, John Lennon, Cat Power. . . .

You get the idea. It would be hard to find a literate songwriter of the past fifty years who was *not* influenced by Rimbaud. His impact on writers has been even more extensive, from French Symbolists to Dada to the Surrealists, Beats, hippies, punks, post-punks, and beyond. His relationship with the older, married poet Paul Verlaine scandalized Paris; it ended with Verlaine being imprisoned for shooting Rimbaud in the hand. Years later, when Rimbaud was in Africa, he was rumored to be living with a local woman. His work has influenced numerous gay artists and writers of the twentieth and twenty-first centuries, including the late artist-activist David Wojnarowicz, who famously referenced him in his photographic series *Rimbaud in New York*, and the elegant novelist and critic Edmund White, author of *Rimbaud: The Double Life of a Rebel*. In 2005, the French government named the writer and artist Patti Smith a Commandeur in the Order of Arts and Letters (the highest honor given to an artist), noting how much Smith has done to promote Rimbaud's work in the English-speaking world.

Leonardo DiCaprio played Arthur Rimbaud in the 1995 film *Total Eclipse*, based on the play by Christopher Hampton about the teenage poet's volatile relationship with Verlaine, and Ben Whishaw played Rimbaud in Todd Haynes's 2007 Dylan movie *I'm Not There*. The title of that movie (and the Dylan song that inspired it) is a riff on Rimbaud's line, "'I' is somebody else."

There are myriad books and Web sites about Rimbaud. I've

listed what I found most useful. The single best book, in my opinion, is Graham Robb's 2000 biography *Rimbaud*, which is extremely readable and often very funny.

For the most part, I relied on Robb's Rimbaud chronology for this novel. Rimbaud ran away from home several times between the ages of fifteen and sixteen, and I wanted as much as possible to have my time line follow the actual events in his life. But there are some "missing days" during these periods, and I used those as the days when he meets up with Merle in our own time.

I've tried to stick to the facts as much as I could (considering this is a fantasy novel). But I made two speculations based on information I turned up during my research.

The first is that I think Rimbaud might have seen the aurora borealis, or northern lights, in mid-October 1870, when he was sleeping rough during one of his sojourns from home. I found an old newspaper account of the aurora's appearance at that time, and later found another reference to an October sighting of the aurora in Paris, described in a first-person account of the events surrounding the 1870 Siege of Paris. To me, Rimbaud's great, hallucinatory poems "Vowels" and "The Drunken Boat" seem as though they might easily have been inspired, in part, by the aurora's spectral light display.

My second speculation comes from reading several eyewitness accounts of a Parisian policeman who was tortured, then thrown into the Seine on February 26, 1871. Graham Robb's chronology puts Rimbaud in Paris at that time, in or near the area where the event occurred. Of course there's no way of proving that Rimbaud witnessed this, or that it influenced his writing. But again, it was very easy for me to *imagine* him seeing it, and to imagine that it might indeed have fueled some of the violently surreal words and images of "The Drunken Boat."

Arthur Rimbaud's extraordinary, event-filled life didn't end when he stopped writing poetry. He traveled around the world, and spent many years in Abyssinia (now Ethiopia) as a trader and, according to some, a gunrunner for the Abyssinian emperor. But for those adventures, you'll need to read his biographies or Rimbaud's own letters. He died on November 10, 1891, at the age of thirty-seven, of what was probably bone cancer. The previous day, hallucinating from his illness—his leg had been amputated, a grievous fate for someone who was a great walker—he dictated a letter requesting that he be put upon a ship conjured from his delirium, called the *Aphinar*, so that he could return to Egypt.

Please send me the cost of the voyage from Aphinar to Suez, he wrote. *I am completely paralyzed, so I want to leave in plenty of time. Please tell me when I should be carried on board.*

Even with his last words, he was embarking on another journey.

—Elizabeth Hand
August 19, 2011

SELECT BIBLIOGRAPHY

Bertall (Charles-Albert d'Arnoux). *The Communists of Paris, 1871: Types, Physiognomies, Characters*. 1897. [Can be read online via Google Books.]

Bingham, Denis. *Recollections of Paris*. 1896. [Includes Bingham's account of the Siege of Paris; can be read online via Google Books.]

Borer, Alain. *Rimbaud in Abyssinia*. Translated from the French by Rosemarie Waldrop. William Morrow, 1984.

Clayson, Hollis. *Paris in Despair: Art and Everyday Life Under Siege (1870–1871)*. University of Chicago Press, 2002.

Gibson, William. *Paris During the Commune, 1871: Being Letters from Paris and Its Neighborhood*. 1872. [A first-person account; can be read online via Google Books.]

Horne, Alistair. *Seven Ages of Paris*. Alfred A. Knopf, 2002.

Jeancolas, Claude. *Passion Rimbaud: L'album d'un vie*. Les editions Textuel, 1998.

Lissagaray, Prosper Olivier. *History of the Commune of 1871*, translated by Eleanor Marx Aveling. 1886. [Can be read online via Google Books.]

Mason, Wyatt, editor and translator. *I Promise to Be Good: The Letters of Arthur Rimbaud*. Modern Library, 2003.

Miller, Henry. *The Time of the Assassins: A Study of Rimbaud*. New Directions, 1946.

"An Oxford Graduate" (Markheim, Henry William Gegg). *Inside Paris During the Siege*. 1871. [First-person account of the Siege of Paris; can be read online via Google Books.]

Rimbaud, Arthur. *Collected Poems*. Translated with an introduction and notes by Martin Sorrell. Oxford University Press, 2001.

Rimbaud, Arthur. *Complete Works*. Translated by Paul Schmidt. Harper & Row, 1967.

Rimbaud, Arthur. *Illuminations*. Edition Critique avec introduction et notes par H. De Bouillane de Lacoste. Mercure de France, 1949.

Rimbaud, Arthur. *Illuminations*. Translated by John Ashbery. W. W. Norton, 2011.

Rimbaud, Arthur. *A Season in Hell and The Drunken Boat*. Bilingual edition; English translation by Louise Varèse. New Directions, 1945

Rimbaud, Arthur. *Selected Poems and Letters*. Translated and with an introduction and notes by Jeremy Harding and John Sturrock. Penguin Books, 2004.

Robb, Graham. *Rimbaud: A Biography*. W.W. Norton & Company, 2000.

Ross, Kristin. *The Emergence of Social Space: Rimbaud and the Paris Commune*. Verso, 1988.

Starkie, Enid. *Arthur Rimbaud*. Revised edition. New Directions, 1961.

Steinmetz, Jean-Luc. *Arthur Rimbaud: Presence of an Enigma*. Welcome Rain Publishers, 2001.

White, Edmund. *Rimbaud: The Double Life of a Rebel*. Atlas & Co, 2008

Whitehurst, Felix M. *My Private Diary During the Siege of Paris*. 1870. [Another first-person account that can be read online via Google Books.]

ACKNOWLEDGMENTS

First and foremost, as ever, my gratitude to my agent, Martha Millard, sole proprietor of the known universe's only full-service literary agency.

To my editor, Sharyn November, an incalculable debt of thanks for encouraging me to write this book, and staying with me during the years it took to complete it.

To my copy editor, Kathryn Hinds, my heartfelt thanks on an extraordinary job.

To William Sheehan, who read several drafts and offered suggestions for improving each one.

To my brother, Patrick Hand, who helped me reconnoiter Washington, D.C., after too long an absence from the City of Trees; William Roesing, who shared his knowledge of the C&O Canal, and walked with me there; David Streitfeld, who prescribed the proper dose of Auden when needed; Judith Clute, who pointed me to Rimbaud's house in Camden Town; and my late friend Russell Dunn, Rimbaldian comrade in arms for thirty-seven years.

To Arthur Rimbaud, Jean-Michel Basquiat, and Bob Stinson, *shantih*.

Most of all, my love to my partner and compass, John Clute, who traced Rimbaud's footsteps with me along Royal College Street and beyond.

Born in San Diego, ELIZABETH HAND grew up in Yonkers and Pound Ridge, New York, before heading to Washington, D.C., to study playwriting and anthropology at Catholic University. For a number of years she worked at the Smithsonian's National Air and Space Museum, but in 1988 quit her job to write full-time and moved to the coast of Maine, where she lived in a 400-square-foot lakefront cottage with no indoor plumbing or running water (it now has both, and is her office).

She is the author of twelve novels and three collections of shorter fiction. Her book *Generation Loss* won the inaugural Shirley Jackson Award for best work of psychological suspense. She has also received two Nebula Awards, three World Fantasy Awards, two International Horror Guild Awards, the James M. Tiptree Jr. Award, and the Mythopoeic Society Award. She is a longtime reviewer and critic whose work appears regularly in the *Washington Post*, the *Village Voice*, Salon, and the *Boston Globe*, among others. She has two children and continues to live in Maine, where she is at work on her next novel.

Her Web site is www.elizabethhand.com; she can be found on Twitter as www.twitter.com/Liz_Hand; and blogs at lizhand. wordpress.com